Black President:

The World Will Never Be the Same

Black President:

The World Will Never Be the Same

Brenda Hampton

www.urbanbooks.net

Urban Books, LLC
300 Farmingdale Road, NY-Route 109
Farmingdale, NY 11735

Black President: The World Will Never Be the Same

ISBN 13: 978-1-62286-484-3
ISBN 10: 1-62286-484-0

First Trade Paperback Printing May 2017
Printed in the United States of America

10 9 8 7 6 5 4 3 2

*This is a work of fiction. Any references or similarities
to actual events, real people, living or dead, or to real
locales are intended to give the novel a sense of reality.
Any similarity in other names, characters, places, and
incidents is entirely coincidental.*

Distributed by Kensington Publishing Corp.
Submit Orders to:
Customer Service
400 Hahn Road
Westminster, MD 21157-4627
Phone: 1-800-733-3000
Fax: 1-800-659-2436

1

First Lady Raynetta Jefferson

There I was, Raynetta Marie Jefferson, sitting with my guests at the U.S. Capitol, waiting for my husband, the president of the United States, to arrive and deliver the State of the Union Address. To my right were three wounded soldiers and several activists from the Black Lives Matter movement, a movement that had become even more relevant over the years. To my left was a father who had recently lost his two-year-old daughter to gun violence, a gay couple who were still fighting for equal rights, and two former senators who wanted to hear how my husband intended to deal with global warming. All of these issues he would address, and we were only minutes away from his arrival.

I sat in a peach linen suit with black, high-heeled shoes on. My eyes scanned the historic, impressive, and symbolic place where the U.S. Congress convened almost every day to create and execute our nation's laws. The American flag hung high behind the wide, wooden podium, and the crowd consisted of numerous elite congressmen and women who probably considered today's event a party. Smiles were plastered on plenty of faces, back pats and handshakes were freely given. Fakeness infused the air, and as the smiles and waves came my way, I reciprocated. Mean mugs were also on display, and a slight roll of my eyes was given to those who simply annoyed me. Many of the angry Republicans had voiced their disapproval and outrageous opinions about my husband and me to the media. On almost every news network, we were ripped to shreds. More so Stephen, but as the saying goes . . . when you hurt him, you hurt me. And by now, everyone knew an enormous amount of information about us—rightfully so, considering our new status.

The first thing we were attacked for was my inability to conceive a child. The "people" wanted to know why. I'd heard it all from A to Z, and according to those who claimed to know me well, the reason I couldn't have children was because I was a promiscuous black woman who had had four abortions that damaged me for life. Others claimed I had given up a child for adoption, and one congressman called me a belligerent, mentally ill cunt who had murdered my firstborn child. That was just the tip of the iceberg, and needless to say, politics had gotten real ugly. I wasn't prepared for any of this, but I followed my husband's lead. He wanted this, not me. He believed that he could somehow make a real difference in people's lives, but the truth was, he had major problems of his own. Big problems that had us on the brink of divorce, plenty of times.

Simply put, I was not a happy camper. I had valid issues with Stephen—issues that stemmed from adultery to his sharp, nasty tone toward me. My mother-in-law was another problem, and between the two of them, I wanted to pull my hair out. She was the only one who had a grip on her controlling son, and no doubt about it, he was a powerful force to be reckoned with. I wasn't sure where things were headed between us now that he was leader of the free world. I suspected that things would take a turn for the worse, but I stayed because there were benefits and perks for being the FLOTUS. From the house, to the maids, the money, the attention . . . I had a lot to be thankful for. I still didn't know if all of this would be worth it, but for now, I put on my game face and went with the flow.

My eyes were fixed on my mother-in-law, Teresa, who sat several rows in front of me. I hated to be in the same room with her, and after our conversation earlier, she should've felt privileged to sit this close to me. We'd gotten into a heated argument about what *she* wanted me to wear tonight. In her opinion, peach wasn't a suitable color for the first lady to wear. I needed to wear something dark. I couldn't help but to sit there and revisit our prior conversation where, yet again, she tried to tell me what to do.

"Peach doesn't mesh well with light-skinned women," she hissed. *"And the last time you wore that suit it was too tight. Your hips are too curvy, and when you button your jacket, it squeezes your big breasts. You need to wear something that'll hide your assets."*

"I'm very proud of my assets, and I haven't worn my peach suit in almost three years. To me, it looks fine, so I'm not quite sure where you're going with this."

Teresa didn't bite her tongue—neither did I. She took an opportunity to simplify things for me.

"Pay attention and I'll tell you where I'm going. You are now first lady of the United States, and you're not going to embarrass my son. He has worked too darn hard for this, and the last thing he needs is for the media to weigh in on a tacky-ass suit that doesn't fit his wife. I know you have something else better to wear. It would please, not only me, but him too, if you would wear something more suitable for this occasion."

"Really, Teresa? At this point, do you think I give a hoot about what the media thinks of me? No matter what I wear, they're going to talk trash about me. And,

quite frankly, if you don't like my suit, then you know what you can do."

"Watch how you speak to me or else . . . I'm warning you, and don't you dare wear that suit. Put your hair in a neat bun or something, and don't let those long strands dangle in your face. That style looks too ghetto, as does those thick lashes you wear sometimes. Wear the ones from MAC, if you must wear them at all. They look much better."

"I'm sure they will look better, and I'll consider doing all that you say, if you will consider wearing a clown suit tonight. Trust me when I say it would be very fitting."

I heard a gasp, but decided to end our call on that note. Teresa was treated the exact way she treated me. I blamed her for many of the problems Stephen and I had. He didn't know how to put her in her place, and even when he tried to, he always wound up feeling guilty about it. We all were at war with each other, and, now, he added everyone else's problems to the mix. I wasn't sure how he intended to pull this off, but plenty of his supporters trusted that he could. That was because they were on the outside looking in. They had no idea who Stephen really was, granted that he was a confident, intelligent, and well-prepared man. He presented himself that way, but many people didn't know that he had become broken and very bitter behind the brutal election process. Never in his wildest dream could he have imagined the blatant disrespect by people who were determined to bring him down. He was hurt and confused by the hatred. Being referred to as a "nigger," "monkey," "dumb-ass politician" . . . Comments like that truly disturbed him and set him off. He did his best to conceal his anger and stay cool, calm, and collected. But a person could only take so much. I kept telling him to walk away and forget about this, but the naysayers and haters fueled him. He became more ambitious, more motivated, and was determined to win. The pressure was unbearable, but after being bloodied, bruised, disrespected, and counted out by the media, he won. I definitely had to give him credit for that, and what woman in her right mind wouldn't want to be by the side of a winner?

With disappointment trapped in her eyes, Teresa searched me from head to toe. She cracked a tiny smile, and when I turned my head, pivoting in another direction, I heard her whisper my nickname, "Ne-ne." Referring to me by that name was inappropriate, so I ignored her.

"Ne-ne," she whispered again. I knew she was trying to annoy me, especially when she kept at it. "Ne-ne, Ne-ne, do me a favor. Give that young man behind you my business card."

The lady in front of me was nice enough to take the card from Teresa's hand and pass it to me. I pretended as if I didn't know what it was.

"Your mother-in-law wants you to give her card to the person behind you," she said.

"Oh, okay. Thank you."

I took the card but continued to ignore Teresa. I didn't bother to give the card to the gentleman behind me, and maybe next time Teresa would think before calling me Ne-ne in public.

"By the way," said the woman in front of me, "you look amazing tonight. Your makeup is always so flawless, and I would die for bouncy hair like yours. Every time I see you, you look so perfect. I told my husband that I don't know how you do it, but you do it very well."

"I'll just say that I have a lot of help. But thanks. You look nice too."

We laughed. I totally appreciated her compliments. It took a lot of hard work for me to look a certain way that was satisfying to me, even though I considered myself a very beautiful woman. I didn't know what Teresa's problem was, but instead of worrying about me, she should've been concerned about that wig she wore, slipping off her head. It had gray streaks in it and was cropped on the sides and back. A sway of bangs covered her forehead, and the silver accessories, along with the square-framed glasses she wore, made her appear to have a *little* class. The dark green suit, however, didn't work. I couldn't help but to laugh as I thought about her trying to tell me how to dress.

For the next several minutes, I conversed with the numerous people in my row. They had issues that needed to be seriously addressed. Many were angry, and we all kept taking peeks at the individuals in attendance who constantly caused gridlock and refused to get anything major done. They had set the tone, and it had gotten to a point where this country was too divided. Things had gotten worse since our last black president, and I wasn't sure if Stephen would be able to fix any of this mess. I certainly didn't want to make his job more hectic, so, for now, I smiled for the cameras, supported his endeavors, and made the best of a more-than-sticky situation.

The two-minute warning came, and it wasn't long before everyone stood at the call of "Mr. Speaker, the President of the United States!"

From a short distance, my husband, Stephen C. Jefferson, entered with the majority leaders of the House and Senate, and members of his new cabinet following closely behind. Loud applauses exploded, whistles blew, and nearly everyone was on their feet, with the exception of a few who pretended to be engrossed with cell phones. Overall, though, it appeared to be a joyous occasion as Stephen made his way down the aisle, shaking hands with new friends and foes. Many rushed to take pictures with him, especially women who had followed him on the campaign trail to here. I had a front-row seat to the thirstiness, but a part of me couldn't blame women for being excited or maybe even obsessed with my husband. He was the full package; charming as ever when he wanted to be. Had already been named as one of the sexiest men alive, and that title alone caused his ego to skyrocket. His six-one frame was stacked with muscles that bulged through his tailored navy suit. Hazel eyes were like a magnet that instantly drew everyone in. His rich milk chocolate and smooth skin glowed, and his pearly whites were in full effect. Minimal facial hair suited his chin, and his high-fade haircut, with a polished finish on the sides, was trimmed to perfection. Looking at him work the crowd truly took my breath away. I only wished that things between us were as good as we pretended them to be. I regretted that our lives were in shambles, but I lived for today, not tomorrow. Today, I was proud. I held my head up high as the cameras panned the room, constantly stopping at me to monitor my reaction.

I clapped my hands even when I looked at Teresa who seemed to be putting on quite a show. She rushed over to the edge to give Stephen a kiss on his cheek. The cameras flashed; she loved every bit of it. He kept it moving. Hadn't looked my way once, but maybe I missed it. I had fixed my eyes on the congressman who had called me a belligerent, murdering cunt. Stephen told me not to trip, but I was so mad that day, I could have set that fool on fire. Some people didn't understand how much negative words hurt. It was my responsibility to pretend as if they didn't, but deep down, some of this crap cut like a sharpened knife. Stephen had no idea how bitter I was about being forced into this. If anything, I hoped that this was a turning point.

Exhibiting much self-confidence, and what some may prefer to as swag, Stephen strutted toward the podium, flashing an abundance of smiles. He shook hands with the VP, Tyler McNeil, and then extended his hand to the Speaker Roy J. Robinson, who was an angry white man with deep wrinkles and numerous age spots on his face. It pained him to shake Stephen's hand, and from all of the negative interviews Roy had done, Stephen knew he had to watch his back. Nonetheless, this was one of the highlights of his life. A little boy from the rough streets of St. Louis wasn't supposed to be here. A fatherless child wasn't supposed to excel like my husband had, and many people counted him out when he found himself hanging with the wrong crowd in college and got arrested. That incident was his wake-up call. He wanted more out of life and started doing things to improve himself, as well as his community. It wasn't long before he ran for office in his district and won. And after five years in Congress, representing his loyal—and disloyal—constituents, he decided to make a move that shocked many. We had plenty of doubts about this day becoming a reality, and to say I was shocked by his many supporters would be an understatement.

"Thank you!" Stephen shouted as he spoke into the mic. "A big thanks to you all for being here!"

Applauses continued to erupt for at least two or three more minutes. Some had already taken their seats and many more had begun to. I was sure the cameras were on me, so I remained standing and looking in the direction of my husband. Finally, his eyes connected with mine, and he delivered a slow nod. Many eyes traveled to me, and then to Teresa who started waving her hands in the air.

"Yes!" she shouted. "Thank you, Jesus, thank you!"

I slightly pursed my lips, hoping that she would go somewhere and sit her ass down. She wanted the attention to be focused on her, but I was glad that things had shifted back to Stephen who had started to speak.

"To all of America tuned in, Speaker Robinson, Vice President McNeil, and members of Congress, I want to thank each and every one of you for being here today as I provide specifics about the state of our union. I am encouraged by the American people, and I'm hopeful that our best days are before us. But first, we have some work to do. Work that will require us to eliminate our personal differences, put aside political posturing, and begin to work in a bipartisan fashion to handle serious business for the American people.

"The last thing I wish to do is step on any toes around here, but the first thing I must do is ask for complete respect from all of you whom I intend to work vigorously with to get things done. There were many missed opportunities with past presidents, but now, we're on, what I'd like to think of as, a new playing field. We must roll up our sleeves and do exactly what the American people have elected us to come here and do. And any member not completely on board with putting the concerns of the American people first, I ask now that you seek another profession or you will be forced out of the way by people who are seeking to take your places and come here to work."

Cheers erupted from the Democratic side, where many congressmen and women stood and applauded. On the other side sat Republicans with smug looks on their faces. Evil eyes were narrowed at Stephen, while others texted away on cell phones. It pained me to witness the blatant disrespect; Lord knows we had been here and seen this playbook before. But Stephen C. Jefferson was a different breed. He didn't tolerate bullshit, didn't often think before he spoke, and had gotten to a point where he didn't care about being politically correct.

"I regret being petty sometimes, but the second thing I must ask is for all cell phones to be turned off and put away. There is a time and place for everything. Now isn't the time, and out of respect for the people who elected us all to be here, I'm asking for your undivided attention."

Some responded with boos. "You can ask for whatever you want," shouted a congressman who sat near the front. "Doesn't mean you're going to get it. You're doggone right, this is petty! Hell, *you're* petty!"

There was a long, sharp silence. Many people gasped, heads shook, and mouths dropped wide open. Smiles could be seen too, but none wider than Speaker Robinson who had glee in his evil eyes. I could see the fire in Stephen's eyes too. However, the smirk on his face implied that he had prepared himself for this moment. I wasn't sure how he was going to respond, but I inched slightly forward, crossed my fingers, and held my breath, knowing that Stephen was about to put that sucker in his place.

2

President of the United States, Stephen C. Jefferson

From the second I walked in, I could feel the heat. I could sense that everyone wasn't on my team, even before today. But politics as usual, I bravely stepped into my new role as commander in chief, observing as many others lived up to their unfortunate roles too. I expected whispers today. Expected that some would ignore me. Expected that those who ran to every media circuit that they could, dogging me out, would stand before me today with smiles on their faces and vigorously shake my hand. Many also wanted pictures. I happily smiled for the cameras and patted plenty of backs, telling them what a great job they've done. A great job making a mess of this country, and it was idiots like Senator Greg Brassley, who had just interrupted me, and Speaker Robinson, who played a huge part in getting us to where we are today.

Many Americans were fed up. They were unhappy and deeply discouraged with Congress. I'd heard about it every single day while on the campaign trail. I'd read numerous letters that addressed people's concerns about the legislative branch of the federal government, and this fool, Senator Brassley, had the audacity to sit there and challenge me tonight. Just for a few seconds, I contracted my eyes, staring him down like prey. I was well aware of the plan, and since another senator had gotten away with this bullshit before, lashing out at me was now fair game. The sly grins on plenty of faces said so, and I could hear Speaker Robinson cackling underneath his foul breath while sitting there, looking as if he had sucked on a sour lemon. Others sat in disbelief, but little did they know, I came totally prepared. This was a new era, and I intended to use my bully pulpit to silence fools who had no business being here in the first place.

With all eyes zoned in on me, I moistened my thick, soft lips with my tongue, then cleared a small lump that felt stuck in my throat. No question, I was slightly nervous, but my closest advisor told me to never let them see me sweat. The smirk on my face remained locked in place, even when I asked Senator Brassley if there was something he needed to get off his chest.

"It appears that you have something vital to say, so by all means, stand up and express what is ailing you. Only a fucking coward remains slumped in his seat with his head hung low, and I'm sure you didn't interrupt me in an attempt to be petty."

If someone dropped a pin, you could have heard it. Half of the attendees looked as if they weren't even breathing, and I was being eaten alive for sure.

"Proceed, please," Senator Brassley said with a beet red face. Embarrassment was written all over it, and whoever put him up to attacking me, they needed to search the Grand Old Party for someone who could really handle the job.

"Are you sure it's okay for me to proceed? I mean, you are free to speak up, but it is rude when *your* president is talking. All I ask is that you wait until I'm finished. Then you can join others in the spin room to say what exactly is on your mind."

"Mr. Jefferson, let's move this along," Speaker Robinson said in a grouchy tone from behind me. He coughed to clear his throat. "Ma . . . Many of us don't wish to be here all night, and I'm sure that you have plenty of other things on your agenda to do."

The smirk on my face vanished as I swung around to correct him. "For the record, Mr. Robinson, only my closest confidants can refer to me as Mr. Jefferson. You, sir, need to address me as *President* Stephen Carter Jefferson, *Mr. President* or as *President of the United States.* I will not answer to any other name, so tuck away the names you all call me at the country club and save them for whenever I make my final departure from the White House. With that being said, now, I will proceed."

Before I turned around, my VP stood and slowly clapped his hands. The loud clap echoed, causing numerous other Democratic leaders to stand and clap too. Many Republicans sat stone-faced and didn't budge. I mean, if looks could kill, I'd be the first dead president on Capitol Hill. I laughed it off, and in an effort to amuse the crowd, I expressed my sympathy for Speaker Robinson's nasty cough.

"Let's all pray for his speedy recovery, because not only does his cough sound horrific, but he looks terrible too. We should all be able to agree on that."

The crowd burst into laughter, especially when I turned to the Speaker to say I was just joking. The expression on his wrinkled face remained flat, and for the rest of the evening, all I heard were grunts, moans, and groans coming from behind me as I delivered my speech. It lasted almost an hour, and after it was over, I sat in the backseat of the motorcade with a person I sometimes felt was my number-one enemy. My wife, Raynetta. She placed her hand on top of mine, squeezing it.

"You did well," she said with a sly smirk on her face. "I was real proud of you tonight, but you need to back away from the slick talk and present yourself as being more presidential. I know you can't help yourself, but you know all they're talking about on the news right now is how you conducted yourself."

"And all we're talking about in this car is about how much you're starting to sound more like my mother every day. It's really not a good look for you, baby, and since you despise her so much, I think you may want to rethink your ways."

She hated when I compared her to my mother, but the truth was, they had a lot in common. In some ways, that was good, some ways bad. But I picked her, so, now, I had to deal with her. I gave her credit for standing by me, when need be, but Raynetta tricked me into marrying her. She knew she could never have children, and when she told me she was pregnant, I wanted to do the right thing. I was somewhat in love with her, but then there was a side of me that just wasn't ready to commit to anyone. Unfortunately, I did. Then, I found myself creeping behind her back and doing things that no married man should do. When she found out about my affairs, she made me feel guilty for betraying her. The way I saw it was, we were both at fault for the mess we created. And even though too much damage had already been done, I still needed her to stand by me through this journey. I had a certain image to portray. Being happily married was one of them.

Feeling insulted by my words, Raynetta remained silent. She refused to attend a private party with me at the White House, and as we debated the issue in the Oval Office, she tore into me.

"Don't you ever compare me to your crazy mother again." She paced the plush, wheat-colored carpeted floor right next to the presidential seal while I sat on the striped sofa that was fitting to my taste. Gold-colored leather chairs were next to the sofas that faced each other, and the same gold was on much decor around the room, including the wallpaper and silk curtains that draped from the circular windows. As Raynetta continued to rant, I massaged my forehead that started to ache.

"I am *nothing* like that woman, and do you know that she had the nerve to call and tell me what to wear tonight? Shame on her. She got her face cracked when she heard everyone paying me compliments. But no matter what other people say, it would be real nice to hear you say something nice every once in a while too."

"You look nice and thank you for representing tonight. I have no complaints about how you look, and at some point, you have to ignore my mother and stop letting her get underneath your skin."

"I can't help it. She's a thorn in my side. The only reason she hates me is because there won't be any grandchildren. There's not much that I can do about that, unless we decide to adopt."

I was in no mood to talk about this. What I wanted was to make my way to the party, but Raynetta insisted on having a pity party of her own. Thankfully, it was interrupted by a knock on the door. When I looked up, Tyler came inside. One hand was in his pocket, the other hand he used to rake through his blond hair. He was two years younger than I was, and at thirty-six years old, he could pass for a preppy young man who was fresh out of college. He was smart as a whip, had politics embedded in his brain, and came from a family where every single person had been in public office or still was. Those were several of the reasons why I chose him to be my VP. He was sharp and prepared for anything. But the way he raked his hair was always a sign that he was nervous about something.

"Are you guys attending the party or not?" he asked. "Some of the guests have started to arrive."

"I'll be there shortly, but I think that Raynetta is going to sit this one out."

"I may, then again, I may not," she snapped.

"Well, either way, I want to prepare you guys for what to expect tonight."

Tyler walked over to the Resolute desk, a desk that had been in the Oval Office since the late 1800s. He turned my laptop computer toward us, using a remote to change the screen. The first words we heard were, *"What a disgrace this president is."*

"I've never been treated that way by anyone," Senator Brassley said with fake hurt in his eyes. *"And where was the respect for us? Have you ever heard any president use that kind of language on the House floor and speak like that to the Speaker?"*

"No, I haven't," the news reporter said, adding his two cents. *"I don't know how anyone can work with that guy. He seems to be a real jerk. He's very arrogant and comes across as a narcissist. I worry about his temperament, and I'm convinced that the American people will quickly grow to regret their decision for electing another black president. Douglas Franklin was a much better candidate. He would have won the election, had it not been for our ridiculous voting laws that allow some people to vote without the proper identification."*

The entire panel went on and on about me. So did Raynetta.

"See, I told you this would happen. All the good things you talked about tonight don't even matter. They're focusing on all the negative stuff. You can pat yourself on the back for giving them another reason to hate you."

Tyler spoke up before I did. "There is nothing that Stephen can say or do to make certain people like him. Today was a good day, but let's not go to this party and indulge in talk about Senator Brassley or Stephen's critics. Keep all conversations short, especially with members of the media who will attempt to get the two of you stirred up."

"They won't be getting me stirred up because I won't be there. I'm going to take a shower; and then I plan to enjoy the comfort of my bed. I'll see you, Stephen, when the party is over."

Raynetta strutted toward the door in all of her sexiness. Her curves were perfect, her body didn't have an ounce of fat on it, and her ass was round enough to make any man's steel rise to the occasion. As beautiful as she was, I often thought about what our daughter would look like. Raynetta's hair was always so feathery, thick, and long. There was never one strand out of place, and her light skin glistened like tiny diamonds were embedded inside of it. I couldn't ask for a better-looking woman to be by my side, and I had to admit that we were a very attractive couple. But that wasn't enough. I wanted kids—a daughter or son to build on my legacy. I wondered who our son would resemble the most, but after thinking about it for so long, eventually, I pushed those thoughts to the back of my mind and lived on.

After Raynetta walked out, I stood and reached for my jacket that was hanging on a chair. I covered my crisp white shirt that tightened on my shoulders, biceps, and chest. I then secured my leather belt that felt loose around my thirty-four-inch waistline. With Secret Service in tow, I swiftly walked beside Tyler as we made our way down the corridor and into the Blue Room where many of our guests were invited to come. The room was filled to capacity. Everyone seemed indulged in heavy conversation and laughter. I spotted my mother from across the room. She always knew how to mingle, or should I say, fit in. A small crowd surrounded her, and she appeared to be speaking about something very interesting. There were also several individuals there from my administration. Many had their spouses with them, while others didn't. Some of the guests who sat with Raynetta tonight were there, as well as numerous people from the media who were invited to cover the event. I vowed that my administration would be transparent, and that the media would be granted access to everything that happened around here. But transparent I would not be. There were certain things that I wanted no one, including my wife, to know about.

I shook hands and conversed with several people who applauded my speech tonight and seemed delighted to see me. That included my mother who I finally stepped up to, giving her a hug.

"It's about time," she said with a wineglass in her hand. She giggled as she looked at the people around her. "I thought the president of the United States had already disappeared."

They laughed, but I ignored my mother's so-called sense of humor.

"How long are you planning to stay tonight?" We stepped away from the others to talk. "And you know you shouldn't be drinking any alcohol, right?"

"Well, it's not like they have cherry Kool-Aid around here. This wine will suit me just fine. Besides, I've only had one drink. That sure as heck won't send me back to AA."

"I hope not. Just be cautious and you already know why."

"I do, and I thank you for being so concerned about me. By the way, where is that conniving wife of yours? I hope she's somewhere changing those tight clothes she had on. Did you see how tight that skirt was on her big tail? That's ridiculous."

I peeked over my mother's shoulder, waving at Tyler's wife and another woman from my administration. Tyler advised me to keep all conversations short tonight, and since I didn't appreciate the route this conversation was going with my mother, I hurried to wrap things up.

"I wish you wouldn't speak of Raynetta that way because she can't help it, Mother. Her backside just happens to suit me, and it always looks very inviting in anything she puts on. Now, if you don't mind, I need to go and mingle with other people."

"I don't mind, but the only reason you married her was because of that ass. If she had brains to go with it, she'd be fine. Unfortunately, she's lacking in a very important area. A man of your caliber deserves better."

Without replying, I walked away from my mother with a slight frown on my face. I got tired of hearing her nasty comments about Raynetta, and telling my mother how I felt, over and over again, hadn't done much good. I wasn't going to allow her comments to frustrate me tonight. I felt so much better when I started conversing with several other guests.

"Do you mind if we take a picture with you, Mr. President?" said one of the wounded soldiers. "If I don't take one, my daughter will never believe I was actually here."

We all gathered to take pictures, and several others rushed over to take photos on their cell phones as well. I shook more hands, and when I spotted Tyler near the doorway that led to the Red Room, I excused myself from the people I was speaking with, making my way toward him. After several steps in his direction, a reporter reached for my arm. She was a black woman, no more than five-three or -four inches tall, but made to look taller in her silver high heels. Her long, wavy hair was pulled away from her round face and clipped in the back where much of it fell past her shoulders. Her caramel-colored skin glowed, and her doe-shaped eyes were enhanced with thick liner, extended lashes, and shimmery eyeshadow. I had seen her nightly show on MSNBC, and I was slightly taken aback by some of her negative comments about me.

"Mr. President, do you care to elaborate on your behavior tonight?" she asked. "Many people felt as if your comments, especially about Speaker Robinson, were inappropriate."

"A lot of things that I have said, done, and will continue to do, will be deemed as inappropriate. I'm not here to please Mr. Speaker, and if you care for me to elaborate more on the state of our union, then schedule an exclusive interview with me."

I proceeded to walk away, but the reporter halted my steps when she reached for my arm again.

"I would love to schedule an interview with you, but when, Mr. President? When can I interview you and your lovely wife?"

"Tomorrow. Schedule it for tomorrow."

She cocked her head back and widened her eyes, as if she was surprised. "Tomorrow? I need a little more time to plan accordingly for an exclusive interview with you. How about one day early next week?"

Giving it no thought at all, I gazed at the reporter, remaining firm in my decision. "Tomorrow. If not then, I'll make the opportunity available to someone else."

I walked away, again, only to hear her say, "Thank you, Mr. President. I'll see you tomorrow. But I need to know one thing. Will any questions be off-limits?"

"No," I said without turning around. "Your show, your call."

I stopped to speak to the man who had lost his daughter to gun violence. After promising him that I would do everything in my power to change our gun laws, we departed. I finally caught up with Tyler who was standing next to my chief of staff, Andrew McAllister. He was also one of my advisors; he managed my schedule and decided who was appropriate for me to meet with. Andrew was sharp-minded like Tyler was, but he wasn't as clean-cut.

He dressed rather slouchy, and his too big shirts always gathered outside of his slacks. The suspenders he wore never matched anything, and his dark-brown hair always looked as if he slicked it down with grease.

"Chanel Hamilton," I said, extending my hand to Andrew's, shaking it. "I'm doing a live and exclusive interview with her tomorrow night. Find out what you can about her, relay her interviewing style to me, and tell me what to expect."

"I can tell you what to expect without doing any research," Tyler said. "She's going to hit you with a bunch of got'cha questions, and she'll attack you like a pit bull in a skirt. I don't recommend that you conduct your first exclusive interview with her, and as a matter of fact, I'm totally against it."

"I agree," Andrew added. "Especially not after what happened tonight. Allow news about your State of the Union Address to spin for about another 24 to 48 hours. Then, I'll schedule an interview with you and Mr. Davidson on CNN."

"Sorry, but no thanks." I shot down their recommendations. "I prefer to interview with Ms. Hamilton, tomorrow night."

Andrew held out his hands, pleading with me. "I mean, gosh, Stephen, what am I being paid for if you refuse to listen to my advice? I have my reasons for doing things, and we all know that Chanel Hamilton is not that good at what she does. Mr. Davidson is my final choice."

"She may not be good at what she does, but her show gets good ratings. Numerous people who I want to reach watch her, and they think she is as good as it gets."

"I beg to differ, but a lot of people who you'll need to impress watch CNN."

"No matter what news channel I appear on, they'll all tune in. And there is only one person I'm interested in impressing tomorrow night. By now, you should know who she is."

We all turned our heads to look at Chanel Hamilton. She was speaking to my mother, and when they pivoted to look in my direction, I responded with a nod, then walked off to converse with other guests.

Later that night, I went to the Master Bedroom where Raynetta lay sound asleep in nothing but her silky skin. The canopy bed she lay in was draped with white sheer fabric. Part of the thick comforter was tucked between her legs. The room had a slight chill, so I folded the comforter over her body, covering it. I then planted a soft kiss on her forehead and quietly closed the door behind me.

People often wondered where presidents slept, and I'd be the first to admit that it wasn't often in this room. The simplicity of it didn't do much for me, and I guess the most intriguing thing about it was the historic nature of it. Besides that, it wasn't like there was much action happening between Raynetta and me, so many of my nights were spent in the Oval Office where I lay back on the sofa and fell asleep while meditating or listening to jazz music thump through the speakers. That was where I'd spent the night, and by six o'clock in the morning, my prayers had gone up, workout was done, and I was in the shower, preparing myself for a new day.

With my eyes closed and soapy suds and water rushing down my milk-chocolate skin, I was in deep thought. Reality was starting to kick in, and after what had transpired on Capitol Hill last night, I predicted that I had my work cut out for me. According to my schedule, that was also posted online, I had a ten o'clock meeting with a few members from my administration, a one o'clock luncheon with several members of Congress, a two-thirty meeting with my secretary of Defense, and a five o'clock brief meeting with the VP. What wasn't on my schedule was my early-morning briefing, my meeting with the press, and my interview with Chanel Hamilton. My press secretary, Sam Dotson, insisted that it would be best if I handled questions from the media today regarding my State of the Union Address that had many people up in arms. So, dressed in my navy silk suit and black leather shoes, I headed back to the Oval Office. My cologne wafted through the corridor, and people parted like water in the Red Sea as they stepped aside and watched me. Like always, Secret Service was close by, and so was Tyler. He met me right at the Oval Office doors, and we went inside for an early-morning briefing provided by the director of National Intelligence.

For some, to hear the kind of shit that was going on around the world, as well as within our own country, it could be depressing. There were times when I cringed, flinched, and even scratched my head as I listened in to the top secret information. I thanked the director for his time, and right after he left, so did Tyler. I sat at the Resolute desk, right between the American flag and the Presidential flag, thinking about how troublesome things had gotten. My hands swayed across the desk, and just for a moment, I wanted to make sure this was no dream. I started to read several letters from the American people that Andrew classified as highly important. I smiled at a few, laughed at others, and agreed with many. But right as I was reading a letter from an eleven-year-old girl who had been battling cancer, there was a knock at the door. I lifted my head and in walked Raynetta, dressed in a cream-colored pantsuit.

"I was surprised that you didn't wake me last night," she said. "I had been waiting on you all night, as I always do."

"By the time I got to the room, you had fallen asleep. I came here to get a little work done, and I fell asleep on the sofa."

"That's what you always say. Before I get my day started, is there anything important that I should know about? I hate to be out there mingling with people and don't have answers."

"Get used to it, because I can't share everything with you. The only thing you need to know about is our interview this evening with Chanel Hamilton. I'm not sure how busy your schedule is today, but be here no later than six."

Her mouth opened wide. "Interview? Why can't you conduct the interview alone? I hate being in front of the camera like that, because I very well may say the wrong thing."

"You won't, especially when you already know the protocol. When I want you to stay silent, I'll kiss the back of your hand. When you want me to elaborate more, pat my leg. When I want you to add more to the conversation, I'll wink. And when either of us gets bored with the interview, we're supposed to pat our feet on the floor."

Raynetta rolled her eyes, then sighed. "I don't know what you've gotten us into, but I sure hope it's all worth it. Have a great day, and try your best not to hurt anybody."

"I won't, but I'm sure you will."

Raynetta chuckled a bit as she left my office, closing the door behind her. I continued to read the letter; it truly broke my heart. Many people thought that the presidency enabled me to play God. In no way could I ever fill His shoes, but I intended to do my best, even with my many flaws. Thinking of my flaws, I rubbed my hairless, smooth face that had been smacked with aftershave. My hazel eyes shifted to my cell phone that sat near the edge of my desk. Vera Walton, a woman I had met while on the campaign trail, had been texting me on my private phone. She had been named Teacher of the Year, and many would say that her reputation was stellar. We had hooked up a few times, but when I became president, I backed away from her. Hadn't replied to one single message, and in her last text message she wasn't exactly happy about it. She referred to me as a phony-ass Negro and threatened that the world would soon know what I was all about. I never suspected that my encounter with her would get out of hand, but if things got too hectic on that end, she would be dealt with.

Several minutes after noon, I followed Sam to the Press Briefing Room where everyone stood as I entered. The room was somewhat narrow, but was packed wall-to-wall with reporters who came to get updates, question me, report, and listen to what I had to say. With Sam standing behind me, I stepped up to the podium with a serious expression on my face. The media wasn't always nice to us around here, but this time, I was there to speak for myself instead of allowing Sam to do it.

"Good afternoon, everyone. I'm sure that many of you may have questions about my State of the Union Address to Congress and to the American people, but please make your questions brief and precise. I do have a busy schedule today, so my time with the press is limited. Besides, I'm sure that many of your questions will be answered tonight during my exclusive interview with Chanel Hamilton. Be sure to tune in—I expect it to be interesting."

I made a gesture to a reporter in the front row who anxiously waved his hand while I was speaking.

"Thank you, Mr. President. I watched your State of the Union Address last night, and in conjunction with many Americans, I thought you sounded a bit harsh toward members of Congress. While we've certainly had our problems with them, to suggest that they put away their cell phones was a bit much, don't you think?"

"At the end of the day, it all boils down to a respect thing. And if you or anyone else thinks that my request was too harsh, then you're in for a rude awakening because I will require that all members of Congress do way more than that. I get that—"

"Bu . . . but you're not paying their salaries. The American people are. How can you put forth such demands and expect for them to play by your rules?"

"They will do so, and you're about to play by my rules too. Do not interrupt me while I'm speaking. Doing so will get you ignored."

I turned to my right, calling on another reporter. Appearing nervous, she stood and cleared her throat.

"Mr. President, first let me say that I enjoyed your speech last night. But why call Senator Brassley a f-ing coward and go after the Speaker? You said it was a joke, but there seems to be much tension between you and Speaker Robinson. Is there, and if so, how do you expect to work with him in order to get things done?"

"This is the last question that I will answer about my tone, so here is my answer. Get used to it and don't expect for me to bite my tongue. I will work with anyone who works with me. If they choose not to, and prefer to cause more gridlock on Capitol Hill, then I'm going to roll right over them. The American people expect me to get things done while I'm here. I'm not going to waste time with idiots who have issues with the color of my skin, and if you've listened to Speaker Robinson's comments about me, then you know why our relationship is what it is."

She quickly followed up, "Are you insinuating that he's a racist?"

"I have my own opinions. Make yours based on facts and common sense."

More hands waved in the air. My eyes shifted across the room to another reporter who stood to address me.

"Mr. Jefferson," he said, but I quickly interrupted him.

"Again, for future references, and just so we're all on the same page, please address me as President Stephen C. Jefferson, Mr. President, or President of the United States. Thank you."

The reporter straightened his black-framed glasses, then wiped a sheen of sweat from his forehead. "I apologize, sir, but, uh—"

"No, not sir, but *Mr. President*. Next time, come better prepared and I'll answer your question when you're ready. You seem flustered so I'm moving on."

Many members of the press appeared shocked by my bluntness. But the way I saw it was like this. From day one, people needed to know that I wasn't going to be treated unfairly. I wasn't going to allow inappropriate things to be said about me or the ones I loved. I intended to stand up to ridiculous comments that were said by professionals who should know better. And even though some people felt as if the president should always take the high road, I felt differently. Every man needed to defend himself. I had no intentions of sitting back and being bullied by people whose ultimate goal was to break me.

I had already answered several more questions from *some* reporters who acted as if they had sense. I called on one final reporter before wrapping this up.

"President Jackson, I mean Jefferson, you touched on this briefly in your speech last night, but do you have more specific plans on what to do about ISIS? Over the years, this terror group has expanded. I would like to know how you intend to go after their leaders and put an end to their organization."

I started to walk away from the podium after he referred to me as President Jackson, but since it was the last question, what the hell?

"In closing today, I really wish that all members of the press, who should be privileged to be here today, would do your homework and come prepared with informative questions that the American people deserve answers to. I've wasted time answering 16 out of 20 questions that weren't even relevant to issues that really matter. ISIS is, indeed, a threat. We are putting forth every effort to shut them down. It wouldn't be wise for me to provide specificities, because many of the things we discuss are top secret and shouldn't be conveyed to the world. It is my—"

"But you said that your administration would be transparent, didn't you?"

A hard stare was given to the reporter who interrupted me. I blinked, then lifted my hand in the air. "Good day, everyone. Until next time."

I walked away, ignoring a bunch of more questions that were being fired at me. And when Sam and I were away from everyone else, he reached out to shake my hand.

"Good job, Mr. President. I love your style, and I hope that I can do as well as you did in there."

"You will. Trust me, you will. But sometime today, or tomorrow, let me know who the female reporter was in row seven, seat two."

Sam halted his steps, turning to me with a puzzled look on his face. "That's uh, uh, I can't remember her name. But is there a reason why you want to know her name? Did she offend you?"

"No, nothing like that. I just want to have it for my own personal reasons, that's all."

He nodded, then proceeded down the corridor with me. I couldn't help but to think about how messy things were about to get.

3

First Lady Raynetta Jefferson

As hostess of the White House, I had a busy day. I was in attendance at several social events that I worked with my staff on to put together. Then I joined some of the children who were here to tour the facility. I didn't mind keeping myself busy, and I made sure that my staff kept my schedule as full as possible. That way, I wouldn't get in Stephen's way. I could be a real B at times, but, at least, I knew it. Then there were times when I just didn't want to be bothered. Like tonight, with this interview that I wasn't looking forward to. We had already put ourselves out there for the American people. What else did they need to know about us? What else did Stephen have to say, and how many questions did he need to answer? I almost changed my mind about joining him, but I felt much better after I ate something. The chef prepared chicken and rice for me. It was seasoned to perfection, and I topped it off with dessert, which was a slice of apple pie.

I left the kitchen and returned to the Master Bedroom, where my closet was. It was a tiny closet, and many of my clothes and shoes had to be put in another room. I wanted to look real nice tonight, so I opted for a light-blue dress with rhinestones around the neckline. My jet-black hair was parted through the middle, and wavy curls fell along the sides of my face. I didn't wear any jewelry, aside from my wedding ring. My black heels gave me more height, and I sprayed on a dash of sweet perfume before joining my husband in the White House Family Room.

When I arrived, three cameramen were already there. Part of the room was being staged for the interview and the news reporter who was going to conduct the interview stood by the fireplace, talking to my assistant. I had watched the reporter on TV before, and I found myself turning the channel because of her snippy attitude. But there she was, looking dolled up and ready to go. The short red dress she wore melted on her curves and revealed her shapely legs that were bare. Like always, her hair was pulled away from her face and curls flowed down her back. I was surprised by how beautiful she was in person, but her looks didn't intimidate me one bit. I strutted over to her with my hand extended and a welcoming smile on my face.

"Hello, Ms. Hamilton," I said. "How are you?"

Within a few seconds, the direction of her eyes traveled from the tips of my shoes to the top of my head. Jealousy was visible in her eyes, and fakeness was upon us. I was gifted at reading people so well. And, quite frankly, that was one darn good gift to have, especially in a place like the White House.

"I'm doing well, Mrs. Jefferson. Thanks for asking, and I hope you're ready to get started. My cameramen are almost done. I was just speaking to your assistant about certain issues you may not want to discuss. I spoke to the president yesterday; he set no limitations on what I can ask. I want to clear that with you as well."

"Whatever he says goes. We're an open book, but I hope that your questions revolve more around things that may be beneficial to the American people, instead of personal questions that revolve around us."

"There will be a mixture." She looked at her watch. "Do you know when we can expect the president to join us?"

"I'm here," Stephen said, swiftly coming through the door, looking fabulous as ever. He damn sure took my breath away, and from the way Ms. Hamilton's eyes popped out of their sockets, I could tell that her horny little self was pretty impressed too.

His masculine cologne followed him into the room, and tailored suits, along with the seriousness in his eyes, always made him look ready for the cover of *GQ* magazine. With his clothes off, *Playgirl* magazine would be more fitting.

"I know I'm a few minutes late, but never too late," he said.

His eyes were locked on Ms. Hamilton. If anyone could read my husband, it was me. There was lust trapped in his eyes, and whenever he double licked his lips, it was an indication that he was ready to taste something. Possibly those loud red lips of hers that were covered with gloss. I had to sway his attention in my direction, and I did so when I cleared my throat. He spoke to everyone else in the room, then reached for my hand and escorted me over to two chairs that faced Ms. Hamilton's chair.

"Mr. President, we should be ready in five, no more than ten minutes," the cameraman said. "I'll give a two-minute warning, and then a countdown."

After we took our seats, Ms. Hamilton joined us. She crossed her legs, and while sitting with excellent posture, she studied a few notes. Stephen leaned in close to me, but his very narrow eyes were zoned in Ms. Hamilton's direction. He was slightly slumped in the chair, with his index finger resting along the side of his face. My eyes traveled to his crotch area where I noticed an enlarged muscle that wasn't there before. I mean, what in the hell was he thinking about? I was so sure that the other individuals in the room witnessed the hungry look in his eyes, and when I glanced at my assistant, she almost looked speechless.

"Excuse me, Ms. Hamilton," I said, getting her attention. "Can you tell me how long you anticipate this interview will be?"

My question snapped Stephen out of his trance. He sat up straight, then crossed one of his legs over the other.

"Chanel," she said. "Please call me Chanel, especially during the interview. It will probably last for about forty-five minutes or so, depending on the length of your responses. There will be no commercial interruptions, and we're going to roll this straight through."

I looked at Stephen. His eyes were fixed on her lips as she spoke. "Keep your comments brief and to the point," I said to him. "The faster we wrap this up, the better."

"I agree," he said, then sat up straight and tugged at his jacket.

The cameraman gave the two-minute warning, and shortly thereafter, he lifted his fingers, counting down from five. The numbers also appeared on the screen in front of us, and when zero flashed, the screen was replaced with Chanel's beautiful face.

"Good evening," she said, presenting a pleasant smile as she looked directly at the camera. "Thanks for joining us. I have the pleasure of sitting here tonight with the first lady, and president of the United States, Stephen Carter Jefferson. Much has been said about our new president, but I look forward to delving into a conversation that will help us all better understand the mission of our new commander in chief. We all want to know how he intends to work with a very difficult Congress, and then we'll discuss some more personal issues that plagued him while on the campaign trail. So thank you both for inviting me to come here. I was totally shocked by the invite, Mr. President, but very ecstatic that you chose me to conduct your first exclusive interview."

This was breaking news already. I didn't know Stephen had chosen her to do this. I didn't have to wonder why, and from the hunger in his eyes, it was obvious. I grinned at him without showing teeth. My hands were clenched together, and I had already begun to tap my foot on the floor as a gesture to hurry this interview the hell up. He looked straight-ahead at Chanel, giving her his undivided attention.

"I've seen you on the news before and I applaud your style," he said. "Couldn't think of a better person to conduct my first interview, and no offense to you, but I don't mind starting off soft, then going hard."

WTF! My eyes bugged from his comment, but when Chanel giggled, so did I. I guess both of our minds were in the gutter, then again, Stephen's mind was there too.

"Hey," Chanel said, jokingly, "just because I'm a woman, that doesn't mean I won't go hard on you, Mr. President. There are plenty of questions that the American people still have, and in such a short period of time, you've caused quite a stir. Your performance in the Press Briefing Room today has been played over and over again on TV. What, exactly, are you trying to prove, and do you think that kind of tone is going to help you in any way?"

"If you had an opportunity to watch my press conference from earlier, you would know that it shouldn't be referred to as a performance. It was what I consider reality. I intend to keep it real around here, and I'm not here to kiss ass or make a whole lot of friends. Nothing or no one will stand in the way of me doing the job the people elected me to do. I can't express that enough, and the only thing that I am out to prove is things can and will get done when we put aside all of the unnecessary rhetoric and partisan bickering, and get serious with the business of the American people."

"Many presidents have said some of the same things before. What makes you so different? Why do you think it's going to be easy for Republicans to work with you?"

"I'm not like any other president that we've had before. And all I can say to you is sit back, watch, learn something, and pay attention."

Seemingly caught off guard, she played it off by chuckling a little. "Ahh, okay. But, uh, what do you say to reporters like Austin College, and others, who felt kind of dissed by you today? Would you like to use this opportunity to apologize to them?"

"No. But what I will say to all of them is get my name, as well as my title, right, when using it."

Looking more uncomfortable, Chanel shifted in her chair. She went on to ask Stephen three more questions about his performance today. I could sense that he was getting irritated with her. His tone had gone up a notch. I hoped that she noticed the warning and moved on.

"Thus far," Stephen said, bluntly, "I'm not feeling the purpose for this interview. I'm going to advise you to get to the real questions or turn those cameras off so I can go get some rest with my lovely wife."

At that point, my teeth started to show. I smiled harder, especially when he winked at me. That was my cue to chime in.

"I know exactly what my husband is saying, Chanel, and our time is very valuable. We all have to get serious about the challenges that face our nation. My husband's so-called performance in the Press Briefing Room should not be breaking news. Poverty is on the rise, many of our children are going to bed hungry, our country is close to being at war, infrastructure is a big concern, and many Americans are still without jobs. There are so many things that we need to focus on, and during my husband's term, we're going to do whatever we can to make this world a better place."

"We do have our issues, no doubt. But speaking of children, when are the two of you planning to have some? Now that the election is over, are the two of you planning to get started, or is it true that you are unable to conceive?"

Stephen lifted my hand and planted a soft kiss on the back of it. That was my cue to stay silent and allow him to take charge.

"All of those reports that you heard were false. We have talked about having children, but right now, we don't see where a child can fit into our busy schedules. Since my father wasn't there for me, it is extremely important for me to give my children all of the attention he or she may need. As president, I wouldn't be able to do that. Raynetta would be an awesome mother, but she too is incapable of devoting her time to a baby right now. Whenever we're ready, we will make the announcement. But I can assure you that it won't be anytime soon."

"But other presidents and first ladies before you have managed to juggle work and family. There has to be a balance, and I don't think any family has ever lived in the White House without children."

"Again, I would ask that you do your homework, because, to my recollection, there were, at least, five presidents who resided here without children. George Washington, James Polk, Warren Harding, James Buchanan, and Andrew Jackson. I'm surprised that a smart woman such as yourself didn't know that."

Chanel swallowed, then went on to ask Stephen several questions about gun control, women's health, race relations, and foreign policy. That was an easy area for any new president to trip up on, but he was thorough and knew the subject well. I guess all of those nights he'd spent in the Oval Office studying had paid off.

"Well, that almost sums it up," Chanel said. "But I am curious to know two more things. First, what are your thoughts about our first black president?"

"Outstanding man who faced a great deal of unfortunate opposition, but was still able to move his agenda forward and improve this country in a major way. History will recognize him as one of the greatest presidents ever. I can only hope that I am as successful as he was, even with all of my imperfections."

"Imperfections? Care to elaborate?"

"Something that we all have, including you."

"Yes, I do, but okay, Mr. President. One last, fun question. You were recently named one of the sexiest men alive. How does that make you feel, and Raynetta, feel free to chime in too? How do you feel about your husband having that status?"

I jumped right in before he did. "Sexy can be defined in many different ways. I don't know who created such a list, but I would definitely like to have a conversation with the woman, or man, who can make that judgment, based on his outside, not his inside. Nonetheless, he is very sexy and is also married to a sexy woman."

"That she is," Stephen said. "And even though I'm flattered, being sexy isn't going to get the job done that I came here to do."

"No, it won't, and only time will tell if you will be successful." She gazed at Stephen, then shifted her eyes to me. "This has been fun. I hope we get a chance to do this again, and thanks, again, for allowing me this opportunity."

We both shook her hand, and when the cameras turned off, I jumped up from my chair, caught that bitch by surprise, and let her have it.

"I didn't appreciate your question about Stephen and I having children. You know good and well that I've had some issues. I don't care to discuss why, and to be frank, it's none of your damn business."

Without saying anything else, I marched out of the room, leaving Stephen and my assistant behind. Minutes later, he came to the bedroom, where I had already taken off my clothes and gotten in bed.

"Wow," he said, standing next to me. "I'm surprised you let her get underneath your skin like that. Usually, you're more in control of yourself. I really don't think that was a wise move for you."

"And it wouldn't be a wise *move* for you either, if you know what I mean. If I had a condom, I would have passed it to you on live TV. You may as well had stripped her naked right in front of me and screwed her brains out. I know that there are times when you can't seem to keep that thing of yours under control, but by all means, Stephen, try your best to show me a little respect."

"Yeah, well, you know how I am, Raynetta. I'm the worst man you could have ever married, and you've always had plenty of good options."

"As a matter of fact, I do have options, as well as choices. So do you, and if you intend to hold the highest office in the land, and chase ass while doing it, that's up to you. Eventually, you'll go down. But just so you know, I won't be going down with you."

Stephen responded with a shrug. He removed his jacket, then placed it on the back of a chair. After glancing at his watch, he sucked in a deep breath, then released it.

"I'm not ready to turn in yet. Besides, I have some work to do. See you in the morning, and I hope you get some rest."

I didn't bother to reply. I turned sideways in bed, then picked up a romance novel that was already on the nightstand. For the next hour or so, I indulged myself.

4

President of the United States, Stephen C. Jefferson

Tyler and I sat in the Oval Office, watching the media go crazy over my interview tonight with Chanel Hamilton. Snippets that didn't follow through on my whole conversation were played, and everyone from politicians to panels weighed in.

"You sure do know how to turn up the heat," Tyler said, smiling and loving every minute of what was going on. "I don't think I've ever seen anything like it."

"Yes, you have. It's called foolishness, and it's been going on for years."

He laughed, then plopped down on the sofa and yawned. "You may be on to something, but switching the subject, I need to step away for the weekend and go see about my father. He's back in the hospital. My mother says he's not doing well."

"If that's the case, why wait until tomorrow? Why not leave now?"

"Because I wanted to make sure everything was squared away with you and your first exclusive interview. You've had a long day, and I can assure you that things won't let up around here."

"I don't expect for them to, but I do expect for you to go see about your father. Leave now, and be sure to call and let me know how he's doing."

Tyler nodded, then stood to leave. He shook my hand before making his way to the door.

"Before you go," I said, halting his steps, "stop by Andrew's office and tell him I need to see him right away. If he's not in there, shoot me a text."

"Will do, and enjoy the rest of your evening."

"You too."

This time, I walked over to the sofa and sat. My feet were propped on the table in front of me, and my hands were clenched together behind my head. Minutes later, there was a knock at the door before Andrew came in.

"Is everything okay?" he said, nervously wringing his hands together. "Tyler sounded like something was important."

"No, everything is fine. Come have a seat and relax."

Andrew flat-footedly walked into the room and sat on the sofa across from me. "What can I do for you, Mr. President?"

"Two things. I need a new private cell phone, and the other phone needs to be disconnected. I also need for you to get Chanel Hamilton here tonight. I had some issues with our interview, and I want to speak to her, in private, about my concerns."

"She was kind of nasty toward you in that interview, but you and the first lady handled yourselves well. The feedback is definitely in your favor, and the American people remain on your side."

"That's good to know, but I have so much on my mind that I need to say to her. More than anything, I want to make sure that nothing like that ever happens again."

As usual, Andrew got on it right away and honored my request. And almost forty-five minutes later, while I stood by one of the windows looking out, my senior secret service agent, Ben Harrisburg, entered my office. Chanel followed closely behind him, looking like a high school girl who was in deep trouble.

"Thank you," I said to Ben. "Shut the door behind you and allow no one to enter my office."

Giving no response, he exited. I walked around my desk and invited Chanel to have a seat. She walked slowly to one of the chairs, then crossed her legs after taking a seat.

"I'm not sure what this is all about, Mr. President, but please allow me to apologize for upsetting your wife. I didn't know that she had issues with having children, and had I known for sure, I would have scratched that question from my list."

"Listen, I'm going to say this one time and one time only. You don't have to pretend with me. I would appreciate if you wouldn't lie to me either. Many insiders, including you, know my wife's history and are well aware of why she's unable to have children. The horrific rape she endured years ago was quite painful for her, and she has always had a difficult time talking about what happened to her as a teenager. I was surprised that you made a decision to venture there tonight, and, quite frankly, I'm disappointed. I had more respect for you than I do for some of the other journalists. That's why I gave you the opportunity to do the interview. While I do think that it went well, I do believe that there was a major misstep on your behalf."

A shameful look washed across her face. "I agree, and I deeply apologize. Sometimes I get caught up in the moment and can't help myself. All journalists look for a story line that makes people crave for more information. I saw an opportunity and took it. I don't mind apologizing to your wife, and the next time I see her, I most certainly will."

"Please do. And just so you know, there won't be a next time. I will never allow you to interview me, or her, again. I will listen to my advisors and seek someone who has less fire in their eyes and a bit more experience."

Chanel's eyes grew wide. She looked taken aback by my comments, as well as hurt. "Mr. President, my apology was very sincere. I've worked as a journalist for almost ten years, and I assure you that I am proficient at what I do."

I shrugged. "Proficient, maybe. Completely professional, not always."

"Different words, with similar meanings."

"Depends on who you ask."

"Let's ask the dictionary. Do you have one?"

"As a matter of fact, I do."

I walked over to the built-in bookshelf and removed a dictionary that was placed up high. I tossed it to Chanel, already knowing that the meaning of both words were, indeed, similar. She opened the dictionary and started to read the definition.

"Proficient," she said with her finger scrolling the words in the book. "Competent or skilled in doing or using something. Well advanced, may I add, and the synonyms are: skilled, skillful, expert, experienced, blah blah blah, and professional. So, there you have it, Mr. President. You were wrong, I was right."

"Soooooo, let me get this straight." I walked toward her, stopping only a few feet away. "Competent or skilled in doing or using something, huh? Does that apply strictly to a certain profession or do other things apply as well?"

She slowly closed the dictionary, then swallowed hard. "This dictionary is very limited, but I'm sure that one doesn't have to be in a certain profession to be skilled or competent at what they do or use. They could be competent and skilled at doing or using anything, right?"

"Could be, but would you like to provide me with some more examples?"

"I would, but I think that your wife, the first lady, would have serious problems with that."

I shrugged again, watching as she nervously stood in front of me. In an attempt to cover more of her pretty legs, she pulled on the bottom half of her dress to lower it by a few inches.

"She may have a problem with it, but then again, maybe not."

"Well, I have a problem with it, and I . . . I think I'd better go."

Without hesitating, I led the way to the door.

"Wait a minute," she said, causing me to stop dead in my tracks and turn around. "Wha . . . What would make you think that your wife wouldn't have a problem with me showing you examples of how skilled and competent I may be at using something?"

"Because, in her heart, she believes that no one is more competent at doing anything better than her."

"She may be wrong about that."

"I prefer that you show me how wrong she may be, not tell me."

Chanel stepped forward and proceeded to show me by pressing her body against mine. She looked up at me, puckering for a kiss. I slightly lowered my head, and within seconds, we were engaged in an intense lip-lock that caused our hands to roam. I caressed her shapely ass with my hands while she gently massaged my rising muscle, sampling it. It was rock-solid hard and expanded more with her touch.

"Mmmm," she moaned as I grinded a little while holding her close to me. "This," she backed her mouth away from mine, "this could get real, real ugly. Would you recommend that we quit while we're still ahead?"

I was about to answer, but when the door flew open, we both snapped our heads to the side. I was surprised to see my mother standing there, squeezing her chest as if she was in severe pain.

"Lord Jesus, noooo," she shouted. "Talk about being in the wrong place at the wrong time! Please tell me there is something wrong with my eyes."

With a frown on my face, I released the gentle hold I had on Chanel's ass. She jumped away from me like I was contagious. The hump in my pants was still visible, and when my mother looked at it, she shielded her eyes with her hand.

"Jesus be a fence right now," she cried out. "I need you to stand between me and my son, before I reach out and knock the hell out of him."

I ignored her and rushed past her to see where in the hell was Secret Service. When I yanked on the door, I saw Ben casually strolling down the corridor, drinking a soda. He sped up his pace after he saw me standing with a twisted face.

"Is everything okay, Mr. President?" he asked. "I told Oscar to stay here while I went to go get a soda. Where did he go?"

"Not sure, but I gave an order, and you didn't follow it. I need your resignation letter by tomorrow, and you can tell Oscar that I need his too. If you motherfuckers can't protect me from my own mother, then you don't deserve to be working here."

I went back into my office and slammed the door. My mother was saying something crazy to Chanel, but I quickly silenced her when I asked both of them to exit.

"Not tonight, Mama, and, Chanel, we'll talk soon."

She didn't hesitate to leave, but my mother stood with her mouth wide open, gazing at me with a twitching left eye.

"Don't you dare start this mess up in here, Stephen. I came here to congratulate you on how well you handled that interview this evening. I didn't expect to come here and find you dancing and doing the nasty with the devil. That woman is worse than the one upstairs in your bedroom. Do you not have any sense at all?"

"Mama, I'm going to say this to you one more time before I call Secret Service to get you out of here. Not tonight. Not tomorrow either, and please don't view this as disrespect."

She pouted and put her hand on her hip. "How else am I supposed to view it? You're threatening to throw me out of here—after all that I've done for you?"

I walked back to the door, opening it. Ben wasn't there, but another agent had taken his place.

"My mother needs to find her way to the front door. Please see to it that she gets in her car and makes it home safely."

The agent entered the office, and when he reached for my mother's arm, she snatched it away from him.

"Don't touch me!" she shouted. "I'm leaving, but I *will* be back. I'm not done talking to you yet, and after tonight, we have a lot to discuss."

Maybe so, but that conversation wasn't going to take place tonight. After she left, I sat back on the sofa and dropped my head back, closed my eyes, and thought about many ways that I could show Chanel how competent and skilled I really was.

The following morning, I was in the workout room with Andrew who badly needed to exercise. His T-shirt barely covered his potbelly; sweat poured down his red face as we jogged side by side on different treadmills. My press secretary, Sam, took the easy route today. He was lifting tiny weights while watching the news.

"Your new phone and the numbers you requested to be locked in will arrive before eight o'clock this morning," Andrew said, unable to catch his breath. "Also, the other phone has been disconnected. I ordered a new phone for the first lady as well. She complained about not being able to hear clearly on her phone."

"That's fine, and thanks for taking care of that for me. You did have Chanel Hamilton's phone number locked in, didn't you?"

"Yes, sir. All of the numbers you requested are locked in."

He pushed a button to lower the elevation level on the treadmill.

"I don't know how you do this every morning," he huffed. "I haven't had a physique like yours since . . . since never. And I've seen you eat some fatty foods. What do you do? Jog in your sleep?"

I laughed, but kept jogging with my shirt off and basketball shorts hanging at my waist. My all-black Jordans were more than comfortable, even though they were somewhat worn.

"I do eat fatty foods, but I also take good care of my temple. If you're going to be advising me around here for the next several years, I want you in good shape. It's important to be healthy. Helps us live longer lives, and your health is important to me too. So crank up the treadmill again and let's get finished."

Sam heard me talking to Andrew about how important it was to stay fit. He needed some work too and tried to make a quick exit before I got to him.

"Fifteen more minutes, Sam," I said, slowing down on the treadmill. "Plus, before you go, I need to know if you obtained that information for me."

He nodded as he walked up to me. "Yes, I did. I forgot to tell you. The reporter you asked about, her name is Michelle Peoples. She's been a reporter for the past six years, has three children and a husband whom she doesn't know is on the down low. Her parents have been married for almost thirty-five years, and she has two sisters who work for the government. I can get more information about her, if you would like for me to."

I stopped the treadmill, then reached for a towel to wipe sweat from my face. My initial thought . . . too many additional headaches so she was scratched.

"That won't be necessary," I said. "All I wanted to know was her name, just in case I needed to recommend someone else for an interview."

"I see. I'll let you know which reporters I think are easier to connect with, but first, I need to get a good feel for them. Some of them ask a whole lot of questions, and you, Mr. President, are fueling them and giving them much to work with."

"Yes, I am, but that's not a bad thing. And if you can't handle yourself in the briefing room, let me know. Every time I see you, you look to be sweating bullets. Always dabbing your wet forehead, taking deep breaths, and fidgeting. If you're going to represent me, you need to gain some confidence. I like you, Sam, a lot, but I don't have time to come in there and do your job for you every day."

Sam looked as if his feelings were bruised. I didn't mean to hurt his feelings, but he was out there speaking for me. He needed a backbone. If things didn't get better, he would be reassigned elsewhere.

"I totally understand your concerns, sir. I'm working on it. Allow me a little more time to get familiar with the flow of things."

"Will do. Feel free to review my notes on your desk. If you have any questions or concerns, let me know."

Sam exited, leaving me alone with the slacker. Andrew had gotten off the treadmill, and stood on the mat to watch TV.

"All they talk about is you, Mr. President. I'm not sure if that's a good thing or a bad thing, especially since I never hear them speaking about the vice president."

"That's because their issues are with me, not with him. I hear them speaking about him, but not much."

"Not much at all, which makes me wonder why. I hope I'm not out of line by asking if you trust him. Do you?"

I didn't hesitate to answer. "No."

"Do you trust me?"

"No."

"Why not?"

"The truth is, I don't trust anyone. In an environment like this, trust can get you hurt, disappoint you, or make you want to kill somebody for betraying you. I learned that from the streets of St. Louis, so therefore, words like 'trust' are left out of my vocabulary."

Andrew appeared shocked by my answer. He slowly nodded, then wiped his wet face with his T-shirt.

"I know that's how you feel, but speaking for myself, you can trust me. I have no reason, whatsoever, to betray you, and as a matter of fact, I've always admired the heck out of you. You're the kind of man this country needs. I'm behind you every step of the way. I'll always be honest and upfront with you, and if you ever don't like or appreciate my advice, feel free to tell me to go to hell. I promise I won't take it personal."

"Good, Andrew. Go to hell with that speech, and no matter what you say, I'll never trust yo' ass."

We both laughed and spent the next thirty minutes or so finishing our workout and talking.

In less than an hour, I had showered, changed, and prepared myself to have breakfast with Raynetta who sat across the table from me, still bitter about the interview. Her face was tight, and without a drop of makeup on, she looked real pale.

"Did you sleep well?" I asked.

"As a matter of fact, I didn't. I tossed and turned all night, thinking of a whole lot of other stuff I should have said to Chanel for crossing the line. But you handled everything for me, didn't you?"

She evil-eyed me from across the table while sipping from a glass of orange juice.

"Yes, I did. Handled it like I always do."

"I wouldn't go that far, but I did appreciate your reply to her. We are two very busy individuals, especially now. But at some point, I think it may be good for us to adopt."

There she goes venturing down this road again. I told her before that I didn't want to adopt. I wanted my own children, but that wasn't going to happen.

"Adoption doesn't work for me. Maybe one day I will change my mind, but please don't get your hopes up."

"I never do, Stephen. Besides, you're the one running this show, right?"

"As long as you know, that's all that matters."

"What I do know is, if you're running this show, you'd better call your mother and tell her to stop worrying me about what I should be wearing as the first lady. I think she sits at home all day, just to watch me on TV and see what I'm wearing. I'm going to blow her away when I attend the next important function with my fur coat on in seventy-degree weather. That'll give her something to talk about, as well as the media."

I didn't bother to comment because I felt that Raynetta was pushing for an argument this morning. I quickly downed my coffee, told her to have a good day, and then got up from the table. I had another long day ahead of me . . . hours and hours of meetings and plenty of conversations. On my way back from the Pentagon, I started getting numerous calls and text messages about what Raynetta had worn to an outdoor function at the White House.

"Is she okay?" Andrew asked, sounding concerned. "She had on a long fur coat with a wool suit underneath it. It was warm outside today, and she . . ."

I sure as hell didn't take her comment from earlier serious, and I was sure she wore that mess to tick off my mother. Maybe even me too.

"She's fine. I'll talk to her when I get there."

The second Andrew started to speak again, my mother's number flashed across the screen. I didn't feel good about having her removed from my office, so I told Andrew I would check-in later.

"Yes, Mama," I said, answering her call.

"Unfortunately, you married a woman who is a hot-ass, embarrassing mess. Do you know what she had on today?"

"I've been told. She wore it just for you."

"Is that why she kept waving at the TV?"

"Don't know, don't care. But since you called, I do want to make sure you're okay after my door hit you in the back." I chuckled a bit, she didn't.

"Come on, Mama. Where is your sense of humor at? Did you lose it?"

"The only thing I'm going to be losing is a son, if you don't get focused and wind up embarrassing the hell out of me. I'm no fan of Ne-ne, trust me, but that reporter who was seconds away from spreading her legs in the Oval Office is not the one. I can't stand to watch her on TV, and how dare you stick your tongue down her throat, after the way she treated you in that interview."

"All she was doing was her job. And what you walked in on last night was nothing. We were just kidding around."

"Excuse me, but I'm a grown-ass woman, who may be old, but I can damn sure see. I'm warning you, Stephen. This time you're going to wish that you had listened."

"Maybe so, but just so you know, I apologize for the Secret Service thing. I was kind of upset that Ben left his position and no one was out there to watch my door."

"I don't blame you for being upset; you should be. Secret Service don't give a shit about protecting a black man, and they were lucky that it was just little ole me strolling through the West Wing. If anything ever happens to you due to them slacking, there will be a price to pay."

"What you gon' do, Mama? Hit them with your purse or kick them with those high-heeled shoes you wear?"

"First, I'm going to tell you how ridiculous you sound, using words like 'gon'.' Then I'm going to polish my Glock 9 over here and put it to good use. Don't underestimate me, Stephen. You already know how I am."

"I do, more than anyone." I heard a beeping sound on my phone; someone else was calling. "Someone is trying to reach me, but before I go, do me a favor and back off Raynetta. You're putting me in a bad position, and I already have enough to deal with."

"I'll think about it, but in the meantime, tell her not to wear cream when she's outside visiting with children. I saw her yesterday morning, and she looked awful. I called to tell her about herself, but—"

"You're not listening to me, Mama. I'm sure you must have mistaken her for someone else, because she's a beautiful woman and you know it. Please, stop hating."

"She may be beautiful on the outside, but she is one ugly and rotten woman in the inside."

"No offense, but sounds like somebody else I know. Bye, Mama. Talk to you soon."

I could hear my mother's voice still ranting as I ended the call. The other caller had hung up, but since it would be awhile before I got back to the White House, I dialed out to call someone who had slipped into my mind a few times today.

"Chanel Hamilton speaking," she said.

"Tell me something good, before I go into my next meeting."

"What? Who is this?"

"Nobody's voice is like mine, and you should be ashamed of yourself for not recognizing it."

"I guess I should be, Mr. President, and your voice is definitely smooth. What a surprise this is."

"It shouldn't be; after all, it's not like you can just pick up the phone and call me. I figured you'd want to hear my voice today, so I pulled a few little tricks to help you out."

"I love surprises, but what would make you think I wanted to hear from you today? I've been extremely busy, and, to be honest, you were the last person on my mind."

I chuckled at her . . . cuteness. "I'm sure I was. And I can only hope that the next time I call you, you'll sound a bit more enthused. Enjoy the rest of your day, and don't forget to give me a little shout-out on the news tonight."

"You can be sure that I will."

Within the next few hours, I was making my way down the corridor with Andrew when he received a call from Tyler. We made a swift exit into another room and quickly placed his call on speakerphone.

"How's your father?" I asked. "I expected to hear from you by now, and we were starting to get a little worried around here."

"He's receiving the best care, so I'm positive that he'll be okay. I'll be flying back in tomorrow night, but if there is anything that you need me to do before then, please let me know. I already cleared my schedule for a few days, but things are going to be hectic when I get back. My wife, Gena, is being a pain in the ass, and my daughter has a severe cold. She's been asking for me to come home all day."

"Well, see about your family and don't worry about your schedule. Andrew will fill in where he can, so we're good."

"Thank you. See you guys soon."

Andrew and I left the room, then headed to another one where we had a long meeting with the secretary of Health and Human Services. The Affordable Care Act was still going strong, and we were now looking for ways to draft a plan that would enable Americans to purchase insurance across state lines. The meeting lasted for three long hours, but we were finally prepared to present something to Congress and see if they could come up with some kind of legislation that would pass both Houses. We shook hands, then left the room together. As Andrew and I were side by side, he walked swiftly to keep up with me.

"As you know, Mr. President, it's almost time for you to meet with some of the leaders from other countries. I know you've spoken to some of them already, and they congratulated you on winning the election. But if you don't mind, I want to allow myself more thought on which leader I should invite to the White House first. I think that it's important for them to come on our turf, instead of you going on theirs."

"I agree. Let me know what you ultimately decide, and be sure to let me know when you feel it's appropriate for me to visit Capitol Hill again. I'm eager to do so, and I hope it will be soon."

"It will be. Very soon."

Andrew called it a night, and I intended to do the same after I went into my office and watched Chanel on the news. As expected, she and a few other reporters talked and laughed about Raynetta's fur coat.

"She looked ridiculous," one female reporter said. "I also thought that she came across rather snide in the

interview too. No first lady should acknowledge her sexiness, and there is something about her that I really don't like."

A black reporter let her have it. *"I wonder if Sally would be saying the same thing if the first lady was a white woman? Forget about the fur coat. What is it about her that you don't like, and you have never had the pleasure of meeting her before?"*

"Seeing her is enough for me—"

From the look on the reporter's face, I could sense that a feud was about to begin.

"Seeing her? Really? I get it. She's too black for you, right? You wouldn't—"

Chanel interrupted. *"Okay, ladies, I have to move on. I want to show some clips from the interview. Then you all can tell me your thoughts."*

The clips played, causing Sally and a few others to shake their heads.

"First, let me say that I think you did a magnificent job," one redheaded male reporter said to Chanel. *"This is not the kind of man you can easily converse with, and being around him can be very intimidating. But you handled yourself well. I thought that his strongpoints were on foreign policy, and his weak points were when he started rambling about how well he intends to work with Congress. We've heard it all before, and I think he's in for a rude awakening. At some point, he started to sound very naïve."*

Chanel nodded, then turned to another reporter who appeared hyped to weigh in. *"What was your take on the interview, Claire? What were the high and low points to you?"*

"I didn't have any low points at all, and we need to stop speaking about the president like he's the scary black man in the room. This president comes across as strong, powerful, and he definitely has a lot of tenacity.

I do think you're going to see some changes on Capitol Hill, and I believe that he's going to force a lot of people to take a look at themselves and finally get some things done. The first lady is very likable, and even on the campaign trail, many women connected with her. It was a joy to watch the entire interview, and when you asked about him being named as one of the sexiest men alive, I was tickled pink by both of their answers."

Chanel laughed. "I'm sure that you and many other people were. As for me, I had highs and lows. I think President Jefferson really wants to get things done, but a part of me is concerned about his tone. It can be a bit brash at times, and his temperament may wind up being too much for the American people. I didn't welcome the idea of him trying to tell me how to do my job, and he made the same mistake with the media earlier that day. On a positive note, I admire him a lot. I want to give a huge shout-out to him, and to the first lady, for reaching out to me—yes, little ole me, for an exclusive interview."

She winked at the TV, causing everyone to laugh. I closed my laptop, giving thought to what Chanel had said, but sticking to my guns that would, eventually, rock the White House like they had never seen it been done before.

5

First Lady Raynetta Jefferson

Sometimes, many people failed to give first ladies the credit we deserved. They thought that we often sat around twiddling our thumbs, baking cakes and cookies, tending to kids, and putting up with our husband's shit. The truth was, it took a very strong woman to be in this position. One who knew when to speak and when not to. One who played by her own rules instead of the rules that were already prepared for her. One who let no one tear her family apart, even when she knew that things on the home front weren't always perfect. And one who didn't need her husband's arms around her every single night to make her feel loved and safe. The bedroom was often lonely and cold, but only a superstrong woman could survive this and endure the madness that transpired in this place for many years.

The good thing about being a first lady was, unbeknownst to many, we knew more about this little White House than some of the senior staff members who worked here did. As hostess, we kept tabs on visitors, luncheons, events . . . all of that good stuff that kept us busy from day to day. Therefore, I didn't have to ask Stephen why Chanel was in his office last night. I also knew that her visit was cut short and interrupted by his mother. A smart woman knows these things, and we understood that millions of women loved men in power, especially sexy ones like my husband who could charm the panties off women just by looking at them. That's what he'd done to Chanel. I could see her melting in the chair during the interview. He broke her down, minute by minute. She wanted him; he wanted her. I was well aware of that, and when it came to my marriage, there were often very little surprises. Little surprises, but big secrets, especially on my behalf, pertaining to lies I'd told him about my inability to have a child. I knew it was wrong, but I felt as if this was payback for him not giving our marriage his all.

Displaying my attitude toward him this morning was enough. I gave him a tiny hint that I knew how desperate he was to lay that bitch, Chanel, on her back. He could lay her down wherever he wished—in a filthy alley for all I cared. The only time we would ever have a problem was if a baby popped up. That would send me over the edge and cause me to do things that no first lady should ever do. Now, while I was strong, I still was human. I cried when I had to, got angry when I felt it was necessary, and even threw tantrums when I really wanted to get my husband's attention. I even threatened him from time to time, but when all was said and done, I realized that this was the life I'd chosen, and if I ever wanted to walk, I could simply do it.

My schedule was loaded with fun, as well as interesting things to do today. But around six o'clock that evening, I had some important, personal business to tend to. I sneaked away from Secret Service, who were slacking anyway, and had my personal driver take me to an address I had written on a card. Within the hour, he parked inside of a parking garage where plenty more cars were parked too. I was escorted upstairs by him, and he observed our surroundings, making sure the coast was clear. After he knocked on the door, we waited. Moments later, a woman with short, layered hair answered. Her swollen eyes implied that she'd been crying, and her brown skin looked kind of dry. She wore a long silky robe with leopard prints all over it. Her feet were bare, and she seemed a bit nervous as she looked at me.

"Vera Walton?" I said, making sure I was at the right place.

"Yes." She widened the door. "Please come in."

I told my driver that I wouldn't be long, but he insisted that he wait outside the door for me. I certainly didn't mind that, especially since I didn't know what kind of foolishness I would walk into when Vera reached out to my assistant last week, telling her that it was imperative that we spoke. After three more phone calls, I decided to return her call. She informed me that she needed to speak to me about Stephen, so there I was, in the flesh, eager to hear what she had to say.

"Thank you for coming," Vera said as she stood by the door next to me. "I honestly didn't think you would come, but I want you to know how very important this is. So important, that you may need to have a seat."

I looked around at the cozy little apartment that needed an interior decorator to add a touch or two to it. The loud colors didn't blend well together, and the sectional was too big for the small space in the living room. Bookshelves were to the right, and a dining room set for two people was to the right. I hoped that Stephen hadn't spent much time here, and if he had, what a shame.

I wiped a little fuzz from the couch before taking a seat. "There. You now have my attention, so please tell me why you asked me to come here."

Vera took a seat as well. She crossed her legs, then released a deep breath. "Several months ago, I started having an affair with your husband. I was introduced to him by the mayor, who presented me with an award. I never expected for things to go as far as they did, nor did I expect to experience these deep feelings that I have for him. Everything was fine, until he was elected president. He stopped calling me, stopped responding to my text messages, and I haven't heard from him since. His phone number was recently disconnected, but even before that, I decided to reach out to you. I wanted to put this behind me and forget about him, but I can't. The reason why is because I'm pregnant. Pregnant with his child, and I don't know what to do about it."

I gazed at the teary-eyed woman with little sympathy. She hadn't shocked me not one bit, and as I had said before, I was prepared for little games like this.

"First, let me say that I am so sorry that my husband is ignoring you and stressing you like this. He has a tendency to leave women's lives in shambles, but the baby thingy has really shaken me up. I don't know how you came to the conclusion that the child you may be carrying is his, especially when you've had at least four or five different sex partners this year. Just so you know, I've done my research, and I've discovered some very troubling things about you. You didn't think I would come here without investigating you, did you, and what I found out isn't exactly pretty."

She shifted in her seat and started to fidget with her hands. Could barely make eye contact with me, but made an attempt to enlighten me with her so-called truth.

"I don't know what you discovered about me, but I have only been with your husband this year. I have a very good reputation, and you can ask anyone who knows me what kind of person I am."

"I did ask, and like I said, the information I received was troubling. If you say that the only man you've been with this year is Stephen, I can only tell you that I don't believe you. I can, and will, start naming names, if you push me to do it."

She wasn't backing down and insisted that Stephen had been her only lover.

"That's a lie, and you know it," I said. "Greg Collins can back me up, Richard Nelson can, Benji Lewis, Byron Foster, and Marshall Alexander. I don't know if they wore condoms like my husband did when he screwed you, but I do know, for sure, that if you are pregnant, that child is not his."

With bugged eyes, Vera remained silent. I waited for a response, but the truth was, she didn't need to say anything else. She had wasted my time. Thought she was on to something, but the only person she was about to embarrass was herself.

"As you sit there in deep thought," I said, "keep in mind that if you speak to anyone about this nonsense, or decide to go public, you will only hurt yourself. You've been awfully busy behind closed doors, and I don't think that you really want a woman like me to open those doors and allow the world to see what actually goes on inside."

Anger crept on her face—I must have finally touched a nerve. "You can do or say whatever you wish, but trust me when I say, Stephen will hurt behind this too. My insides still drip with the substantial amount of semen he put inside of me, and I don't care how much you try to deny it . . . This baby growing inside of me belongs to him."

Deciding not to waste any more time with this, I stood and tucked my purse underneath my arm.

"If your insides still drip with my husband's semen in you, then I recommend that you take a long, hot bath. Your medical records revealed to me that there is no baby, and not even a bootleg doctor can help you make this story true. You should have planned this out more carefully, Vera. Have a pleasant evening, and all the best to you."

Vera sat like a quiet mouse as I exited her apartment. My driver was still at the door waiting for me, and the second I returned home, I marched to the Oval Office to find Stephen. Secret Service was at the door, but the agent allowed me to go right in. I saw Stephen sitting behind the desk with several papers scattered in front of him. A piece of paper was in his hand, along with a notebook that was ruffled around the edges. He looked well rested, as if he had gotten twelve hours of sleep, even though I knew he'd gotten less than three or four.

"Didn't mean to interrupt you, but I wanted to make you aware of a small problem that I managed to work out for you. Feel free to thank me later, but in the meantime, since you decided to ignore Miss Vera Walton, she decided to reach out to me. She informed me tonight that she was with child, but before I paid her a visit, I asked a certain someone from your administration to dig up a little information for me. To make a long story short, Miss Teacher of the Year is a whore. She was about to shut you down and embarrass the hell out of both of us. That's no longer going to happen, and you can take a deep breath because she never was really pregnant. In closing this conversation, you, Mr. President, are a piece of work. I don't have time to watch your back, especially when I need to watch mine."

I stood, waiting for a response. But all Stephen did was stare at me while leaning slightly to the side in his chair.

"Do you have anything at all to say to me?" I said. "Or are you going to just sit there like you didn't hear a thing I said?"

"Thank you," he said, then lifted the paper to read it again.

I reached out, snatching the paper from his hand. "Thanks? Is that all I get—a lousy, insincere thanks?"

He held his hands out, appearing very nonchalant. "What else do you want me to say? You leave me speechless, as you did with the fur coat incident, but I'm not going to entertain your nonsense. Pertaining to Vera, had you told me she called you, I would've handled things myself. I would have told you she couldn't have been pregnant because I wore a condom and didn't even come. I would've told you that she was not going to be a problem for either of us, because with a rap sheet like hers, she wouldn't dare put herself in the spotlight. But thanks again, baby, for always doing what you do best, which is jumping to conclusions without having all of the facts."

I was totally put off by this . . . this . . . I didn't know what to call him right now, but since my *kind* words didn't seem to have an effect, I had to simplify them for him. I moved in closer to his desk and bent over so I could be face-to-face with him, showing my gritted teeth.

"The fact is, you slut-bucket-ass Negro, you shouldn't have been there in the first place. Now, I'm going to say this one time and one time only—hopefully, you'll be able to step into the light and comprehend. You hold one of the highest positions in the world. It is going to require you to be focused, sharp minded, alert, and on your knees, praying for direction every single day. The second you slip up, the white man is going to be watching so he can kick your dumb ass out of that chair and replace it with his. This is the big leagues, sweetheart, and simple-minded niggas don't belong here. Every—"

Stephen shot up from his chair like a rocket. "I don't have to listen—"

"Yes, you do! Now, sit your ass down and shut the hell up until I'm finished!"

He didn't sit, but folded his arms in front of him with a mean mug on his face, allowing me to continue.

"Unfortunately, if you do not change course and get a grip on yourself, just like all of the other black men who go up and come down because of the almighty free pussy, you *will* regret it. I encourage you to get your mind right and stop screwing around with these gimmie-what-you-want-for-a-pork-chop hoes. And by all means, if you must cheat on me, please up your standards. But keep in mind that if, or when, you lose it all, *I* will be the one to gain the most from your misfortune."

Having nothing else to say, I marched toward the door, hoping that my friendly advice to the president would, eventually, sink in.

6

President of the United States, Stephen C. Jefferson

It seemed like the days were getter shorter, due to my lack of sleep. There was too much to get done in one day, and if I slept for eight hours, I felt like I was missing something. I'd thought about what Raynetta had said, but most of it went in one ear . . . and out the other. All she ever wanted to do was argue, and who in the hell did she think she was, talking to *me* like that? It totally angered me, and if she thought that was the best way to get my attention, she was sadly mistaken. Hell, I knew she wasn't happy, but at this point in our marriage, there wasn't much that I could do to make her thrilled about anything. Well, maybe one thing, but she already knew that adopting was out of the question.

Doing the norm, I prayed, exercised, showered, got suited up, and prepared myself for the day ahead of me. Tyler was back, and by seven o'clock, he was in my office, speaking on the issue that had occurred with the Secret Service.

"Ben and Paul reached out to me about what had happened," he said, sitting with his legs crossed while on the sofa. "They want their jobs back, but that'll be up to you. I told them the least they could do was come here and apologize to you this morning."

"Apologize?" I said, sitting across from him. "I don't need an apology. One of these days, I could be dead in my grave because of those two. Will they be able to apologize to me then?"

"No, they won't be able to, but they are two of the best agents that we have. They've been here for years and have done a great job protecting other presidents."

"Maybe some, but surely not all. I don't like to give second chances, especially when it comes to playing with my life. The truth is, no one should be able to enter the White House and come straight through those doors over there without being stopped. It makes no sense that my mother was able to do it without one hand being laid on her. While she has clearance to come here, she doesn't have clearance to enter this room without approval."

There was a knock on the door, and when Tyler yelled "come in," Ben and Paul entered.

"Good morning, Mr. President and VP McNeil," Ben said, suited up as if he still had a job. Dark shades covered his eyes, but he removed them. Paul said good morning as well, and they both stood to the left of me, offering their sincere apologies.

"This is a total embarrassment, sir, and I assure you that, if given the opportunity to work for you again, nothing like that will happen on my watch again. We deeply apologize, but just for a few minutes, Paul was called by another agent to handle another important matter."

"That's correct, Mr. President," Paul said, speaking for himself. "I had only been gone for no more than five minutes. I knew Ben would be back shortly."

It was my turn to chime in. "There is nothing or no one around here more important than me, and that is in no way an insult to the VP. It takes less than ten seconds for someone to open that door, raise their gun, and blow my fucking brains out in here. The positions you guys hold have to be taken more seriously, and I'm not about to lose my life over a gotdamn soda. No question, what the two of you did was reckless. It was an embarrassment to all of us, and I'm not ready to offer your jobs back yet. Allow me to sleep on this for a while. My chief of staff, Andrew, will be in touch soon."

They both thanked me for my time, then left the room. Tyler remained there with me, and shortly thereafter, Andrew came in to discuss my schedule.

"In reference to the conversation I had with you yesterday about meeting with some of our allies, I still haven't gotten all of that together yet. However, due to what some view as a race war in our country, many leaders are uneasy. I think it would be wise for you to strengthen our relationship with Africa and join the U.S. ambassador when he returns there in a few days. Our economic and trade relations with South Africa remain strong, and this trip would allow you to reinforce the U.S. commitment to expanding economic growth and investments with new leaders."

"I agree," Tyler said. "And even though there needs to be much more work done here to help lower racial tensions, the message we want to send to the world is very important."

"It's not like the two of you have to pull my teeth out in order for me to visit Africa. I would love to. To my recollection, only three or four sitting presidents have been there, and I do think it is equally important for us to reinforce our commitment to their new leaders, as well as others. We have to continue to strengthen our relationships. Over the years, the United States has lost a lot of respect, and I'm willing and able to meet and listen to any leader who strives for the betterment of all people."

"Good deal, Mr. President," Andrew said. "I'll make the announcement soon. Be prepared, by Wednesday, to head out on Air Force One."

"I will be ready, and I hope the Secret Service will be too. Going forward, I want all new agents, so get on finding professionals in the field who can protect me and my wife."

"You're not going to reconsider rehiring Ben and Paul?" Tyler said. "I thought you told them you would think about it."

With a straight face, I didn't hold back. "Fuck Ben and Paul. No one will be allowed a second chance when it comes to my life, and there really is nothing else I need to think about. I'm strapped regardless, and it's a damn shame that it has to be this way in the Oval Office."

Seemingly in shock, they both nodded, then left my office. I was looking forward to going to Africa. I expressed my enthusiasm to Chanel while speaking to her around noon that day. I also thanked her for the shout-out the other night.

"You're very welcome, Mr. President. I only wished that I could say more."

"I think you said enough, but that's just my opinion, of course."

She laughed, then hit me with a question that I suspected was coming soon. "Sooo, when am I going to see you again? I enjoy these little five-minute conversations we have, but it would be nice to see you face-to-face again."

"I figured you would ask, but *I* get a chance to see you almost every evening on the news."

"Well, that may satisfy you, but it doesn't satisfy me. And by the way, I'm glad you enjoy watching my show. On purpose, I tend to speak to and about you a lot."

"Trust me, I've noticed. It seems as if you can't get enough of me. But before our five minutes are almost up, I have another job for you. Many members of the media will cover my trip while in South Africa. I want you to be there, on special assignment, if you will. Air Force One will take off at eight o'clock, Wednesday morning. You need to be on the plane by six, or, at least, way before the cameras arrive to view my departure. I'll make sure that you get Top Secret Clearance, and you'll be issued a Secret Service Credential's pass, only for this trip."

There was a lengthy silence before Chanel spoke up. "That will be difficult for me to pull off. I can't just drop what I'm doing and take off for a special assignment. My boss may have a problem with that, and I'm sure someone else from our network will be assigned to cover you while you're there."

"Not interested in anyone else, and that will be made clear to your boss. No is not an acceptable answer, so I expect to see you on Wednesday morning when I enter Air Force One. Until then, have a nice day."

I had hoped to have a nice day too, but around three in the afternoon, things took a turn for the worse. Tragedy struck again, as two men armed with assault rifles stormed into a day care facility, taking out every person in the main office and several kids who were on the playground. Pandemonium erupted at the White House, like I had never witnessed it before. Everyone was on edge, including me. I was mad as hell, and as my phones kept ringing, I couldn't help but to shout at Andrew who called to see if I had eaten something for dinner.

"Hell, no, I haven't had dinner! To hell with dinner, Andrew! You know, as well as I do, that those people didn't have to die! This shit is crazy, and what in the hell is it going to take for Congress to get off their asses and do something about gun laws in this country? These shootings used to occur every other week. Now, they're happening every other day! It's time to say fuck the NRA and do more to keep the people safe!"

"I agree, but you know what many leaders will say. This has nothing to do with gun laws. It's all about the persons pulling the trigger and their state of mind. I wish—"

"No, I wish you would shut the hell up and listen to me. I want an emergency meeting scheduled with the leaders in Congress tomorrow. Invite them here, or make arrangements for me to be on Capitol Hill. This shit is not going to continue to happen on my watch. It's time to stop taking baby steps and take giant steps to get this done!"

I slammed the phone down, ending my call with Andrew. Minutes later, my cell phone rang. My mother's number flashed on the screen, but I didn't answer because Raynetta had come through the door with a somber expression on her face.

"No knock, no announcement, no nothing, huh?" I said, marching over to the door to confront Secret Service. I pulled the door open, barking at one agent who stood outside. "Wha . . . Why was she able to walk into my office without being stopped?"

He appeared confused. "Be . . . because she's your wife, sir, and I didn't think—"

"I don't give a damn who she is!" I shouted near his face. Veins popped out of my neck—I was too mad. "Do not allow *anyone* to enter my office without acknowledging who they are first! Not her, not the VP, not my mother, nor my dog, if I had one! Do . . . you . . . understand?"

He nodded and didn't even flinch as I got in his shit. "Yes, Mr. President, I do understand. I will relay that message to the other agents as well."

"Thank you!"

I walked back into my office, slamming the door behind me. Raynetta's eyes were bugged. She looked at me, shaking her head.

"I'm not going to even start with you today, but you need to calm down. I promise not to walk in here again without announcing myself, and trust me when I say it's not that serious. But what is serious is what happened today, as well as the overwhelming murder rate in this country. Gun control should be your administration's top priority. I don't understand why stuff like this continues to get swept underneath the rug."

I plopped down in the chair behind my desk, then rubbed my aching forehead. My chest continued to heave in and out; I started to take deeper breaths to calm myself.

"It will be our priority, and I'm going to ask the American people, once and for all, to stop allowing special interest groups to control what happens in this country and vote against any Congress member who continues to put their needs before the people's. The truth is, I can't govern this country all by myself. I have to reach out, but I'll be damned if I sit idly by and allow our elected officials to do nothing. Those babies on that playground deserve better, and so do the people who were in that office. Those were children, Netta. I saw unedited videos of what happened to them. I saw the expressions on their little faces, fear in their eyes, and cries, as they were being shot multiple times. My heart aches for the parents, and I will reach out to them, soon, to offer my condolences."

"I will do so as well. Be sure to include my prayers and sorrow in your statement to the American people, even though I know many of them are tired of hearing words with no action."

"I agree. Can't say that I blame them for being fed up."

Later that day, along with Andrew, Tyler, and Sam, I watched the ongoing coverage of what had happened today. I was sick to my stomach, and had already released a brief statement that expressed our sympathy and apologies for ongoing inaction. The shooters had been gunned down by the police, but that made no one feel better.

"What a sad day this is," Tyler said, using the remote to turn off the TV. "Several members of Congress will be here tomorrow morning, so I think it's best that we all turn in early and get some rest."

We all shook each other's hands and went our separate ways for the night. I wanted to lay my head on a soft pillow tonight and cuddle in a warm bed with my wife. But my mind was on overload. What happened today was the kind of shit that affected me in a major way. I feared days like this while living in the White House, but I also suspected that this was just the beginning. Maybe I was prepared, maybe I wasn't, but the one thing I was, was a caring human being.

The next morning, I found myself slumped in my chair, after getting very little sleep. My tie had been removed from my neck, and my white shirt was unbuttoned and full of wrinkles. My shoes were off, mouth was dry. I yawned, then got up to tackle another day.

Around nine o'clock, I was already in a boardroom with numerous members of Congress sitting at the table with me. The media was allowed to come inside, and with smiles plastered on all of our faces, I happily shared with everyone the direction I wanted to go in with controlling gun violence.

"I invited each and every one of these congressional leaders to join me today, because these are some, not all, but some of the people who have not taken vital steps to improve our gun laws in this country. Hopefully, some are starting to wake up, before it's too late. We cannot continue on this reckless path, and there has to be a way to protect our Second Amendment rights, while also keeping the American people safe. With that being said, will the media please exit so that the discussions can begin?"

Most of the Democrats at the table were with me on this, so they smiled at the cameras and waved. The Republicans, however, sat like zombies, including Speaker Robinson who had initially refused to attend today's meeting. After the media had vacated, I jumped right in, asking if there had been any legislation drafted pertaining to gun laws that I didn't know about. Everyone sat quietly. In return, I shook my head.

"All I can ask is . . . What are we waiting for? Simply put, this is ridiculous. I can't believe the stronghold so many special interest groups have on you all. It's time to end this and stop making it all about money. I'm looking for solutions. What is the plan? I would like to hear ideas that convey a reasonable way forward."

Yet again, many sat silent. A few whispers followed, and then Speaker Robinson spoke up. "In case you haven't noticed, Mr. Jefferson, there aren't many ways forward. Many of us believe that protecting our Second Amendment rights is the priority, and no gun violence law should affect those who have gone through the legal process to obtain guns and have the right to bear arms and protect themselves. There is no easy fix, and your anger and insults will not encourage us to have a change of heart on this matter."

"Maybe my anger and insults won't encourage you all to have a change of heart, but I would hope that these pictures would." I opened an envelope, then scattered numerous photos of people, from all races, who had been victims of gun violence in this country for the past six months. "There you go. Look at them. Almost nine thousand Americans—dead. From gunshot wounds to the heads, or shots straight through the hearts. Twenty percent of that number pertains to children, so Mr. Speaker, I suggest that you not make this about me, and make this about people who didn't have to die. Others would applaud you and every other congressional leader who decides to take action and get off their asses to do something."

As expected, my choice of words weren't welcomed. They caused others to finally speak up, and, at least, I had everyone talking now. No one, however, louder than Speaker Robinson, whose wrinkled face shook as he spoke and choked on his words as he coughed.

"Just who do you think you are, Mr. Jefferson?" he shouted, then placed his tightened fist in front of his mouth to cover his cough. "You have no . . . no goddamn authority to—"

I quickly cut him off. "*I* am the head Negro in charge, Mr. Speaker, and you *will* respect me!"

"Stop this," Senator Evans yelled with tears at the rim of her eyes. "You're so right, Mr. President, this isn't about you. But you cannot expect to get things accomplished by attacking us and accusing us of not caring about this issue as much as you do. We do care, but like the Speaker said, this is not an easy fix. If it was, it would've been done."

"Let me correct you, Senator Evans, and also educate you as well. I have not attacked anyone who hasn't attacked me. Mr. Speaker went on live television, and in front of all America, he referred to me as a loose cage monkey. It is only behind closed doors that I will remind everyone of this, and in return, tell him that a loose cage monkey can—and will—eat the feathers off an old, white, angry chicken with weak legs to stand on, and destroy him. In one week, and with an all-hands-on-deck approach, we can draft legislation that requires mandatory, universal background checks on all private sales of firearms. We can create a policy that would allow family members or law enforcement to petition courts to remove firearms from individuals in crisis or with mental health issues. Basically, come up with commonsense proposals that will set us on the right path to correcting part of this epidemic. Senator Evans, the floor is yours."

"And the door is mine," the Speaker said, wobbling to his feet. "I have other serious matters to tend to, and as far as I'm concerned, this meeting is over."

"Walk fast, old man, and don't allow the door to hit you on the way out. And anyone else who wants to join him, please do. Just be sure to call a plumber to help him clear his throat so he can speak to me like he has some sense."

Many heads shook, and a few others stood and left. I was surprised that many stayed to provide their input and listen. While we never came up with a joint resolution today, this was a start. We agreed to revisit this issue next week and see what we could do to get the ball rolling on controlling gun violence.

Around eight o'clock, I did the norm. Sat on the sofa in the Oval Office with my head tilted back and eyes closed, meditating. Instead of jazz music wafting through speakers, I had the speakers up loudly, tuning into news with Chanel Hamilton.

"It was another chaotic and unproductive day at the White House as the president and Speaker Robinson exchanged several harsh words. It's no secret that there is no love lost between the two, but many say that this was unlike anything they had ever witnessed before. We were informed by several people inside of the administration that things got overly heated, and the Speaker was thrown out. Racial slurs were being used, and at one point, Senator Evans allegedly picked up a chair and threw it. We reached out to Senator Evans for a comment, but she has yet to respond. The

president, himself, hasn't responded either, and we've been informed that Speaker Robinson has no plans to ever return to the White House again."

"Bullshit," I whispered underneath my breath. I then lowered the volume with the remote and dimmed the lights. Tonight, I needed a bed, so I headed to the Master Bedroom to get as much rest as I could, before my trip to Africa in the morning. Thankfully, when I crept into the bedroom, Raynetta was in a deep sleep. I planted a soft kiss on her forehead, stripped naked, then got underneath the warm covers, turning my back to hers.

7

Newsroom Contributor Chanel Hamilton

The president must've been totally out of his everlasting mind. Then again, so was I. I couldn't believe that I had dropped everything to accommodate him on this trip, but my presence wasn't too obvious because there were numerous people on board Air Force One who were fortunate enough to take this trip to Africa with him. Unlike some of the other journalists who had already taken their seats in the press quarters, it was my first time on a plane like this. I wasn't even sure if I should call it a plane. It was more like a luxurious hotel with dining rooms, offices, a boardroom, and kitchen. I was far from the presidential suite that was near the front of Air Force One, and I was informed that it even had a workout area. TVs were mounted everywhere and security was on top of everything. I was so excited, also a little nervous, about this whole thing too.

Why? Because having feelings for the president of the United States was a big deal. Yes, there were plenty of women who probably had fantasies about him or wished that they could one day meet him. But I had been super close to him. Had touched the man's package and tasted his tongue. I couldn't stop thinking about him, and there was no way for me to avoid a man who was the main subject on the network I worked for every single day. I had never been involved with a married man before, and as far as relationships go, well, I hadn't had many. My life was too busy. No man would put up with me spending twelve-to-fourteen hours at work. I loved my job, especially when it enabled me to be a part of something like this. I was thankful to the president for allowing me this opportunity, and the interview with him and the first lady had already opened some other doors for me.

Many of us crammed our luggage, duffle bags, and laptops into several compartments. Our section was rather busy and noisy as well. That was, until the president appeared near the front section of our area with his chief of staff behind him.

"Welcome, everyone," he said without looking in my direction. "Thank you all for being here. Once I get things settled in and take care of some minor business, I'll come back for conversation and questions. Until then, make yourselves at home, eat heartily, and enjoy the long ride."

Just for a split second, his eyes connected with mine. He turned to walk away, leaving many of us feeling exuberant and eager to have another casual interview with him.

Almost an hour later, Air Force One was off the ground and on its way to Africa. The press area was still very noisy, and the reporter I sat next to was known for rambling on and on. She had a lot to say about the president, but all I did was keep my mouth shut and listen. I already talked about him enough on my show, and there were times when I purposely pretended as if I was not on his side. The truth, I was. I loved everything about him and his brash comments, boldness, his arrogance . . . none of those things bothered me one bit. Unfortunately, I hadn't voted for him, though, and I was starting to regret it.

"I loved the interview you did with him," the reporter, Mandy, said. "But if I was given that opportunity, I would have challenged him on way more things than you did.

It's going to take someone brave to stand up to him, and I don't blame Speaker Robinson for walking out on their meeting. You said he was forced out, but I heard he and other members of Congress left."

"You know there are always two sides to every story, sometimes three. And sometimes, we say whatever to get people to tune in. I've received a lot of praise for the interview, and because of it, I'm looking forward to a generous promotion when I get back."

That surely kept her quiet for a while. Jealousy was written all over her face, and she had directed her negative comments elsewhere. Not having much sleep, I tucked a pillow close to my neck, then leaned my head to the side. Within minutes, I was out.

What seemed like hours later, I cracked my eyes open to dim lights inside, darkness outside. I couldn't believe I had slept this long, and when I looked around, several others were asleep as well. Mandy was reading a book. I stole her attention to inquire about what I had missed.

"Did the president return? I didn't hear a thing; this ride is so smooth."

"You didn't miss anything. He hasn't returned yet, and it is rare that we ever see or hear from the president while on here."

"I guess he's busy, but if you don't mind, I need to go to the restroom. Can you move aside?"

She stood so I could get out. It took every bit of two minutes for me to handle my business, and right after I came out, I was met by security.

"I need you to come with me," he said.

Several people looked at me as if I had been caught with drugs. All I did was shrug, as if I didn't know why I was being asked to follow him.

"Chanel, are you okay?" one reporter asked.

"Yes, I'm fine. I lost one of my bags earlier. Maybe they found it for me."

"Oh, okay. That's happened to me before too."

I kept it moving behind security, and after a lengthy walk in the other direction, I was finally face-to-face with the president again. I swore before God that the magazine who had named him one of the sexiest men alive had gotten it right. He looked even sexier while sitting in the dim office, with recessed lighting, shirt unbuttoned, tie pulled away from his neck, and no shoes on his feet.

"Anything else, Mr. President?" Security asked.

"No. Thank you, John. That will be all."

John left the room, closing the door behind him. I stood in front of the kitty-cornered, wooden desk with a tight skirt and wrinkled blouse on. My hair was now in a ponytail, and there was very little makeup on my face. I only wished that I had more time to get myself together, but the slight smile on his face implied that he didn't seem to mind.

"Have a seat," he said, directing his eyes to the leather sectional that sat several feet away from his desk. A wide-screen TV was mounted behind the sectional, and only one reclining leather chair was in front of his desk.

I backed up to the sectional, taking a seat. He immediately joined me, facing me as we began to converse.

"You must've been tired," he said. "I had someone check on you earlier, but they said you were out like a light."

"Fortunately, I was. I needed that sleep, and I'm sure that you need to get some too."

"I do, but sleep can wait."

"It shouldn't have to. It's the most important thing your body needs."

"Could be, but do you mind if I tell you what else my body needs?"

I swallowed hard before speaking. "For some reason, I get a feeling that you're going to show me, instead of tell me."

"I just may do that. Besides, who needs to talk when we both are in professions that require us to talk all day long?"

"Yeah, that's exactly what I was thinking."

I leaned in a little farther than he did to steal a kiss. Our tongues danced for a while, and then I reached out to do something that I couldn't wait to do. I unbuttoned his crisp, white shirt, peeling it away from his buffed chest that was solid as a rock. My hands rubbed all over his chest, before I moved them to massage his back. His body was cut and carved to perfection. The honeydew taste of his lips had me locked in a trance. I didn't dare look into his eyes yet, but when I had the courage to, they lured me right in. I quickly surrendered myself to him by leaning back on the sectional and staring deep into his eyes that spoke volumes to me without him ever saying one word. He blinked, then lowered his lips to my neck, delicately licking it up and down. His pointed tongue traveled south, and requiring access to my firm breasts, he yanked on my blouse, causing buttons to pop and my blouse to tear open. The light purple bra I wore stood in the way. But after unlatching the front of it with his teeth, he went all in, treating my nipples as if they were precious black diamonds. His tongue twirled in slow, rhythmic circles around them, making them wet and sticky. I was very much caught up in the moment, and when a high arch formed in my back, he secured his arm around me, carefully bringing me closer to him. My body felt limp . . . weak in his strong arms, and my pussy had already started to rain.

"Mr. President, help me, please," I whined. "Help me make my fantasies a reality, and let me show you how much I want . . . need this."

Helping me in a major way, he lifted me from the couch, still holding me in his arms. I wrapped my legs around him, and we made a quick transition from his office to the presidential suite. I was surprised by how modern and sleek it was, but the last thing on my mind was the décor. He laid me on the bed with a tufted headboard and began to remove his clothes. My narrowed eyes scanned down his impeccable, chocolate body that made a little of my saliva drizzle from the corner of my mouth. The size of his package was jaw-dropping, and after he stripped me naked, he crawled on the bed, giving me the royal treatment. I shuddered uncontrollably from the feel of his thick, wet lips planting delicate and sensual kisses all over my body. I tried to calm myself, but the feel of his velvety tongue venturing from one hotspot to the next took my breath away. I couldn't believe this was happening to me, especially when he wrapped my legs around his waist, then cracked my secret code with his lengthy, extremely hard, muscle. My stomach tightened; I held my breath and relished the feel of him maneuvering his way in. It was everything that I imagined it to be . . . and so much more. I clawed at the soft, cotton sheets, begging him to pinch me somewhere . . . anywhere, so I would know this was real.

"Pinch you?" he whispered in my ear while stroking me at a tranquilizing pace. "You'll know it's real when I make you come all over me."

No questions about it, he was in command. He lifted my legs, kissing them tenderly, before placing them over his broad shoulders. The pace increased and rhythm changed, right after he journeyed a little bit deeper. At that point, tears welled in my eyes—he was just that good to me. I couldn't take my eyes off of him; his eyes were locked on me as well. He reached for my hands, placing them over my head and clenching them with his as we rocked our bodies together. I was completely stuffed with his goodies, and as he methodically worked his magic stick in and out of me, I knew I would never get enough of this. Mr. President was a smooth lover, and I had never met a man to smack it up, flip it, taste it, and rub it down, all at the same time, like he did. My juices boiled over, and sweat rained on our naked bodies that made sweet music for almost the entire night. I wasn't sure how we were going to keep this a secret, but we would soon find out that cameras—even on Air Force One—revealed everything.

8

Vice President Tyler McNeil

I had gotten ahead of myself, but I didn't sweat it because this was how the game of politics was played. I think every vice president had a desire to actually be the president, and not too many were comfortable being the second man in charge. I was bored to death. Thus far, Stephen hadn't utilized me in a way that I thought he would. He boldly took charge and hadn't listened to any of my advice. That angered me to a certain extent, and to be honest, who in the hell wanted an egotistical black man calling all of the shots? I surely didn't, and neither did the American people. Yes, the majority had voted for him, but that was all in the plan. Many Republicans voted for a Democrat just so Stephen and I would win. I couldn't run against him, because Democrats never would have switched their votes for me. Since the Republican Party had diminished over the years, we had to create a new playbook. We had to get on the ticket with a vulnerable Democrat and profess to the American people that we shared the same views as the Democratic Party did. It was the only way for us to eventually push our conservative agenda forward. Once Stephen was dead, or impeached, I would be in power to finally take this country back. It was time, and after plotting for several years, it would be done.

With my hands dipped into my pockets, I raked my blond hair while pacing the floor in front of my grandfather's chair. Speaker Robinson was also in the room smoking a cigar, and our dedicated former Secret Service agent, Ben, was there as well. My grandfather, Christopher J. McNeil, was one of the wealthiest men alive. He had the *real* power, and in no way was he happy about Stephen being president.

"Africa is where he belongs," my grandfather said while scratching his snow-white beard. "He needs to stay there and take some of these other idiots who are destroying our country with him."

"If it wasn't for me being dismissed the other day," Ben said, kissing up to my grandfather, "Mr. President wouldn't be coming back from Africa. He'd be dead."

My grandfather slammed his hand on the table. "Well, thanks to you and that goddamn soda, that won't be happening. Now, we have to wait and come up with a new plan, since he requested all new Secret Service agents."

I regretted Stephen's request, and I thought that Ben's and Paul's apologies would be enough. I had to let my grandfather know that I didn't have anything to do with Stephen's decision. "That slob Andrew is in the process of hiring new agents. And you can bet that he is going to dig deep into their backgrounds and make sure they are fitting for the job. Getting to Stephen will be more difficult now."

My grandfather slowly nodded. "You're damn right it will be, and the more I think about it, Ben, get the hell out of here! Shoo and don't come back! You've let me down, and no one, ya hear me, *no one* on my team lets me down!"

My grandfather's whole face was beet red. He was livid, and his cold, blue eyes stared Ben down as he exited the room with his head hanging low.

"Fucking idiot," my grandfather barked, then fell back in his chair. He crossed his legs, then darted his finger at me. "We don't have much time to waste. The longer that nigger stays—"

"Grandfather, I get your point. I already know what I have to do, and it starts with getting Stephen to trust me. In order for him to even consider me as his VP, he already has some kind of faith in me. We all knew that this would take time, and it would seem a little suspicious if something happened to him his first sixty days in office. Maybe it's a good thing that Ben didn't kill him that day. His mother saved him when she showed up—I had no idea she'd be there. I was surprised by Chanel Hamilton being there as well."

Speaker Robinson whistled smoke holes into the air, then laughed. "That little pretty black bitch was there to fall on her back and get some yum-yum. She's on that trip to Africa too, and if you ever want to disrupt a coon's life, all you have to do is feed'em some good pussy. She's going to help us accomplish what we want, and so is that loudmouthed mother of his. The first lady will be beneficial too, just wait and see."

"That might be true," my grandfather said, "but don't you dare sit there and refer to that woman as first lady. First ladies don't conduct themselves like she does, and, quite frankly, they don't look like her. I have nothing nice to say about that angry woman. Every time I see her, I want to puke all over myself. I will be more than delighted when she's packing her bags and is on her way out of the White House."

"Rest assured," I said even though I sort of liked the first lady, my issues were with Stephen, "she will be out. But I don't want any of us to underestimate Stephen, especially you, Roy. He's a very intelligent man, with weaknesses I think we can tap into. I do, however, fear that some Congress members may start to listen to him.

Are you positive that you have the Republican Party in line? While in that meeting yesterday, I saw some members of your party wavering a bit."

"They can waver all they want, but the votes will never add up in the president's favor, unless I want them to." He leaned back in the chair with a smirk on his face. "Now, when I tell you two not to worry, I mean it. We won't have to lift a finger to cause the president's demise. The truth is, my brother from another mother, Stephen C. Jefferson, will eventually destroy himself."

"I'll drink to that." My grandfather held up his shot glass of whiskey, then clinked it against ours. He gave me a stern look while tightly cuffing his hand. "Squeeze his balls and make him scream like a bitch. I want him to regret ever wanting to be president and for even thinking that he could be. And when you have his balls in your hand, drag him back to the streets where he belongs and pay one of those other coons twenty bucks to blow his fucking brains out."

"Ten dollars," Speaker Robinson said. "I'm sure you could get one of them to do it for ten."

We all released hearty chuckles, knowing that Stephen's downfall was imminent.

9

First Lady Raynetta Jefferson

I hated when Stephen was away from me. His trip to Africa lasted five long days. The only time I'd gotten a chance to see him was on TV. We spoke twice, that was all. It seemed that his trip had gone well, very well, especially when I tuned in to Chanel Hamilton's show and discovered that she was also in Africa. I predicted that she would interview Stephen again, but during her reporting, she seemed to only cover information that had been passed down from other journalists. Not once did I see a close-up between the two, but that didn't mean much. The revealing moment came when Stephen entered our bedroom in silence. It was almost nine o'clock at night; I was in bed reading.

"So, how did it go?" I said, observing him as he strolled in front of the bed with his suit jacket thrown over his shoulder. His shirt was halfway unbuttoned and his high fade needed a trim.

"It went well. Better than I expected, but the African people still have a lot of issues. Mainly because of a corrupt government, but who am I to judge when our government is no better?"

"Right. Same story, different country. What else did you do?"

He yawned, then came over to my side of the bed. A soft kiss was planted on my forehead, before he started to remove his shirt. I could smell his masculine cologne, and I thought I would be able to smell *her* perfume, but I didn't.

"Too much to talk about tonight. We'll talk more in the morning. For now, I need a shower and some rest."

Stephen removed his shirt, then laid it across a chair. I figured that my observing eyes on him made him a little uneasy, because he went into the bathroom, closing the door behind him. Minutes later, I heard the shower come on. We hadn't made love in God knows when, but tonight, I was in the mood. I placed the romance novel I was reading on the nightstand, then proceeded out of bed. My silk nightgown clung to my sexy curves that not many men could ignore. I removed my gown, laying it on the bed. In all of my nakedness, I sauntered toward the bathroom and entered. The room was filled with steam—Stephen loved to take scorching-hot showers. I could barely see him standing in the shower, but I could smell the black peppercorn body wash he used to lather his body. The closer I got, I could see him facing the wall. His muscular, stallionlike frame from the backside took my horniness up a notch. I hurried to enter the shower, then wrapped my arms around his waist. He seemed startled and quickly pivoted to face me.

"I thought you could use some company," I said in a soft tone.

He stared at me for a few moments, and then removed my arms from around him. "I don't mind if you stay, as long as you're good with it."

"If I wasn't *good* with it, I wouldn't be here."

Without replying, he turned his back toward me again. He started to wash his body, but this time I helped. My hands massaged his tight muscles, but as I reached around to touch the most impressive muscle on his body, he moved my hand away from it.

"Not tonight," he said without turning around. "I'm tired. Need some rest."

I pressed my body against his, hoping that after he felt my hard nipples and firm breasts brushing against his back, he would have a change of heart.

"I'm tired too," I said. "But I assure you that this won't take long."

I planted a trail of kisses against his back, but as I made a move to squat, he turned to face me. His package hadn't increased a single inch. To say I was surprised would be an understatement. I was shocked that he didn't appear turned on by me anymore.

"Raynetta, I have too much on my mind tonight, and that doesn't include sex," he said, towering over me. Our eyes remained connected; I figured that he could see the pure disappointment in mine.

"Why isn't it on your mind? Why are you rarely ever in the mood anymore, and what in the hell am I supposed to do if my husband refuses to have sex with me?"

"You're supposed to wait until he's ready and not take it personal."

My brows furrowed as I cocked my head back in awe. "Wait? Are you kidding me? How can I not take it personal, especially when I have a gut feeling that you weren't too tired to explore other *things* while in Africa?"

Stephen reached for the faucet to turn off the water. "We're not doing this tonight. As always, I have a busy day ahead of me. And for the last time, I need some rest."

He stepped around me to get out of the shower. All I could do was shake my head as I watched him reach for a towel and tie it around his waist. He exited the bathroom with me following closely behind him. In no way did his rejection feel good, but I refused to let him see how much his actions really hurt me.

"You know what?" I said with a grin on my face. "If you're not in the mood, I surely am."

I opened the drawer, pulling out my sex toy, which was a chocolate dream, multispeed vibrator . . . plopped on the bed, opened my legs wide, then flicked it on. Stephen looked at me as if I had lost my mind.

"Wha . . . What in the hell are you doing?"

"What does it look like I'm doing? You're a smart man, and I'm sure you can figure it out. First ladies have needs too."

I positioned myself and sighed from relief after carefully inserting the sizeable, pleasing instrument. Anger and a little bit of shock appeared on Stephen's face as he watched me. I started to moan a little; it was obvious that he had seen enough.

"I hope you're enjoying yourself," he said, walking to the closet.

"Oooh, baby, you better believe that I am. Yes! Yes! Yes! I aaaam."

Stephen hurried into a pair of sweatpants and a T-shirt. I continued to display how excited I was, and just as he'd made his way to the door, I expressed my enthusiasm. He couldn't resist watching me as I heavily breathed in and out, trying to catch my breath.

"That's right," he said as if he was upset. One would have thought that he was witnessing me in bed with another man. "Release all that fakeness, and remember that I do know what you really sound like when you're overly thrilled about something being inside of you."

Okay, maybe I was overdoing it, but what the hell? I clicked off the vibrator, then looked at him with a satisfying smile on my face. "I'm glad you remember what I sound like because I don't. But, until I can recall what it used to feel like, my new friend will suit me just fine. Good night, Stephen. See you in the morning, and don't forget to dim the lights."

I fluffed my pillows, then turned on my side to get comfortable.

Morning was there in a flash. My schedule was crammed with things to do today, but I had to somehow or someway squeeze in a visit to Chanel Hamilton's office. While I suspected that she and Stephen had gotten close on his trip, I wasn't exactly sure how close. My assistant, Claire, was doing a little digging for me too, but she hadn't come forth with any information yet. Either way, I wasn't going to wait. I needed to know something, and the one thing I knew about slick women was, they were always willing to talk. Chanel would definitely let the cat out of the bag. She came across as the kind of woman who would shout her business to the world. Then again, I was sure that Stephen told her to keep everything hush-hush. He never appreciated his business being out there, and now that he was president, I was sure that he encouraged her to remain tight-lipped. He surely remained that way with me, and he skipped breakfast this morning, just so he didn't have to elaborate on his trip. I grabbed a few pieces of toast and coffee. And while going over my schedule with Claire, I told her it was imperative for me to squeeze in a meeting with Chanel.

"I'm not sure if you will have time," she said, looking at my schedule. "You have a very tight schedule today. I just don't see where we can squeeze it in."

"We need to make time. If I have to cancel lunch, that'll be fine with me. She and I have some unfinished business to discuss. All I need is fifteen or twenty minutes with her."

"Okay. I'll call her office to see if I can make that happen." Claire looked at her watch. "As for now, we have to get going. It's almost nine thirty. You're supposed to be at the homeless shelter in less than an hour. Are you ready?"

"As ready as I'm ever going to be."

As usual, we left the White House with Secret Service in tow. Many of the agents were new. They were nearly glued to me. I could barely shake people's hands, and when a little girl reached out to hug me while at the shelter, one of the agents attempted to pull her away from me.

"It's okay," I said, displaying a frown. "No need to be so aggressive."

He backed away, allowing the little girl to get closer to me. She held wilted daisies in her hand while thanking me for coming to see her.

"These are for you." Glee was in her eyes. "My mom said that you would like them, and they go well with your yellow dress. It's so pretty, just like you are."

I accepted the flowers and smiled. "Thank you for the flowers, but I'm nowhere near as pretty as you are. What's your name?"

"Anastasia."

She swayed from side to side, showing much happiness as I complimented her. She looked to be about five or six years old. Her thick hair was brushed into a ponytail, but was very kinky. The dress she wore looked as if it hadn't been washed in ages, and her white shoes had black scuff marks all over them. I volunteered my time to feed the homeless, but it pained me to see so many homeless children there with their mothers. Anastasia introduced me to her mother who looked as if life had been very hard on her. Bags were underneath her eyes, her hands were real hard and dry when I shook them, and her hair too was a mess. I didn't want to question why she had been living in a shelter, but one of the workers mentioned to me that she and Anastasia had been abused by the mother's boyfriend. Feeding them didn't seem like it was enough. I wanted to do more, and when I returned to the car, I discussed it with Claire.

"I know that everyone makes their own choices in life, but what we witnessed back there should not be. We continue to protect and lookout for the wealthy, and it's a darn shame. A measly check and food vouchers will never be enough to help change those people's situations, but decent-paying jobs and a good education will. But as you already know, schools are closing, teachers are being laid-off, and many jobs don't pay enough. I truly hope that Stephen and his administration can do more to help homeless people. Meanwhile, please contact the shelter and see to it that by the end of the week, Anastasia and her mother have a roof over their heads and the mother has a job. Can you handle that for me?"

"I will do my best."

"Please do."

I sat in silence while looking at the wilted flowers in my hand and thinking more about the homeless. I said a prayer for them, and then prayed for myself as I entered Chanel's office. She was on the phone and didn't look happy to see me.

"Someone very important just came in," she said. "I have to go, Ciara, talk to you soon."

Chanel laid the phone on her desk, then stood to greet me. Her office was surrounded by glass, and we both noticed several individuals peeking in to see what was going on.

"I was quite surprised when I received a phone call from my boss, telling me that you were coming here. I'm not exactly sure what you'd like to discuss, but tell me now if I should close my blinds and allow us some privacy."

"I think that would be a good idea."

I watched as Chanel sashayed over to each window, closing the blinds. She wore a gray pantsuit that showed her hourglass figure. Her hair was brushed back into a ponytail that was full of curls, and her makeup didn't allow any blemishes to show. I had never been jealous of any woman Stephen had been with, but there was something about Chanel Hamilton that made me feel as if the competition was real steep.

"All done." She walked over to her cluttered desk, barely sitting on the edge of it and crossing her arms.

"Thank you," I said politely. "Normally, I don't waste time with women who I suspect are after my husband, but this time I couldn't resist. Why? Because I kind of like you. I think you have an amazing and rewarding career, and I would hate for you to mess it all up by getting involved with Stephen."

A noticeable purse of her lips appeared. "So, you came here to warn me . . . or threaten me? Which one?"

"I didn't just threaten you, did I?"

"No, but let's not pretend that you came here to save me from ruining my amazing life-slash-career. You couldn't care less about me, and you made it clear, after our interview, that you really don't like me."

I snapped my finger. "That's right, I did. And you made it clear during that same interview that my husband could have you at the snap of his finger. My gut tells me that your trip to Africa turned out to be something *real* special. I hope I'm wrong, but I can't help that I'm good at recognizing . . . Well, I hope this is appropriate for me to say, but I do recognize whores when I see them."

Chanel chuckled, then straightened her face as she took a few steps in my direction. "Whores don't have three sex partners after living on this earth for thirty-two years. A whore does not save herself until the right man comes along, nor does a whore care about the kind of man whom she spreads her legs for and allows to enter her. After careful thought and much consideration, I made an adult decision because I felt as if Stephen was so deserving of me. I mean, he took me to a place I had never been before, and what a passionate and experienced man he is. I'm a little disappointed that he's married to a ghetto drama queen, but I guess every man has flaws. Even our president."

This time, I inched forward, chuckling too. "The one word I will take from that crap you just said is experience. They say experience is the best teacher, and you, my dear, will learn, starting today, that a passionate man in the bedroom will diss the hell out of you once he leaves it. You will also learn that if you take another step forward, his ghetto, drama-queen wife will knock you on your ass and stomp you with the heels his money paid for. I hope you thoroughly enjoyed yourself in Africa, and before I go, I must gift you with a scrapbook for your memories. Keep them close to your heart, because I assure you that Stephen will never screw your trifling ass again."

I reached in my bag, then dropped the three-by-five scrapbook with four pages in it on the floor. I turned to exit, but stopped in my tracks when Chanel fired back at me.

"How much do you want to bet that Stephen *will* come to me again, especially after what I put on him? I doubt that he'll *ever* forget it, so you'll have to swap that little scrapbook for an eight-by-ten with many more pages for me to fill because he *will* be back."

Without turning around, I responded. "See, you just proved me right about whores. You all stay confused and are very delusional."

I left Chanel's office, waving at those who waved at me. One reporter kept hounding me about my visit, but to silence her, I encouraged her to set up an interview with me in the near future. She was ecstatic about that, but I wasn't doing much smiling on my end. I was torn up inside. Couldn't get the thoughts of Stephen having sex

with Chanel out of my mind. Then I thought about how
he rejected me last night. That angered me even more. I
couldn't even gather myself to attend my next meeting,
and while in the car, I had to shed a few tears. The path
Stephen and I were on was dangerous. I was starting to
dislike him, and I just didn't understand his ugly ways.
Arguing with him all the time hadn't done much good,
but something about confronting him made me feel
better. I couldn't wait another minute to do so.

The second we returned to the White House, I marched
down the West Wing, heading for the Oval Office where I
knew Stephen was in a meeting, thanks to Claire. Secret
Service was nearby, and one agent stopped me as I
approached the door.

"The president is in an important meeting with a few
members of his administration, with the vice president
and chief of staff. He asked not to be interrupted, but he
should be finished within the hour."

"I thank you for telling me, but I need to see my husband, now. Please move away from the door so I can go
inside."

He shook his head. "Sorry, ma'am, but I can't do that.
I've been advised not to let anyone go inside."

I ignored the agent I had never seen before. When
I touched the knob, he grabbed my hand, squeezing it
tightly.

"Sorry, Mrs. Jefferson, I can't."

I snatched my hand away, then lifted my finger to his
face. "Keep your hands off of me and move out of my way.
If you don't, I will have you thrown out of here so fast that
you'll regret not—"

Just then, Florence, from Stephen's administration,
opened the door. She said hello to me, but I moseyed
right on by her, entering the Oval Office. Stephen and
Tyler sat across from each other on the sofas. Andrew

stood next to Stephen, and three other people stood near the chairs. It appeared that the meeting was close to being over. Stephen glared at me; he could instantly tell I wasn't happy.

"I need a moment with my husband."

My eyes shifted from one person to the next in the room. Stephen looked past me, focusing on the Secret Service agent behind me.

"I apologize, Mr. President, but she wouldn't listen to me when I said you were in an important meeting and she couldn't go inside."

The direction of Stephen's eyes traveled to me. "We're not done with our meeting, so whatever is on your mind will have to wait."

"You love keeping me waiting, don't you? Well, I don't like to wait, so please allow your meeting to resume in about ten or fifteen minutes."

"My meeting will resume now. We'll talk when I'm finished, Raynetta, and as you can see, this is very important."

I looked around at everyone staring at me with bugged eyes. A few mouths were dropped open too, but I didn't care. *I* was the priority. It was time for Stephen to treat me as if I was.

"I have no problem having this conversation in front of your staff. If you want me to, I will. If not, I suggest you make the right decision and ask everyone to leave."

I figured that stubborn bastard wouldn't see things my way. The smug look on his face said it all, along with his tone that went up a few notches.

"Out, Raynetta, now!"

I moved closer to the sofa where Stephen was, appearing as calm as I could. "I'll get out after I say this. If you ever screw that bitch again, I will slice your throat, cremate you, and send your remains to your enemies around the world. Don't put me in that position, 'cause if you do, you *will* regret it."

Like always, Stephen didn't appear moved by my threats. Didn't blink, didn't flinch. The others were in shock—I heard loud gasps. Tyler also said something, but I was too busy digging into my purse for a switchblade. I quickly pulled it out, causing more of a reaction when I reached out, pressing the sharp blade against Stephen's neck. This time he blinked and attempted to back away from the blade.

"Oh my God," one lady said. "Somebody, do something!"

"Plea . . . Please put that away," Andrew pleaded. "It's not necessary."

I ignored them all and kept my eyes focused on Stephen while caging him in his seat. "Did you or did you not understand what I said?"

He didn't respond, just stared at me with pure anger trapped in his eyes. By then, Secret Service was in the room. Two agents grabbed me, and one of them snatched the switchblade.

"Everybody out!" one agent shouted. "Clear the room!"

Everyone left the room in a rush, leaving Stephen, the Secret Service, and me all by ourselves.

"Release her," Stephen said, then got off the sofa. He hadn't shown one bead of sweat and barely looked at me as he casually walked over to his desk. He opened the drawer, then placed what looked to be a nine millimeter Glock on top of it. His eyes narrowed as he glared at one of the agents. "I don't know what it will take for me to get the protection I need around here, but do me a favor and clock out for good."

The agent took a hard swallow. "Mr. President, allow me an opportunity to tell you how your wife was able—"

"Out!" he shouted. "O-U-T!"

Speechless, both agents left. I didn't feel good about this, only because I knew this wasn't their fault. Whenever things calmed down, I intended to clear things up. For now, I had Stephen to deal with.

"I am so sick and tired of you." He was blunt. "I'm dealing with a country that is possibly on the brink of war, gun violence issues, racism, cyberattacks, poverty, lack of jobs, a failing educational system, a Republican Party that is threatening another shutdown . . . and you have the audacity to run up in here threatening me over sex I'm having with someone else. How petty is that, especially when all you have to do is open your mouth and speak your truth, Raynetta. 'Cause when you do, you'll finally understand why I'm not in the bed with you and I prefer to be in bed with others. I will speak no further than that, but sit on that shit for a while, and then come back here when you're ready to correct your lies. Until then," he lifted the gun from his desk, cocked it sideways, and aimed it at me. "Understand that I *will* blow your brains out before you can ever cut my throat and cremate me. My mother has the authority to bury me, and whenever that time comes, I will be laid to rest in one piece."

I was slightly tongue-tied and somewhat caught off guard. Did he know I had been untruthful with him about not being able to have a child? If he did know, why hadn't he said anything? I needed to figure out how to approach this situation, so for now, just for now, I surrendered and gave him a win when I abruptly left his office.

10

President of the United States, Stephen C. Jefferson

What a day this had been. And just when I didn't think things could get any worse, Tyler rushed into my office telling me that there was a hostage situation in Wisconsin that involved an entire police station. Much gunfire had already erupted; several cops were dead. And a train had derailed in Illinois, causing very serious injuries, and a major bridge collapsed, sending cars crashing into the murky water. An effort to save lives was underway. I hated days like this, but sadly to say, this had become the norm. Inaction was the cause of many of these problems. Tyler agreed with me.

"It's time for you to extend your hand again to Congress," he said. "You can't get much done without them, and you'll have to find common ground with Speaker Robinson. Getting through to him is your only way. You may want to start with an apology."

"Apologize for what?" My face was twisted—No, he didn't just insult me. "If anything, he should be apologizing to me. Apologizing to the American people for years and years of inaction. Apologize for being at those lobbyists' beck and call. My list can go on and on, but you can be sure that I will *not* be the one apologizing to him."

Tyler released a deep sigh, as if he was frustrated. "I think it's the right move. And there have been other presidents who have had to do the same thing as you.

They made a decision to put the country first, and all I'm asking is for you to take your own advice about partisan bickering and figure out a way to work together."

"You work much better with Congress than I do, so I just may do what *one* other president had to do during his term, which is rely on his VP who has the right skin color to seal some deals. Meanwhile, I do understand what you're saying. It is important for me to keep on trying, even though I know how many members of Congress feel about me. I'll have a talk with Andrew this evening and request that he set up another meeting for me on Capitol Hill."

"Great. I'll join you as well, and we will all work hard to get things done. On another note, is the first lady okay? I've never seen her behave that way. What woman was she referencing?"

"I don't care to speak on that right now. All I will say is the first lady is fine. She will be much better, once she deals with her own issues."

Tyler scratched his head, then rubbed his blond hair back in place. "I won't push, but just so you know, we all have marital problems. Gena isn't happy about how much time I dedicate to work either, nor is she happy about any of my female companions. But giving her money to shop keeps her quiet. You should try giving the first lady a sizeable stash. Maybe she wouldn't be as irate and out of control as she seems to be all the time."

"No offense, but you should keep comments about the first lady out of your mouth and refrain from saying anything negative about her. First warning. You should also get with Andrew and Homeland Security to find out why Secret Service continues to fail me. I'm about to get some of my boys from the hood up in here to protect me, and I'm sure you *all* will have a major problem with that."

Tyler cleared his throat, then stood. "Andrew was the one who picked them this time, so don't blame me. I'll go chat with him about that and make preparations for our meeting on Capitol Hill tomorrow. Check in later, and if anything else comes up, I'll let you know. As for the first lady, I get it. Wives are off-limits and so are children."

I saluted Tyler, watching as he left my office. I appreciated his efforts in trying to get all of us to find common ground. Hopefully, one day, we'd be able to do it.

I used the remote to turn on the news, specifically to watch Chanel's show. We'd had an interesting time on Air Force One, but after spending the night with her, I distanced myself from her for the duration of the trip. I had already informed her that she would never be allowed to interview me or the first lady again. I kept my word, and she seemed disappointed. I spent very little time with the press, but the journalist who was up close and personal with me during the trip was an experienced, older reporter whom I had respected for many years. I did, however, see Chanel when she exited Air Force One. I gave her a handshake, thanking her for joining me.

"The president's visit to Africa was well received," Chanel said as I watched the news. *"These are some of the photos while he was there. As you can see, the new leaders appeared very hopeful for progress. While I didn't get an opportunity to have another interview with the president, James Burnashaski did. Tonight, I have the pleasure of bringing you that interview."*

I started to watch the interview, but shortly thereafter, I was interrupted by a knock on the door. Secret Service announced that it was my press secretary, Sam. Right after he came in, so did Andrew.

"Sorry to bother you, sir, but I wondered if you would like to come into the Press Briefing Room tomorrow and speak to the American people. There's a lot going on, and

I, sometimes, think it's good for people to hear directly from their president instead of me."

Andrew added his two cents. "I agree. Just for fifteen or twenty minutes. You can also let everyone know that you'll be visiting Capitol Hill. By relaying that message, you'll come across as the one who is making an effort to get things done."

"Fine. Let's roll with it. And, Sam, you're getting better. I've been watching you in the Press Briefing Room. Keep up the good work and try to smile just a little bit more."

Sam laughed while nodding. "Thank you, Mr. President. Glad you noticed, as I am doing my best."

After receiving a compliment from Andrew too, Sam left the room. Andrew stayed, giving me the scoop on the Secret Service. The incident from earlier appeared to be unpreventable, but it still didn't make me feel good that Raynetta was able to get a knife that close to my neck. I expressed further concerns about that with Andrew.

"You're right," he concluded. "She shouldn't have been able to do that, but no one expected that she would. And while I was very close to you, I wasn't sure if you would be upset with me for putting my hands on her."

"No, I wouldn't have been upset, under the circumstances, and trust me when I say I can handle my wife. But what if she wasn't the one holding that knife? I can only wonder if you would have made a move then."

"I guarantee you that I would have. It's just that I don't know how or when to intervene when it comes to certain issues with your wife. I didn't mind getting you the information you requested in regards to her medical records. And I'm very surprised that she lied to you about being raped. She seemed pretty adamant about speaking to you earlier, and I have to ask, are you, indeed, having an affair? I think I know the answer, based on what I see. But I don't want to jump to any conclusions."

"Nobody's business but mine. Have a good evening. We'll talk more before I go on Capitol Hill tomorrow."

"Fine, but one more thing before I go. Chanel Hamilton has been trying to reach you all day. She asked for your direct line, but I wasn't sure if you wanted her to have it."

"No. And if or when she calls back, tell her I'm busy."

We both turned our heads to look at the monitor that showed Chanel.

"All I know is that I had a wonderful time in Africa. The people were very kind and receptive to all of us. They are confident that the president will go on to do great things for their country, and I am almost certain that he will do some amazing things for this country too."

"Yeah, I guess that's why she voted for you, right?" Andrew said, knowing that she hadn't.

"We all make mistakes, but some mistakes can't be ignored."

I shook Andrew's hand, before he left.

The following day, I was suited up as I made my way to the Press Briefing Room for the second time. The reporters seemed to warm up to me a bit more this time, maybe because of the trip to Africa where many of them saw a softer side to me. Much respect was given . . . until one reporter was called on to question me. Instead of commenting on news that was happening in our country, he decided to attack me for making Africa my very first trip.

"Many Americans saw it as a slap in the face, especially when we have a serious racial divide in this country. You haven't said much about race relations, and as a black president, don't you feel as if you should be doing more?"

"As a black journalist and human being, what have you done to improve race relations—other than sit behind your desk and run your mouth?"

He placed his hand on his chest, as if he was offended. "Excuse me, sir, but I'm not president of the United States. You are."

"And just like me, you too are responsible for doing all that you can to help improve race relations. I want to ask you to name one thing, one single thing that you've done to unite this country. Have you reached out to other races, conducted any meetings, shared your experiences, listened to how others feel about what is transpiring, offered solutions, opened up a dialogue about these issues, met with police officers, state leaders, blogged . . . anything?"

"I . . . As I said, I'm not the president."

"You most certainly are not. That's why I'm here, and you're there. Next question," I said, looking directly at her. "Uh, Michelle Peoples, right?"

Michelle stood with a wide smile on her face, revealing her perfect teeth. Her natural, curly hair was shaped into an Afro that fell slightly above her shoulders. Her slanted eyes were beautiful and her smooth brown skin made me want to touch it.

"Wow, yes, I'm surprised that you knew my name. I feel very important now." Many laughed as she went on to ask her question. "Mr. President, many of our roads and bridges are crumbling, and as you said, what happened yesterday was very unfortunate. Congress has yet to create a comprehensive infrastructure package that will put more people to work and help to save some of our bridges that are no longer as sound as they used to be. Where does infrastructure fall on your list of priorities? Before or after the increasing homeless situation? The first lady mentioned that something needed to be done soon about that. Do you agree or disagree?"

"I wholeheartedly agree on all, and one does not take precedence over the other. The first lady made mention of her visit to the homeless shelter, and I was heartbroken. I'm also aware of the thirty-plus people who lost their lives when the bridge collapsed. We can't allow that to happen again. I will be visiting Capitol Hill today and will put forth every effort to reach out and discuss things of that nature. I expect changes in the weeks and months to come, and I'll definitely keep you all posted on how my meeting with Speaker Robinson goes. Until then, thanks and have a good day."

The reporters continued to fire questions at me before I left, and when Sam and I reached the hallway, I paused. A smile was on his face; he looked to be in deep thought.

"You okay?" I asked.

"I'm fine, sir. Just thinking about how much I love my job."

"That's good, Sam, I'm really glad to hear that. And before I go on Capitol Hill, do me a favor. Stop Michelle Peoples before she leaves and bring her to the meeting room straight-ahead. I'm very impressed with her, and I want to let her know why."

"Row seven, seat two, right?"

I winked. "No. That's where she sat last time. This time, row four, seat eleven."

"Got'cha. Give me five minutes."

Sam walked away, and almost ten minutes later, he came into the meeting room with Michelle Peoples in tow. As expected, she seemed nervous in my presence. The first thing people always wanted to know was if they had offended me.

"No, no, not at all," I said, standing behind a chair. I looked at Sam. "Thank you, Sam. I'll catch up with you in a few minutes."

"Sounds good. I'll be right down the hall."

He walked to the door, closing it behind him. Michelle stood at a distance, still looking confused as ever.

"Mr. President, I don't—"

I held up my hand, interrupting her. "Before you speak, I just want to commend you for always being professional and showing me respect while in the Press Briefing Room. It truly means a lot to me, and I wanted to let you know how much I appreciate it."

Her smile got even bigger. "Wow, uh, thanks so much for noticing, but it comes natural for me. I was so excited about voting for you, and I convinced so many new people to register to vote. You inspired all of us, and I pray that you're successful with moving your agenda forward."

"I hope so too, and thank you for encouraging others to vote. We have to protect our democracy and allow our voices to be heard. And if we really want change, we all have to work real hard for it."

"I couldn't agree with you more. I say the same thing to my husband, as well as to my children. They're young, but they already understand how important voting will be for them, when the time comes."

"Very important, and it's never too soon to school them on world issues. As for your husband, how long have the two of you been married?"

She hesitated a little, but then answered. "For too long," she laughed. "But, actually, only four years. I've known him for almost ten years though."

"You know what I've learned? You can know someone for years and years, but still not know who they really are unless you're willing to search deeper. I've had to do that several times, and I've always been surprised by what I discovered."

Michelle swallowed a visible lump in her throat. "Sometimes, we pretend not to know things just to avoid the hurt."

"Been there, done that too."

She dropped her fidgeting hands by her sides, then released a deep sigh. "I'd better get going. Thanks for inviting me to meet with you. You have no idea how much you just made my day. I didn't mean to venture off into that other stuff, but your comment kind of made me think about some things."

"No problem. And if you ever want to talk, feel free to call me."

She laughed, showing how giddy a thirty-year-old enthusiastic woman could be. "Yeah, right, Mr. President. You know I could never just pick up the phone and call you."

"Who says you can't? I didn't."

Seriousness washed across her face. "I don't know what I would call you to say, but are you serious?"

I stepped forward, holding out my hand. "Let me see your cell phone."

She removed it from her pocket, then gave it to me. I punched in my private number, then gave the phone back to her.

"Okay, that was cute," she said. "I know this is not your real number in my phone."

"Call it and see."

She punched the call button, and when my phone rang, I answered and put the phone up to my ear.

"Hello. I thought you'd never call me, even though I said you could."

Blushing, she hit the end button, then cleared her throat. "O . . . okay, Mr. President. At your request, I will call you if I ever need to talk."

I walked to the door, opening it. "Please do."

We exited together, but stopped before parting ways.

"May I please take a picture with you?" she asked. "If it's a problem, I—"

"No problem. Take your picture."

She held up her phone to take a selfie of us. Very excited, she thanked me again before walking toward the briefing room. I made a right to go handle my business for the rest of the day.

11

President of the United States, Stephen C. Jefferson

Tyler joined me on Capitol Hill, but the first place I headed, with plenty of news reporters following us, was to Speaker Robinson's office.

"Are you expecting a huge fight with the Speaker," one reporter shouted. He was ignored.

"Mr. President, pictures of your mother in a drunken stupor surfaced earlier today. Have you spoken to her? And was it, indeed, her in the photos?"

I ignored that question too, but my thoughts quickly shifted to my mother. I hadn't spoken to her in a few days, and no one around me mentioned anything about pictures being leaked. My administration was starting to piss me the hell off. If this was true, a whole lot of people were about to be without employment. I stepped away from the reporters, as well as from Tyler. Before going into the Speaker's office, I slipped into the restroom to call my mother.

"Yes, darling," she slurred. "And before you say anything, that woman in those photos is not me. At least I think she isn't."

"I haven't seen any photos, but I have a good feeling that tag . . . You're it. I can't believe you've started drinking again. Why now, Mama? Why, when all you ever wanted was to see me doing exactly what I'm doing right now? There is no way for me to do what I came here to do and keep getting hit with setbacks. Your alcohol abuse is going to set me back and cause me to worry about you."

"Don't worry about me. I'll be fine. I just went to a party last night, got carried away, and overdid it. Had I known those nosy-ass reporters would be watching me, I would've left out the back door. I promise that after today, I will not have another drink. I just needed something today to wash down that bad taste in my mouth."

"I've heard it all before. And if you feel as if you need to get some help again, please get it. Call and let me know so I can take you. All right?"

"I said I'll be fine, so stop worrying about me. The person you should be worried about is your wife. What is going on with Miss Ne-ne? She was at a homeless shelter the other day, wearing a loud yellow dress that had her titties busting all through it. The reporter interviewing her could barely keep his eyes off her breasts. You'd better keep your eyes on her, because she's a hot one. With all those Secret Service men around her, somebody is bound to cop a feel from a woman showing all of her goodies like that."

"Mama, please stop talking about Raynetta. She'll be fine. Take care of yourself, and I'll give you a call tomorrow to check on you. I'm headed into an important meeting, so I have to go."

"Okay. And be nice. When I see you on TV, you're always looking so mean. Like you want to hurt somebody, but that's what being with a woman like Ne-ne will do to you. Either way, don't you hurt nobody up there on Capitol Hill, okay?"

"I can't promise you that I won't, but I will promise you that I won't go to jail."

She laughed, and after exchanging the love, we ended the call. I exited the restroom and ran right into Tyler who was outside waiting for me.

"If you don't mind," I said, "I want to speak to Speaker Robinson alone. You can meet with the Majority Whip to see if he can help get some order with the Republican caucus."

"I'll do what I can. Meanwhile, if you need any assistance in there with the Speaker, buzz my phone and I'll be right there."

"I'm sure I can handle Mr. Speaker."

Tyler chuckled as he walked away in his tight-legged pantsuit. I watched him, thinking about how much I was starting not to trust him. Recently, every time he stood in my presence, I got bad vibes. Maybe it was just me, but when he turned around, looking at me with a sly smirk, I sensed, again, that something wasn't right. I walked away, realizing even more that I needed to keep a closer eye on my circle.

Minutes later, I stood by Speaker Robinson's door that had his name engraved on a gold plate. I knocked once, then entered before he invited me to come inside. His leather chair faced the wall behind him while he was leaned back in it. Cigar smoke filled the air, and on top of the mahogany wooden desk was a laptop and a pile of cluttered papers. A fireplace was in front of his desk, and to the left was a sitting area with four leather chairs surrounding a round table. The beautiful crystal chandelier set the entire office off, as well as the thick crown molding that covered every corner of the room. The Oval Office was much bigger, so there was no mistake about who was considered the most important around here.

"You're early," he said, swinging around in his chair. "I thought you would have changed your mind about coming here, especially since I think you're wasting your time."

"Wasting my time or not, I'm here. Are you going to sit here or shall we have a seat over there?" I pointed to the sitting area near the round table.

"No, I reckon that this chair is quite comfortable, and I don't see no reason for me to move my ass. Have a seat in the chair in front of me. It's leather, and I can have it wiped off and polished again after you leave."

Due to my purpose, I bit my tongue, refusing to comment harshly on his bullshit. I then took a seat, crossing one leg over the other.

"Speaker Robinson, I didn't come here to exchange jabs with you, and I've had enough fights in the streets of St. Louis. The issues with our country are more important than the beef we have—"

"Beef?" he said, laughing. "Who said anything about beef? I thought you liked chicken."

My eyes narrowed. If they could shoot bullets, he would have been dead. "As I was saying, the problems we have are bigger than our dislike for each other. I'm here to find out what I can do to encourage you to get your party in line on crucial upcoming votes in the House. The Senate is good, but for several years, the Republican-led House has prohibited us from moving forward. We have to start working on legislation that moves us forward. I'm willing to meet you halfway on anything, but you have to give me something to work with."

He smashed his cigar in an ashtray, then looked across the desk at me with his evil eyes. I could sense how much this man despised me, and quite frankly, the feeling was mutual.

"I thought I made it clear the last time we all got together for one of these ridiculous meetings that I would *never* work with you. You're too dumb, and your attitude is real ugly, *boy*. Those fancy clothes you wear are only a cover-up, and after you remove them, you still have that same ole skin that will never get you anywhere. It's definitely not going to get you anywhere in an institution like this, and just so you know, as long as you reside in *my* house, I intend to have my members block every bill that comes to the House floor."

"So, basically, you're saying to hell with the American people? The color of my skin is going to prevent you from doing your job, and that's all there is to it, huh?"

"You're damn right it is. And, yes, to hell with the American people. The majority of them voted for you, so now they're all going to pay for making a horrible decision. The only thing that will light a fire under my ass is if you step down and allow Tyler to take over. If so, I'll give him gun control. I'll give him infrastructure, more freebees for blacks . . . all of that other wonderful crap you promised on the campaign trail. At the snap of my fingers, I will make my party fall in line, but you'll have to make the Democrats fall out of love with you and your nonsense."

I must admit that I was in awe after sitting in the Speaker's office for only a few minutes. He didn't hold back, and it was good to know where he stood on all of this. I had to clarify a few things, just to be sure that he meant what he'd said.

"So, the bottom line for you is this: As long as I'm president, you will sit there and do nothing. You will make the American people pay for electing me, and you will only make a move if I step down."

"You got it, and it didn't even take you long to figure it out."

"No, Mr. Speaker, the only thing I got is you."

I removed a recorder from the inside of my jacket, showing it to him. Before saying another word, I clicked the stop button, then leaned in close to his desk.

"You have the audacity to call me dumb, but you must be the stupidest motherfucker I know. Within the hour, the whole world will hear exactly what you just said, and they will finally understand why nothing is getting done. I won't be going anywhere, but there *is* another alternative.

If you choose to resign before eight o'clock tonight, this tape recorder stays in my possession. If not, you already know the consequences."

Speaker Robinson looked as if he had stopped breathing. All kinds of flies ran into his mouth—it was opened so wide. He was the one now tongue-tied and was too slow when he reached out, trying to snatch the recorder from my hand.

"Nigga, please," I said, tucking the recorder back in my pocket, then stood. "I need to hear from you or get a fax by eight o'clock. That's plenty of time for you to decide what you need to do, and I know you'll make the right decision to protect this institution."

As I strutted toward the door, Speaker Robinson called after me. I didn't bother to turn around and face the coward.

"You're going to pay for this," he shouted out. "Trust me, you're going to pay!"

"Any cost that I will pay will be well worth it, especially if that means getting you the hell out of here. Pack your bags, old man. Retirement awaits you."

I left with my head raised high. Many cameras flashed at me, and with a smile on my face, I didn't answer one question. My smooth walk was an indication that things had gone well.

When I returned to the Oval Office, I informed Tyler how things had gone down. He was stunned. Near speechless as he paced the floor and raked his hair back while I played the message on the recorder for him to listen to.

"Oh my God," he said. "I . . . I can't believe he said that to you. Didn't he know that . . . How could he not know that you were recording what he said?"

"He was too stupid to realize it. Put his foot right in his mouth, and his own words will be played on every news network if he doesn't resign today."

Tyler looked to be in deep thought. A sheen of sweat covered his forehead, and he kept wiping down his face with his hands.

"This is huge, Stephen. But . . . but I don't know if we should let the American people hear what Speaker Robinson said to you. There could be many attempts on his life, and I don't want you to have any regrets behind this."

I had to laugh. "You have my word that I will have no regrets. If anything, I hope that his replacement will be easier for me to work with. If not, I'll figure out what to do to get rid of that person too."

"There is a chance that Senator Bass could replace him, if he resigns. I don't think he will do it, but then again, I'm not so sure. I need to go find out some more information. I'm sure others are starting to talk, and if I hear anything I'll let you know."

"Please do. I have a quick errand to run, but I'll be back soon."

"Where are you going? I need you here, just in case."

"I won't be gone for long. Just need to take care of something."

Tyler held out his hand. "Do you mind leaving the recorder with me? I want to make a duplicate of it, just in case we may need it."

"No. The recorder stays with me. I'll have duplicates made ASAP."

"Okay. See you when you return."

Tyler rushed out of my office to see what he could find out. I was hyped about what was on the recorder, but the thoughts of my mother weighed heavily on my mind too. I planned to stop by her place to see her, but when Secret Service drove me there, she didn't answer the door. I had a key to let myself in, and after looking around, she was nowhere to be found. I returned to the motorcade, then called her cell phone. Thankfully, she answered.

"Yes, son," she said in a cheerful tone.

"Where are you? I stopped by to see you."

"I'm at a friend's house. Had you told me you were stopping by, I would have stayed home. I didn't feel like being cooped up at home, so I came to Debbie's house to visit her."

"Okay. Tell her I said hello. Buzz me when you get home to let me know you're safe."

"I will do no such thing. Stop worrying about me, please. Now, good-bye."

I felt a little better after we hung up, but she was still on my mind. My thoughts, however, shifted in another direction when I went to Chanel's office to discuss a private matter before her evening program. Looking sexy as ever, she sat against her desk, very delighted to see me.

"So, let me get this straight," she said. "You want me to play that recorder and allow everyone to hear what the Speaker said, even if he resigns?"

"Yes. I told him that I would keep it in my possession, but I didn't exactly tell the truth. Regardless of what he decides to do, I want everyone to know what kind of man has been so-called running things on Capitol Hill. I never want him to work anywhere else again, and right about now, I know that he's trying to figure out a way that he can still prohibit me from moving my agenda forward. As a gift to you, I'm giving you an explosive story to report. Everyone will be tuned in tonight, including other networks that have no access to what you have."

"You are playing real dirty, Mr. President, but I like your style."

"Trust me, you haven't seen nothing yet."

"I'm sure I haven't, but I thank you for looking out for little ole me again. I have to keep asking myself, why me, and not other reporters like . . . like Michelle Peoples?

She's been bragging about a photo she took with you, and I can't help but to notice how your eyes always seem to be looking in her direction during your meetings with the press. Maybe it's nothing, and it doesn't explain why you haven't returned any of my calls. I guess your wife told you about her visit, and I'm slightly annoyed that I haven't heard from you."

Yeah, and she was about to annoy me. "Can we put all of that aside for one night and handle this thing regarding Speaker Robinson? If you don't want to do this, I can find plenty of reporters who will. I just thought—"

She held out her hand, asking for the recorder. "Say no more. The pleasure to serve you would be all mines. After I'm done sharing the good news, I would love to have a celebration with you. Tell me, Mr. President, if that is at all possible."

I wanted everything to flow smoothly tonight, but if I told Chanel that I wasn't down with her celebration, she would trip.

"I'll try my best to call you, but I can't make you any promises because you know the shit will hit the fan tonight."

"Then, what about tomorrow?" She walked up to me and put her arms on my shoulders. "I need to see you again, but I'm not going to beg. I can't stop thinking about what you did to me, and every time I close my eyes, there you are. Have you been thinking about me, or are you too busy to allow me to invade your thoughts?"

Damn, I hated to lie, but the truth was, I hadn't thought much about what had happened between us on Air Force One. There were too many other things on my mind, including Raynetta.

I wrapped my arms around her waist, just to put her at ease. "Of course I've thought about us, but please understand that there is so much going on right now. I

just don't have a lot of free time on my hands, and with
Raynetta on my back, seeing you again may be difficult."

Chanel looked me straight in the eyes while placing her
finger on my lips.

"I said I wasn't going to beg. If you want to make
time for us, you will. Meanwhile, be sure to tune in this
evening, and thanks, again, for giving me what I need."

She leaned in to kiss me, and even though I enjoyed
the taste of her sweet lips, I cut the kiss short. I returned
to the White House almost an hour later. And by 7:30
p.m., I had the Speaker's resignation letter in my hand.
Word spread quickly; it was a total shock to all. Yet again,
my phones rang off the hook, even more so when Chanel
started to deliver the evening news.

*"Chaos has erupted on Capitol Hill tonight, and
Speaker Robinson is in the center of it all. For those of
you tuning in, please beware of the shocking, hateful,
and vulgar words used by the Speaker. I am thrilled that
he has resigned, because there is no place for this kind of
leadership on Capitol Hill. Our president deserves much
more respect than this, and we, the American people,
need to stand by him and encourage our congressional
leaders to do the same."*

Chanel was so good at making people see things her
way. She played the recorder, and not one single news
contributor could sit there and defend what the Speaker
had said. Well . . . maybe one.

*"To me, it sounded as if the Speaker was intoxicated.
And how do we know that message is authentic? I don't
think that any of us should rush to judgment, especially
since we have not heard directly from the Speaker yet."*

*"We have heard from him," Chanel fired back. "He
resigned. He resigned because he had no other choice.
And you'd better believe the message is authentic. I
have a very reliable source who made that recording*

available to me, and there is no secret that the Speaker is a racist. In this day and age, we can't afford to have leaders like him making vital decisions pertaining to our laws."

They all went on and on, chewing up Speaker Robinson and spitting him out. I enjoyed every bit of it, and as I sat at my desk with my hands behind my head, I was delighted to take his call.

"You dirty piece of shit," he shouted. "You said you wouldn't release that message if I resigned! How dare you not honor your word! How dare you, you fucking nigger!"

"I'll be that and then some, Mr. Robinson. And I will also be your president for the next four or possibly eight long years. By then, you'll probably be flip-flopping in your grave."

I hung up, then quickly returned a phone call from Michelle that I missed while watching the news. I was in a very good mood, but by the way she sounded on the other end of the phone, I could tell that she wasn't.

"I know you said that I could call you and talk, and I'm sure you're awfully busy, especially with all that's going on with Speaker Robinson. I . . . I just found myself in an unfortunate situation tonight, and I kind of needed a man's point-of-view in reference to what I've been going through."

No, I really didn't have time for this tonight, but I was good at listening and giving advice. I did just that for the next fifteen minutes or so and was glad when Michelle started to sound better. She admitted to knowing that her husband was on the down low, but she wasn't sure if leaving him was the right thing to do. They hadn't had sex in almost two years, and he spent more time with his lover than he did with her and the kids. "Know when to go" was a piece of advice I'd given her. She agreed.

"I do think it's best that we go our separate ways, and I don't know what I've been holding on for. It's embarrassing, more than anything, and I've always tried to hang in there like my parents have for so many years."

In the moment, I couldn't help but to think about my marriage. I figured Raynetta was still trying to get her lies together, because I hadn't heard a peep from her.

"Years that so many of us would love to have, but we just aren't willing to do the work. I commend those who do it."

"I do as well." She paused. "Good night, Stephen. Thanks for listening. Your advice was much appreciated."

"You're welcome. Rest well."

Our call ended, but several minutes later, Michelle reached out to me again. I had just wrapped up a call with Andrew who expressed to me how chaotic things were tonight on Capitol Hill.

"I'm sorry to bother you again," she said. "But my children are with my parents for the weekend. I'm kind of bored, and would like to go for a nice, long, quiet, and peaceful walk in the park. Care to join me?"

"All parks are closed at this time of the night."

She laughed. "Not closed to the president, and being with you would make it even better. Bring your Secret Service along; we'll have nothing to worry about."

"All I need is one agent, right?"

"Yes, just one. I'll do my best to protect you too."

I hesitated to go, but within the hour, my agent, Bruce, drove me to the park. I saw Michelle sitting on a bench, exactly where she said she would be. I was casually dressed in jeans and a button-down Polo. A cap was on my head, and dark shades shielded my eyes so that no one would recognize me. Michelle stood, and with Bruce following several feet behind us, we began to walk slowly on the trail.

"I can't believe that you actually came," Michelle said with a smile. "And I have to ask, but do you always make yourself available to women like this?"

"I can't say that I do. I didn't mind coming because I needed some fresh air too. Working all the time doesn't do a body good, and every once in a while, I have to take some time out to do simple things like this or else I'll go crazy."

"I wouldn't want you to do that, so any time you want to get away from your busy life, you can always reach out to me. I enjoy peaceful walks like this and the smell of nature." She stopped to inhale. "Along with your cologne, it's enough to take me there."

"Take you where?"

"Farther into the woods over there, where it's just a little darker, and, possibly, a bit more romantic."

"Romantic? What's so romantic about being over there?"

Michelle took my hand, leading the way. Bruce followed, but I asked him to halt his steps as we got closer to an area that was surrounded by very tall trees and a cataract waterfall that offered pure relaxation. Michelle faced me as I was caught up in the beautiful scenery I hadn't noticed before.

"Nice, isn't it?" she said.

"Yes, it really is."

"Sometimes, I just come here late at night to think. A few people join me from time to time, and one couple told me that this is one of their favorite places to come and make love."

"I can definitely understand why."

"I wouldn't know, unless I had an opportunity to experience it myself."

I didn't reply, but Michelle removed my cap, then rested her arms on my shoulders. She couldn't really see my eyes behind the shades, so I removed them before she did. I tucked them in my pocket, then wrapped my arms around her waist, pulling her a little closer to me.

"Let me say this, and I will say no more," she said. "I sensed that there was something about me that you liked during those press briefings, and the look in your eyes said it all. I was, however, shocked that you asked to meet me, and I'm even more surprised that you're here. I will make no demands of you, and I don't want you to feel sorry for me or obligated to speak to me if or when I call you. I understand that you are carrying the burdens of the world on your shoulders, and if we can help each other release some of the stress in our lives for one night, just one night, I'm perfectly fine with that."

I wasn't much of a talker in situations like this, more of a listener. I responded by leaning in, placing my lips on hers. Our tongues danced, and as the juicy kiss intensified, I inched her back to a tree. My hands cuffed her beautiful, smooth face, and I brushed my thumbs against her soft cheeks. While up close and personal, we searched into each other's eyes. I inhaled, so did she. Her firm breasts rose, touching my chest even more. The short, loose dress she wore provided easy access to her goodness underneath it. I removed the straps from her shoulders and planted delicate kisses along the side of her neck and shoulder. With no bra on, her breasts stood at attention. I gently massaged them, and when her dress hit the ground, exposing her nakedness, my hands traced every curve in her figure. I took a moment to explore it, massage it; the healthiness of her ass cheeks required me to venture there for a while. My hands roamed to other places too, like her hotspot that I slowly stirred with my finger, creating a creamy batter inside of her that prompted me to take off my clothes. She waited patiently. And when I pressed my body against hers, her back squirmed against the tree. Her slanted eyes stared me down; she was so damn sexy and pretty. I grabbed at her natural, wild Afro while passionately kissing her again. The sweet taste was still there, and that's when I lifted her legs, opened them wide and positioned myself between them. Her back remained against the tree, and she held on tight when I slipped my protected meat into her, stroking at a smooth pace. I could feel her legs trembling, so I secured them around my back, and began to celebrate what I considered to be a damn good day.

"Stepheeeen," she moaned as I latched on to her breasts while working my goods in and out of her. "I . . . it's . . . Is it okay that I call you Stephen?"

I removed my mouth from her breast, only for a few seconds to answer her. "You can call me whatever comes to your mind. The sound of your sexy voice is like music to my ears."

Michelle called me every name in the book, from "baby" to "sweetheart" to "Mr. President," especially when I turned her around to face the tree and tackled her backside with my fierce tongue, fingers, and lengthy steel. Her healthy cheeks were so perfect as I held them in my hands. We worked our way closer to the waterfall, and I had an even better grip on her cheeks when I lay on my back, guiding her skillful ride on top of me. I could feel the depths of her warm tunnel. The tight grip she had on my shaft and hearing the soothing waterfall in the background made me work harder so we could release our sexual buildup together. It wasn't long before we did. The sound of our voices echoed loudly, causing my Secret Service agent to rush in and make sure things were good. I confirmed that they were.

"All good," I said, shielding Michelle's body with mine. "Ten minutes, and I'll be ready."

With her back facing me, Michelle kneeled in front of me. She wrapped one of my arms around her waist; directed my other hand to her wetness. "Thirty minutes," she countered. "He'll be ready in about thirty or so more minutes."

"Take your time, sir," Bruce said. "I'll be over there waiting."

I was so sure that he was somewhere watching . . . or possibly taking notes. Whatever he was preoccupied with, I took my time with Michelle, stroking, tasting, touching, and licking every part of her sweet-smelling body that I could. In the moment, I felt high. Didn't come down from my high until I returned to the White House, resuming what I now considered a normal life.

12

First Lady Raynetta Jefferson

I had great days, okay, and bad. Today was a horribly bad day, and I had to shed some tears as I sat on the edge of the bed, looking through the numerous photos of Stephen having passionate sex with Chanel Hamilton on Air Force One. Claire had arranged to get the photos for me. She was very disgusted as she handed the envelope over. Like always, I put on my game face, saying that I didn't care, even pretended as if I didn't. But this did something to me. The ugly conversation I had with Stephen did something to me as well. I wasn't sure if he was trying to blame me for his behavior. He told me to speak my truth, and after all this time, maybe it was time for me to just come out and say that I never wanted any children. I didn't know how to say it, so I concocted a lie about being brutally raped by my uncle when I was a teenager. I told Stephen that my uncle had cut my insides with a knife, and the damage he'd done prevented me from having children. Before that, I told him that I was pregnant so that he would marry me. When I was forced to come clean about that, he was devastated. There was no question that a trail of lies and deceit followed me, but Stephen had plenty of issues too. This thing with Chanel was eating me alive. Stephen had served her well; I could tell by her expression in each photo. He too seemed to be enjoying himself, and it had been such a long time since I'd seen that satisfied expression on his face. All I witnessed around here was how unhappy he was. He damn sure wasn't the only one.

Feeling frustrated, I tossed the photos on the night-stand, then headed to the bathroom to splash water on my tearstained face. Stephen had been away all day. I wasn't even sure if he was here now. He was probably somewhere celebrating Speaker Robinson's resignation. That was unquestionably a good thing, and yet again, I felt as if this was a turning point in the right direction for Stephen. He would be able to get many things accomplished with the Speaker out of the way. Then again, I wasn't so sure because many members of the Republican Party hated him with a passion.

Around midnight, I changed into my nightgown, then climbed in bed. I wondered if Stephen would come to bed tonight, and if he did, I intended to clear my conscience and speak my truth. We hadn't had a heart-to-heart talk in a long time. After all that had happened, it was time.

I fluffed my pillow, then lay on my side. My eyes locked on those photos again, and as tears began to well, I shut my eyes, fading into a deep sleep.

The next morning, I woke up to the bright sunrays coming through the window. I squinted, then stretched before looking next to me where there was no Stephen. His side of the bed hadn't been touched. I figured he must have spent another night in the Oval Office, or the Yellow Oval Room on the second floor, where he chilled a lot too. Nonetheless, we had a big day ahead of us. The White House Correspondence Dinner was tonight. I barely had time to figure out what to wear, but before I did anything, I wanted to free my mind and get some things off my chest. I figured that Stephen was already up and probably in a meeting. I reached for my phone to call Claire so she could tell me exactly where he was.

"Can you do me a favor and find out where Stephen is this morning? I don't want to interrupt him if he's in a meeting."

"I'll look into it and call you back in about five minutes."

I laid the phone on the bed and took a deep breath. The direction of my eyes traveled to the nightstand, where I had laid the photos last night. Almost immediately, my heart sank to my stomach—The photos were gone. I jumped off the bed and pulled on the drawer, just in case I put them in there. No luck. I then got on my knees, searching underneath the bed and looking everywhere that I could possibly think of. I didn't think I put them anywhere else, and the more I thought about it, I was positive that I put those pictures on the nightstand. Stephen probably came in last night, without me knowing it, and removed the photos. I hoped that was the case, especially since no one else had access to this room but us.

My phone rang, startling me. I quickly snatched it off the bed to answer.

"His early-morning briefing is done," Claire said. "He doesn't have another meeting until noon. After that, he'll be pretty busy until the correspondence dinner this evening. I'll be there as well. If you need me to reach out to your stylist I will."

"I don't feel like being bothered with my stylist. She sounds too much like my mother-in-law, always trying to tell me what to wear. I think I can handle what to wear tonight myself."

"Okay. If you change your mind, let me know. Meanwhile, after you speak to Stephen, stop by to see me. We need to go over a few things pertaining to your schedule for next week, okay?"

I told Claire that I would stop by her office. Afterward, I took a quick shower, got dressed, and then made my way to the Oval Office to see Stephen. This time, I had no issues with Secret Service. The agent escorted me inside, where Stephen was speaking to his chief of staff. Andrew said hello to me, and then directed his conversation back to Stephen.

"I'll get busy on getting that information to you some time this afternoon."

"If you can do it before then, that would be much appreciated. Thanks for your help. I owe you one."

Andrew left, leaving us alone. I walked over to the sofa where Stephen was sitting and sat across from him. My hair slipped from the clip, falling in front of my face. I swooped it behind my ears, then cleared the tiny lump in my throat.

"I'm not going to beat around the bush," I said. "So are you ready to hear my truth, as you called it?"

"I'm always ready to hear you speak the truth." He glanced at his watch. "But it seems as if you've had a problem venturing there."

"There are times when you've been untruthful too, but this isn't about you right now. It's about me coming clean."

"Coming clean, after you discovered I already knew about your lies? All I need to know is why. Why would you lie to me about something like that?"

"Because I didn't want to lose you. After I told you I lost our first child, you wanted another one so badly. That's all you ever talked about, and I feared that you would divorce me had I told you that I never wanted any children." I paused as I started to get choked up. "I love children, but I just don't have the patience. I fear that I won't be a good mother, and I never truly felt that you were in love with me. I know you married me because you thought I was pregnant. But right after you found out there would be no children, you turned cold toward me. You've been that way ever since."

Stephen wiped down his clean-shaven face, then massaged his chin. "You're right. I have been cold, and after I had Andrew check out some things for me, it's hard for me to even look at you. I'm so angry with you, Raynetta, and there are times when I feel that we just need to end this and be done with it. But now, I'm here. Things have changed, and quite frankly, I need you."

"All you need me for is to continue this charade. But how long do you think it will last? This is very difficult for me, and since I know that you don't love me anymore, I really don't have a reason to stay."

"Who said I didn't love you anymore? I never said that I wasn't in love with you."

"Your actions say that you don't. And the way you screwed Chanel's brains out on Air Force One, it's apparent that you don't have any love for me whatsoever. I'm sure you saw yourself in action, since you removed the photos from our bedroom."

"I assumed we were being 'watched' so I added a little something extra during the festivities. As for photos, I don't know what photos you're talking about. I haven't seen any, but obviously you have."

My eyes grew wide. I didn't know how to respond, especially if I had allowed someone to get a hold of those photos. Then again, maybe Stephen had them and just didn't want me to know. There was no need to panic—yet.

"A man who truly loves his wife wouldn't sit there and say what you just said to me. But, I'm over it. I refuse to keep telling you how to treat me, and showing my disappointment is never enough. In reference to the photos of you and Chanel, they were on the nightstand.

When I woke up, they were no longer there. If you have them, great. If not, you can waste your time figuring out who does."

I got up from the couch, then made my way toward the door.

"The correspondence dinner starts at seven," Stephen said. "I'm sure you'll be there, won't you?"

I didn't bother to turn around. "Dressed to impress and in all of my fakeness, yes, I will be. And please warn your mother about saying anything to me. I'm not in the mood for her insults, and I would hate to slap her tonight."

All I heard was a light chuckle.

Bastard.

I didn't need a crystal ball to see into the future. Hours later at the White House Correspondence Dinner, Stephen and I danced and pranced around as if our lives hadn't missed one beat. We smiled at each other, laughed, and even pecked each other's lips a few times. I burst into laughter at some of the stale-ass, corny jokes someone had prepared for him, but the ones about Speaker Robinson's resignation were quite funny. Those jokes seemed to get the most applause and laughter, but to be honest, our surroundings were no laughing matter. Chanel Hamilton couldn't keep her eyes off Stephen. I noticed that he hadn't given her an ounce of attention. He did, however, give his attention to another reporter who had her eyes locked on him all night. I eased over to Claire, as she stood chatting with several journalists from CNN.

"I need to ask you something," I whispered in her ear. "Step aside from your conversation, whenever you can."

Claire was always at my beck and call; I couldn't ask for a better assistant. She looked fabulous in her tight beige dress that fell straight down her slim figure. Her pale white skin was covered with very little makeup, but her red gloss was pretty loud. I always complimented her long brown hair, and, tonight, it flowed midway down her back.

A few minutes later, she stepped aside and came up to me as I was chatting with Senator Canfield. He had started to flirt; I was pleased when Claire interrupted us.

"The president is one lucky man, and I would trade places with him any day, just to be with you. I also didn't know he was that hilarious," Senator Canfield said. "Who would have thought that he had such a great sense of humor?"

"And who would have thought that you were interested in trying to lay his wife? I don't think your wife would find any humor in that . . . would she?"

Embarrassed, as well as shocked by my comment, his eyes bugged, and he abruptly walked away. I turned to Claire who stood with a smile on her face, shaking her head at me.

"Who is she?" I whispered to Claire. She already knew *who* I was referring to.

"Her name is Michelle Peoples." We both looked in Michelle's direction. "The president was with her last night."

I couldn't help but to think that Stephen sure knew how to pick them as I observed the fit woman with natural hair that was styled in a wavy 'fro. She was gorgeous, and the white, fitted dress she wore had a hole in the back, revealing nothing but skin. Her thick lashes made her eyes even bigger, and her five-inch heels gave her much height. I didn't suspect that a long-lasting relationship between her and Stephen was in the works, so I wasn't that jealous.

"How long was he with her last night?" I questioned.

"For a few hours. In the park, might I add."

"Humph. These whores will lie anywhere for a piece of him. Thanks for the information and don't forget to keep me updated on those photos. I want to know who took them and why."

"I'm on it. But please start locking the bedroom door at night. That way, you'll be safe."

I agreed, and as we continued to chat, I could see Teresa from afar, tossing back several drinks. The media had been all in her business. For the past week, she had been the subject of breaking news. Stephen was too busy indulged in political talk tonight, and all I kept hearing about was Speaker Robinson resigning. Stephen hadn't noticed his reckless mother yet. And unfortunately for me, she was heading my way.

"Where does she get money from to buy a dress like that?" Claire asked while sipping from a glass of wine. She was referring to Teresa's black dress with gold studs around the neckline and slits on the side. "Michael Kors, isn't it?"

I winced and rolled my eyes. "Don't know, don't care. I never denied her classiness on the outside. It's the inside of that woman that irks the hell out of me."

Teresa swiped her bangs from her forehead, sashaying our way as if she was carrying a million bucks in her purse. She batted her lashes while searching me from head to toe. Her eyes said it all. She hated my purple flowing dress with no sleeves. It tightened at my waist and gave my breasts an extra boost. Cameras flashed throughout the evening on me, and I assumed that, by morning, my picture would be plastered all over the Internet, as well as in newspapers. On a scale from one-to-one hundred, I couldn't be ranked. I knew it, and Teresa knew it too.

"Well, well," she said with a crooked smile on her face. "If it isn't Thelma and Louise over here. What are you two cooking up now? Whatever it is, it better not have anything to do with my Stephen."

Claire didn't bother to respond. She turned to me. "We'll chat later. I'll leave the two of you to discuss who or what we'll be cooking."

Teresa frowned at Claire as she walked away. "You know what, Ne-ne? I don't like that bitch. Sometimes I want to just snatch her white ass up and slap her a few times. I know she's your girl and everything, but she makes my ass itch."

I couldn't resist. "Hot soapy water can cure that. But it may take more than that to cure your alcohol problem. Why don't you put the drinks down and chill tonight?"

"Chill?" She took another sip from the wineglass. "No, I'm having too much fun to chill. I'm also getting a kick out of you watching Chanel Hamilton. Just between us, she is days away from getting a piece of your man. I thought you had him under control, but from what a little birdie told me, that is not the case. All I can say is, you'd better get her. And, you'd better keep your eyes on a few other women in here too. I have a feeling that there are many coochies humming tonight, especially after that stellar performance by my son. He is soooo handsome, and when have you ever seen a tuxedo fit a man like that? As a mother, I've never been more proud of *my* child for always representing."

"And as his *wife,* I've never been more disappointed in *your* child. He—"

"Oh my," a cameraman said, interrupting us. "You ladies look spectacular tonight. Do you mind if I take a picture?"

"Sure," Teresa said as she grabbed at my waist, pulling me close to her side. "Ne-ne and I would love for you to take our picture."

Both of us displayed wide smiles as the cameras around us flashed. But once the cameraman walked away, our expressions fell flat.

"The only thing you should be disappointed with is that dress you have on," Teresa said. "What's with all the sheer? I feel like I'm at a ball or something with a wannabe Cinderella who will not get her Prince Charming tonight."

"I may not get him, but the one thing I am going to get is the hell away from you and your alcoholic breath. Don't drink too much more, Teresa. You're embarrassing yourself."

I cut my eyes at her, then walked off. And just as I stepped away, I saw Stephen and Tyler standing next to Michelle Peoples. They were all laughing, so I decided to go see what was so funny.

"I haven't been able to catch up with you for at least an hour," I said, walking up to Stephen. He slipped his arm around my waist, continuing to smile.

"Michelle, you haven't met the first lady yet, have you?" he said.

Her smile was faker than a three-dollar bill. "No, as a matter of fact, I haven't. But I've heard some wonderful things about her."

"Yes, and I've heard some interesting things about you. I'm always eager to know more about the people I meet, and maybe one day, you and I can take a late-night walk in the park so we can learn more."

I knew I was messy, but sometimes, I just didn't care. Stephen's arm slipped from around my waist, and Michelle looked as if she had choked on her spit. She swallowed hard; her eyes quickly shifted from Stephen, then back to me. Tyler was the only one clueless. But the more I thought about it, I doubted that he was.

"Uh, maybe so," Michelle said. "Just let me know when."

"I sure will. Real soon, okay?"

I left her speechless. All she could do was walk away. We all gazed at her backside.

"I guess if my ass was dimple free like hers," I said to Stephen, "you'd be trying to screw me too."

"Enough," Stephen said in a sharp tone. "If you don't want to be here, leave."

I snapped my fingers. "I was just thinking the same thing. Good night, Tyler. I'm sure I'll see you soon."

I walked away, but not before I snatched up a wine-glass with red wine in it and "accidentally" bumped into Michelle. The wine spilt all over her dress, and with her mouth wide open, she quickly blinked her eyes.

"I am *so, so* sorry," I said as if it really was an accident. "Your dress is ruined, but please send it to me in the morning so I can have it cleaned for you."

People were already staring. It was obvious that Michelle didn't want to make a bigger scene. She accepted my apology, but the angry look in her eyes said that she was very upset.

"It . . . It's okay. No problem. I'll get it cleaned soon."

"Are you sure? Silly me, I tripped on something and lost my balance. Again, I'm very sorry."

Just then, several service members came to assist with the cleanup. And since they appeared to have everything under control, I excused myself from the crowd, then walked away. I made my way down the corridor, only to be stopped by Claire who had some information for me.

"I know who took those photos. You're not going to believe who."

"Who was it?"

"Tyler McNeil. The question is, why?"

I had an idea why. But I also had to decide if I should say something to Stephen or allow him to continue to fuck himself. I quickly made a decision to let him sweat a little.

13

Newsroom Contributor Chanel Hamilton

I didn't like this feeling. Stephen had been ignoring me. At first, I thought it was just me, expecting more attention because of what had happened between us. But there was more to it. He seemed to be purposely avoiding me, and even though the first lady knew about us, that didn't seem to be a problem for him from the beginning.

As for tonight, all I was trying to do was get one conversation with him. I couldn't even get that. He had been locked in lengthy conversations all night, not to mention the long, fifteen minutes he spent talking to Michelle Peoples. I was on edge about that too. She was married with three kids. How in the heck was she even on the president's radar puzzled me. Regardless, I carried on and indulged myself in many conversations, trying my best not to pay too much attention to the president.

"Chanel," Jake said, giving me a hug. "You're stunning. My heart keeps beating faster and faster as I look at you. You must allow me to take you out on a date."

Jake was a nerd. Well, a rich nerd, but in no way was I interested in him. We had a lot of fun at the office, but that was it.

"You know I don't do the dating thing, Jake, especially with coworkers. My schedule is too busy, but if I ever decide to change my mind, you'll be the first to know."

He smiled, then kissed the back of my hand. I was surprised when the vice president interrupted us.

"I love your show," he said with his hands in his pockets. "Very informative and so easy on the eyes."

"Yes, indeed," Jake replied. He said hello to Tyler, then walked off to chat with someone else.

"So, you watch my show too?" I said while blushing. "I thought the president was the only one at the White House who watched me."

"No, we all watch you. And, as a matter of fact, I've been watching you all night."

My brows rose—so did my curiosity. "What have you discovered by watching me all night?"

Tyler stroked the fine hair on his chin. "I've discovered a few things. One, that you're super crazy about the president. Two, that you know he's intrigued by someone else. And three, that you're an amazingly beautiful woman who should never play second to another."

"One out of three isn't bad. I don't intend to play anything, though, and I'm more concerned about where this conversation is going."

Tyler looked around to observe our surroundings. "Let's step outside to get some fresh air, shall we? It's a little stuffy in here."

I pivoted toward the door and made my way outside with Tyler following me. There were more people out there as well, but less noise. He reached into his suit jacket to retrieve an envelope. He tapped it against his hand while looking at me.

"I have something in my hand that may, unfortunately, make the news in a few days. It's going to affect you in a major way, and that's why I'm bringing this to your attention. I don't think you want anyone to see this, but that's your choice. It's your reputation and job on the line, not mine."

I hadn't a clue what the vice president was talking about . . . until I opened the envelope and saw photos of Stephen and I having sex. To be blunt, two photos of me with his penis in my mouth, savoring it as if it was the best thing on earth. I was speechless.

"You don't want anyone to see those photos. They are damaging to you, as well as to Stephen. Somehow or someway, you need to speak to him about the harm those photos can cause if the whole world sees them. Raynetta won't be your only problem, and for God's sake, what will your boss say if he knew the real reason you went to Africa? I'll let you handle this little problem, and if you tell Stephen where you got the photos from, or about this conversation, I'm going to handle things on my own. I hope you understand what *that* means."

I swallowed the sizeable lump in my throat, then nodded. "I'll handle it, but I want to be clear. Your objective is to get Stephen to step down, correct? If not, my career, as well as his is finished."

"I don't know if we're both clear, but I'll say this. We're both Republicans. And nothing should suit us better than to have a Republican president in the White House."

I wasn't sure if I agreed with him or not, but I told him I would do what was necessary to keep those photos a secret. Several minutes later, I finally caught up with Stephen. He had just wrapped up a conversation with two Democratic congressmen who applauded Speaker Robinson's resignation.

"Do you have a minute?" I said to Stephen, touching his arm. "I know you're quite busy, but I haven't had a chance to say hello or anything. You also haven't thanked me for putting the news out there about Speaker Robinson."

"That's because you should be thanking me for giving you the story. It would've gotten out there regardless."

"Maybe so, but not how I delivered it. With that being said, if possible, I would like to see you, alone, tonight.

There is an important matter on the rise that we need to discuss."

Stephen hesitated before responding. "I'll see what I can do, but I can't make you any promises."

"I don't expect for you to, but keep in mind that this is urgent. I'm sure you know where to find me."

"Yes, I do. Apartment 14C, correct?"

"Correct."

After he walked away, I left the correspondence dinner almost thirty minutes later. I couldn't stop thinking about those photos, and I pondered how to handle this. I guess that depended on Stephen. I needed him to show a little more enthusiasm about us.

On the drive home, I received a short text message that said: *Be there soon*. That caused a smile to wash across my face. The second I arrived home, I hurried to tidy up a bit and quickly changed into a soft pink silk negligee with black-lace trimmings. The panties were made of sheer fabric; I didn't mind letting my goodies show. I removed the knot from my hair, allowing my curls to fall down my back. I definitely missed my calling as a Victoria's Secret model, and as I glanced in the mirror, I couldn't be more pleased.

Waiting patiently, I fluffed a few pillows on the couch, sprayed several splashes of perfume in the air, and then walked over to the huge picture windows to close the linen drapes so no one could see inside. My apartment was very spacious. The modern décor made the entire place fitting for a magazine cover. I had spent an enormous amount of money to make my place look unique. In no way was I embarrassed by the president coming here. I clicked on the fire in the mounted fireplace, then headed for the kitchen to go pour some wine. As far as I knew, Stephen wasn't much of a drinker. But one could only assume what he was up to in private.

Just as I started to pour the wine, there was a light knock at my door. I tossed back a quick drink and dimmed the lights, just a little, before opening the door. On the other side stood Mr. President, still dressed in his black tuxedo and white crisp shirt with a bow tie. I noticed one of his Secret Service men by the elevator. I invited Stephen to come inside, and when his black leather shoes hit my hardwood floor, I was in awe that he was actually here. He scanned me with those hazel eyes, then shifted them elsewhere to examine the room.

"Nice place," he said. "I expected nothing less."

"Thanks for the compliment, but do you mind if I take your jacket?"

"No need. I won't be staying long."

Did my face just crack or what? Hoping that he would change his mind, I sashayed over to the sofa, inviting him to have a seat. I couldn't help but to think how could he not be turned on by my butt cheeks that bulged through my tiny panties. How could he not be excited about the strawberry fragrance I sprayed all over myself to lure him right in. He didn't appear . . . moved . . . but the night was still young.

Stephen sat on the sofa, crossing one of his legs over the other. I sat as close to him as I could with glee in my eyes.

"I wasn't kidding when I said that we needed to talk about something important." I rubbed the back of his head. His hair was so soft and lined perfectly. "But before we get down to business, do you mind if I steal a kiss?"

"Yes, I do mind. Kissing leads to other things, and I have to get back to the correspondence dinner before too many people notice I'm missing."

"Then, I suggest that we save our talk for another day."

I leaned in to kiss Stephen, but he cocked his head back. A blank expression appeared on his face. "What do we need to talk about that is so important?"

I didn't appreciate his demeanor, but I tried to remain calm. "Right now, there is nothing more important than you spending just a little bit of time with me. I don't get this. Why are you so . . . so cold?"

"If I was cold, I wouldn't have come here when you asked me to. And since you don't have anything important to talk about, then I need to check out of here and get back to the party."

He stood; I did too.

"Fine. I won't ever invite you here again. You will have to come to me, before I ever reach out to you again."

He strutted toward the door as if my threat meant nothing. I followed closely behind him. "Normally, I don't chase Republicans." He turned to look at me. "They chase me."

I stopped, then crossed my arms. "Okay. Now I know what this is about. You're upset with me because I'm a Republican who didn't vote for you, right? Is that what this is about?"

"Actually, it's not. I just told you that I was leaving because you didn't have anything to discuss. I couldn't care less if you voted for me or not. That was your mistake, not mine."

"Maybe it was, but don't hold it against me. I do have your back, but you need to have mine too."

"If having your back means having sex with you when you want to, forget it. I'm good, and I don't need your support in that way."

Enough said, enough done. Stephen had gotten on my bad side, just *that* fast. I opened the door wide, so he could go. After he walked out, I slammed the door behind him, thinking hard about my next move. In no way was I a bad person, but some people were capable of bringing out the worst in me.

14

President of the United States, Stephen C. Jefferson

Chanel was a trip. The only reason I stopped by to see her was to see if she wanted to share with me the reason why she and Tyler stepped away from the dinner party tonight. I saw the two of them engaged in an intense conversation, and since Raynetta said someone had removed those photos from our bedroom, I figured that Chanel knew something about it. But, like always, I turned to someone I was starting to trust, more than anyone. That was Andrew. When I returned to the dinner party, I saw him outside on his cell phone. I walked up to him so we could talk.

"Lauren, I'll have to call you back." He hurried to put the phone in his pocket. "Thank God you're here. I've been looking for you. I called your cell phone, twice."

"I missed your call, but what's up?"

"It's your mother. She's causing quite a scene inside. No one really wants to get in her way, and I'm sure you already know why."

I had no idea what my mother was up to . . . until I went inside and saw her dancing around like an idiot with a red rose in her mouth. People surrounded her while clapping their hands and laughing. Plenty took pictures, and the band assisted in helping her make a fool of herself. She had kicked off her heels, and even though she seemed to be enjoying herself, I had seen enough. I signaled for Andrew to tell the band to cut it. Just for a moment, the music stopped, clapping continued. I didn't want to embarrass myself, but I had to put a stop to this now. With a slight grin on my face, I made my way to the floor, pretending as if I was delighted to do the tango with my mother. I grabbed her in my arms, but looked deep into her eyes to let her know that I didn't approve of her bullshit. The claps got louder, flashes from cameras got brighter. Nearly everyone looked on as we did the tango from one corner of the floor to the other. I eyed the nearest exit, and when I saw it, we danced our way right out of the room. The crowd erupted with cheers and chanted for more. I quickly closed the double doors, turning to my mother who could barely stand. A sheen of sweat covered her forehead, and with a glassy look in her eyes, I was sure her vision was blurred.

"I . . . I don't know what to say to you right now." I looked at her with disgust. "What in the hell are you doing?"

She snapped her fingers and bobbed her head, as if music was thumping from somewhere.

"Don't you dare stand there and look at me like that. I'm the mother, you're still the child. I was dancing, that's what I was doing, before you interrupted me."

"No, what you were doing was making a damn spectacle of yourself. When you snap out of this and see your face plastered on the news tomorrow, you'll see exactly what I'm talking about. It's going to sting."

She threw her hand back and pursed her lips. "So what, Stephen, who cares? These people love me. That's why they can't stop taking pictures of me and following me around. I'm a superstar. A worldwide superstar. As long as they didn't pull out the violins and start playing anything from *Fiddler on the Roof,* I'm cool."

She started twirling around, dancing again. I opened the door to immediately get my Secret Service agent's attention.

"Please get her out of here and take her home. Make sure she's tucked in bed and keep your eyes on her for the entire night."

"Ooooh, sounds real freaky to me." She opened her arms wide. "Come here, suga. Pick me up, carry me home, and lay me in my bed. You can stay the night, if you want to. But just so you know, I will put a serious hurting on you."

She giggled and almost fell when she started spinning again. Bruce escorted her away, eventually having to carry her because she was too intoxicated to walk. I was frustrated as hell. So frustrated and embarrassed that I didn't even return to the party. I said good night to Andrew who was back on his cell phone. And to Tyler who had been watching me and my mother, making sure everything was okay.

"Get some rest," he said, squeezing my shoulder as he walked beside me. "You need to go to your bedroom tonight, hold your beautiful wife, and sleep for as long as you can. I'm sure you'll feel much better tomorrow."

I shook hands with Tyler, then headed to the second floor where my bedroom was. Sleep was exactly what I needed, but when I got to the bedroom and saw Raynetta lying naked in bed, I wanted something else too. She had come clean today—maybe I needed to come clean too. Maybe even tell her that no matter how upset I was with her, I still loved her. I still wanted our marriage to work, and I still wanted her to one day have our child. The least she could do was give me a son or daughter. I truly felt that she would be a wonderful mother. Had every ounce of faith that she would be. I didn't understand why she didn't see that, but I had to convince her to, one day, change her mind. If not, it would be just a matter of time before someone else gave me what I desired to have.

I removed my tuxedo, took a quick shower, then got in bed with Raynetta. As she lay sideways with the pillow tucked between her legs, I moved in close behind her. I wrapped one arm around her waist, squeezing it as I moved her hair aside, planting kisses along the side of her neck. She began to softly moan. Even clenched one of her hands together with mine. A smile crept on her face . . . before she cracked her eyes wide open.

"Stephen?" she said. "Wha . . . Is that you?"

I sucked her earlobe and gave her a huge hint when I pressed my steel against her. "Who else does this feel like?"

She snapped her head farther to the side to look at me. Her hand loosened from mine; her expression fell flat.

"You couldn't be serious, are you?"

"What do you mean? Serious about what?"

"About you and me, we, us, having sex."

"What's wrong with us having sex? The last time I checked, we are still married, aren't we?"

"Is that what it's called when you take it upon yourself to screw other women on Air Force One and in the woods? A marriage? No, my dear, we don't have a marriage. What we have is an arrangement, and a piece of legal paper that doesn't mean a darn thing. Until I believe it does, please don't touch me. Don't put that thing anywhere near me, and stay over there on your side of the bed."

She used her elbow to shove me away from her. I was in disbelief.

"You didn't have a problem with our marriage the other night when you attempted to have sex with me. Why put up a fuss now?"

Raynetta ignored me. She grunted, then pulled the cover over her head. Deep down, I was pissed. I wanted to leave the room, but instead, I turned my back to hers, grunting too. Before I knew it, I was out.

Unfortunately for me, sleep didn't last for long. I was awakened by the constant ringing of my phone. It was a little after three in the morning, so I hurried to pick up the phone to see what was up. All I heard was the urgency in Andrew's voice.

"Mr. President, sorry to wake you, but you need to get to the Oval Office right away."

I wasted no time asking why. All I did was toss the covers aside, put on some clothes, and then I headed to the Oval Office. By the time I reached the lower level, Secret Service was waiting for me. We all walked down the corridor together and into the West Wing. I entered the Oval Office where Andrew and Tyler stood with frightened looks on their faces. My thoughts immediately turned to my mother.

"Wha . . . What's going on?" I asked.

"About an hour ago, there were three attacks on our army bases. Total of fourteen soldiers dead, nine severely injured," Tyler confirmed. "We don't know if the incidents were terrorist attacks or not, but it appears that the three individuals who planned these massacres all worked together. More specific details are coming to us soon."

"From what I gather, it doesn't seem related to terrorism," Andrew said. "These guys may have been American, but we'll know soon."

I released a deep sigh; nothing but frustration showed on my face. Specific details meant that, yet again, I would have to see, with my own eyes, the brutal killings take place. I had to witness fear in people's eyes as they were gunned down, their cries for loved ones, and pleas for God to spare them. This was downright ridiculous.

"What's the status of the attackers?" I asked.

"Dead," Tyler confirmed. "All three were shot to death by other soldiers. One was seventeen, and the other two were twenty-one. They were connected to several hate groups online; that's why I think the incident was related to terrorism. Those same groups are now considering them heroes."

Andrew continued to disagree. I sensed that he and Tyler didn't get along too well. "Many hate groups are formed right here in our own country. We need to stop blaming others for committing these crimes and look in our own backyard."

Tyler fired back, and they kept bickering. It irritated the fuck out of me. "We'll see, as soon as we get more information," Tyler said.

"Regardless," I said, "they are not heroes. Heroes my ass." I turned to Andrew. "Make sure Senator Bass's unproductive self is in my office by noon. I take it that she'll be replacing Speaker Robinson, correct?"

"It looks that way right now," Andrew replied. "But you just never know, especially when it comes to the Republican Party, or should I say, what's left of it. Either way, I'll make sure that she's here by noon."

I sat on the sofa, waiting until more information became available about the killings. And when much of the information was provided to me, no question, these guys were Americans. They were born here, went to school here, trained to shoot guns here, and died here. I was sick to my stomach. Many of the soldiers had fought in wars. They made it home safely from war, but weren't even safe on American soil. Something was definitely wrong with that picture, and shame on us all for allowing this to become the norm.

A few minutes before noon, Senator Bass came into my office wasting no time sitting down and telling me what she could not do.

"I'm not a miracle worker, Mr. President, and as I said to you before, this is no easy fix."

"And as I said to you before, we have to start somewhere. Now that Speaker Robinson is out, I need you to go back to your caucus and have a serious, long talk with them about where this country is headed if we do not do anything about gun control. Let's start there and somehow work our way into creating legislation that can help save lives."

"Don't get your hopes up, but I'll do what I can. In the meantime, I hope you understand that if I make a move on this, I could very well lose my job, come election time. My party will vote against me, and that would be a shame because I've dedicated my life to helping the American people."

"The way I see it, we all have to leave this institution some time. What we accomplish during our time here is what really matters. So, you decide if you want to stay here and do nothing, or start really helping the American people, as you say. And don't stop at gun control reform. Many of the neighborhoods where I come from need manufacturing companies built there, not in China. They need opportunities, not welfare checks and EBT cards. Teachers in those neighborhoods need to be paid well, and we need to fix an educational system that is severely broken. I need to work with a Speaker who is willing to focus on all people, not just a specific few. Do you understand what I'm saying?"

"I do understand, but I hope you also understand that it is not the government's responsibility to keep giving handouts. We are—"

I held up my hand to silence her, deeply frowning. "Handouts? Please don't make me call you anything other than your birth name. I don't know where this 'handout' shit comes from, but the truth is, somebody needs to be handing out something, when you take into consideration the harm this here institution has caused African American families over many decades. There have been laws created to separate our families, to affect the education of our children, to keep us at poverty level, and to deny our equal rights. And let's not talk about this fucked-up judicial system. I could go on and on, but if I do, I will prohibit you from getting off your ass, right now, and go do something about what we've discussed."

Senator Bass's eyes were wide as saucers. "You . . . You're not going to call me names and bully me, Mr. President! I won't have it, and this is not how you get people to listen to you."

"Maybe, maybe not, but I'm angry, Senator Bass. I need your help, not excuses. My approach may be a bit much for some, but if I can recall, there was a decent, kind, very professional black president in office before, and moth-erfuckers still didn't want to work with him. You already know how he was treated, but not this time. There's too much at stake, and with the Republican Party facing a decline, I can only ask that you step up and do what you can to save it. This may be your final opportunity."

She released a deep breath, then stood. "Give me some time to process all of this. I'll check back with you in a week or so to let you know how the others respond."

"I don't have a week or two. Days. Convene with your caucus in the next few days. We need to move, especially on gun control ASAP. I don't have to remind you that we've already wasted enough time."

Senator Bass said that she would get back to me soon. The second she left my office, Bruce, my Secret Service agent, came in.

"George is going to relieve me for the day, sir. My sister's wedding is later, and I wouldn't miss it for the world."

"That's fine. Tell your sister I said congrats."

"Will do and thank you."

Before he walked away, I stopped him.

"Did my mother get some rest last night? I know she was a mess, and I apologize for any inconvenience that may have caused."

"No inconvenience, Mr. President. I tucked her in real nicely last night, and the two of us had enormous fun."

He winked and laughed; I didn't see anything funny. I wasn't sure what he meant when he stressed the words, "enormous fun."

"Do you care to elaborate on how much fun the two of you had?"

He chuckled, again, smiling as if he really didn't want to say. His face turned red, and it was even redder when I rushed up to him, grabbing his throat. I shoved him backward, slamming the back of his head against the wall.

"I need a good laugh, so tell me what in the fuck is so funny!"

With a tight grip on his neck, he couldn't tell me if he tried. All he could do was claw at my hand, trying to get me to loosen my grip. When I did, he bent over and started gagging. Saliva dripped from his mouth; he used his hands to soothe his throat.

"I . . . I was only kidding, sir." He released several hard coughs. "Just joking around, that's all."

"I'm a grown-ass man who doesn't appreciate you joking about my mother. Now, get the fuck out of here and have all the fun you want at your sister's wedding. Travel to her honeymoon with her, and take all the time you need on your new job search while you're at it. After today, there is no need for you to come back here. You're done, and thanks for your service."

"What?" he shouted. "You can't fucking dismiss me! I did nothing wrong, and now we can't even joke around here?"

"No, you can't. And you know what else you can't do? You can't yell in my office and talk shit to me. For the last time, go shake a leg at your sister's wedding and do not come back here."

He tightened his fists and took a few steps forward. I stepped forward too, with the gaze of a cold-blooded killer in my eyes.

"Trust me when I say that you don't want none of this. Leave here alive or exit in a body bag. Your choice."

He ranted some more but was smart enough not to challenge me. I didn't trust him anyway, and soon after he left, I called Andrew back into my office, telling him that it was now time to bring in a few good men from my hood to protect me. He thought I was joking, but he soon found out that joking around wasn't something I did too often.

Later that afternoon, and to no surprise, things got more chaotic. Another unarmed black man had been gunned down, and riots were brewing in several cities. Two police departments were on fire, and the Black Lives Matter organization was in full effect in the streets. Race relations were another matter I had asked my administration to help me tackle, and as I was given an update over the phone, it sounded like a bunch of mumbo jumbo to me.

"Unfortunately, Shelby, all that you're saying to me right now is not enough. Setting up panels, having discussions, making phone calls . . . Come on, you and your team have to do better. The next time we talk, I want to hear solutions about how we intend to unite people. How we can work with police departments and rid them of crooked cops who don't belong there. What we need to do to make good-paying jobs available, and what is the best way to get some of these kids off the streets and into training programs that will be beneficial to them in the long run. I have an array of ideas, but I want to see what you all can come up with too. Let's talk in a few days. Hopefully, by then, you'll have some better ideas on the table."

"I will, Mr. President. I assure you that I will do my best."

That's what they all say, I thought as we ended the call. And if everyone around here was doing their best, shit wouldn't be as bad as it was. I shook my head, then lifted the newspaper in front of me. My mother and I made the front page of almost every newspaper, and all the journalists wrote about was how drunk and unstable she was. Raynetta's dress was also the topic, and many praised her for making good choices when it came to clothes. All of that nonsense rolled off my back, but I sat as if cement was poured over me as I watched Chanel's show later that evening.

"The photos you are about to see are very graphic and sexual in nature and may disturb some of you. In an effort to protect the female's identity, we have blurred her face. You all will recognize the man in the photos as our president, Stephen C. Jefferson. A president who uses our tax-paying dollars to buy women lavish gifts, just so he can spread their legs on Air Force One. This isn't the only woman the president has spent his time with, and we have obtained additional photos of him with prostitutes, as well as strippers. I'm totally blown away by his actions, and I surely didn't vote for him so that he could use his bully pulpit to lure women into the bedroom. What a shame. I can only wonder how the first lady feels about all of this."

The distorted photos were shown, making my face very clear, but Chanel's face totally unrecognizable. Her body looked much thicker, and whoever doctored the photos, they made her skin darker. No photos of me existed with prostitutes or strippers. It was just another lie to get people to tune in, and for Chanel to make me look bad. But lying about a president, especially me, was a bad move. Chanel was taking a big risk. She just didn't know how badly she had damaged herself tonight. I continued to watch, as many other reporters couldn't wait to chime in.

"This is why our leaders can't get things done. If all we have is a president who can't lead Congress but can lead women into his bedroom, then we have a big problem. I'm disgusted because I voted for this guy. He needs to be thrown out of there and replaced with someone who has time to deal with what happened today to our soldiers. And let's not forget about the two officers who lost their lives in those riots today."

"No, let's not forget about the black man who was killed for no reason," another journalist said. *"I hear what everyone is saying about the president, but I'll wait to hear from him before jumping to any conclusions. I'm not sure about those photos, and we all know that photos can be manipulated. And if it is him, I will say that from head to toe, he is truly blessed. That is a tad bit of information I don't mind sharing."*

They chuckled, then Chanel hurried to speak up. *"I can assure you that those photos were not manipulated. That is the president, for sure."*

"Chanel is right. That is, indeed, our president with his mouth all over that woman. I'm appalled."

Just then, the door to the Oval Office flew open. Andrew and Sam rushed in, as if someone had been chasing them.

"We . . . We have a serious problem, Mr. President," Andrew said, stuttering.

"You're damn right we do."

15

Vice President Tyler McNeil

"I told you that pretty black bitch would come through for us, didn't I?" Speaker Robinson said while rocking in a chair. We were gathered around on my grandfather's back porch, discussing Stephen. A fire pit was lit and a chess game was in the middle of the table that was surrounded by the chairs we relaxed in.

"Yes, Chanel definitely put his business out there in a major way," I said. "I didn't think she would do it, but let's see how he responds."

"It doesn't matter how he responds," my grandfather hissed while displaying his white, bushy brows that were arched inward. "The American people won't go for this. Many will ask for him to step down right away, and you need to haul ass back to Capitol Hill and make sure every member of the Republican Party speaks out about this. The more noise we make, the better."

"I will do what I can on my end, but keep in mind that many are still catching hell from their constituents about what Roy said." I looked at Roy. "I can't believe that you never suspected Stephen would have a recorder. And now that you're out, do you think that Senator Bass will be able to keep the majority of our party in line?"

My grandfather quickly spoke up, after spitting out tobacco. "She'd better keep her fat, freckled-faced ass in line, for sure, or else we'll get someone in there who can hold our caucus together. Roy, I'm damn disappointed in you too. It has always been our motive to take down that nigger, not for him to cause you to lose your fucking job. I'm getting nervous about this, and you'd better hope that those photos are enough to shake things up. I must admit that with a physique like Mr. President's, he surely would have been a darn good slave for my kinfolk."

He and Roy laughed.

"For mine too," Roy said, then coughed. "I reckon that the Republican Party will hold it together, no matter who's in charge. And for God's sake, forgive me. I didn't know that bastard had sense enough to be that slick, but I can still do some damage behind the scenes. I intend to still lead behind closed doors, and I already warned every single Republican about the consequences of wavering when it comes to that fool's agenda."

"As long as they know," my grandfather said, "there will be consequences. Remind them of that, Tyler, and thank you for getting those pictures. This is as big as his dick. We are going to use everything we have to our advantage."

"Getting those pictures was like taking candy from a baby. I almost took something else too when I saw the first lady in her nightgown, looking sweet and sexy that night. Luckily for her, I don't screw around with women of her caliber. But she had me pretty darn close to changing my mind."

My grandfather's face tightened. "Just the thought of it makes my skin crawl. And you're doggone right that you don't screw women of her caliber. The blood that runs through her veins is tainted. You don't want to mix it with our blood, and God help you if you ever do."

I chuckled at my grandfather's dislike of *others*; I had heard it for many years. "No worries, Grandpa. I assure you, no worries."

Roy laughed, then started to cough again. Normally, he was able to control his cough, but this time, his hacking got louder and louder. Spit flew from his mouth as he covered it with his fist, and his whole face started to turn red.

"Roy, are you okay?" my grandfather shouted as he jumped to his feet. He grabbed his cane and started hitting Roy on the back with it. I, on the other hand, delivered sharp blows to his shoulder blade with the palm of my hand. It didn't seem to help much, and when Roy tumbled to the ground, my grandfather glared at me with terrified eyes.

"Call 911. Now!"

16

President of the United States, Stephen C. Jefferson

Andrew and I were running around, trying to do some damage control. The first person I went to was Raynetta. She was the one who had those photos. I wanted to know who she got them from, and if there were anymore. She sat stone-faced with her arms crossed, revealing an attitude.

"As intelligent as you are," she said, "you also have some rather dumb tendencies too. I warned you about those photos, but you blew them off as if they weren't a big deal. Claire got those photos for me because I asked for them. Whoever removed them from our bedroom, they took all of them."

"I didn't come here for you to insult me. And why would you ask Claire for pictures like that anyway? I haven't denied anything that I've done, and if you're curious about something, all you have to do is ask. Now, because of your actions, I have a problem. I can't believe what Chanel did, but payback will be a motherfucker."

Raynetta laughed and shook her head. "You can't believe it? Is that what you just said? Well, *I* can believe it. I know a snake when I see one, and it's a shame that you keep missing the mark. I'm sure you will manage to make her pay for what she has done, but how does this look, Stephen? How do you think this makes *me* feel? I just don't get it, and you still have the nerve to arrogantly stand there and not even apologize to me."

"What good is saying I'm sorry going to do for us right now, especially when you already know how much I regret that our marriage is failing? Meanwhile, I have to get control of this situation. Is there any chance that you removed one of those photos, just one, before someone took them all? Maybe you put one in a drawer or hid it somewhere else. What about Claire? Can you find out from her if she has anymore in her possession?"

Raynetta shrugged. "What I had was stolen. I'll give Claire a call, but I doubt that she kept any with her."

"Please call and let me know. I'm going back to the Oval Office so I can prepare a statement in the Press Briefing Room about these unfortunate killings and make mention of those photos. I don't have much time, but anything you can do, other than insult me, would really help."

Raynetta cut her eyes at me before I walked away. I returned to the Oval Office, and as I began to prepare my statement, Tyler rushed in. His shirt was wrinkled, and his hair was spiked and out of place. He appeared severely on edge—sweat spots were visible on his face, as well as on his clothes.

"It's the Speaker," he said, barely able to catch his breath. "He was just rushed to the hospital. Had a massive heart attack, and isn't expected to make it."

I calmly laid my pen on my desk. "Who? *Former* Speaker Robinson?"

"Yes, Speaker Robinson."

I shrugged while looking at Tyler with a blank expression. "I'm curious. What in the hell do you want me to do?"

Tyler blinked his teary eyes. "I . . . I just thought you may want to know. That way, you can release some kind of statement in support of him. He has served in this institution for many years, Stephen. It would send the right message, if you wouldn't mind showing some concern for his status."

I didn't know what to say, other than . . . "Get the fuck out of here. He didn't serve anybody but himself and the wealthy while in this institution. Meanwhile, many Americans continue to suffer. I will not waste my breath on saying anything about him, but I will say this to you. You reap what you sow. If he dies, he dies. His ass was casket ready anyway, and may he finally rest in peace."

Tyler scratched his head and narrowed his eyes while gazing at me as if I had said something wrong. His frown annoyed me, and as he continued to speak fondly of the Speaker, all I did was listen in.

"Maybe you're confused, Stephen. You fail to realize that Roy has done a lot for this country over the years. He has made some very tough decisions and has put up with a heap of crap from other presidents, as well as from members of his own party. It will be a sad day on Capitol Hill if he dies. None of us can deny that."

"I can, and I will, because it will be a joyous day in the White House. Now, if you don't mind, I have an important speech to prepare. If you want to prepare one on Speaker Robinson's behalf, feel free to do so, and deliver it after I'm done."

Tyler didn't like my response. He abruptly left my office, and minutes later, Andrew came in to inform me about Speaker Robinson as well. He too felt as if I should acknowledge the Speaker's situation and offer my condolences.

"The one thing I am not is a phony. I will not stand at that podium today and recite loving words about the Speaker that do not apply. I will not mention his name, and if I decide to, I will offend his wife and children. You don't want me to do that, so please get out of my office and go tell Sam that I will be speaking to the press this afternoon."

He nodded. "Will do, Mr. President. I apologize for interrupting you."

I liked Andrew a lot. He knew when to push and when not to. And the second he left my office, I got a call from Raynetta.

"One," she said. "All Claire has is one. I don't know why she held on to it, but you are welcome to it."

"Thank you. And just so you know, I *am* sorry."

Raynetta ended the call without responding. Minutes later, I obtained the photo from her, and then continued to prepare my speech. My mother called in the midst of me finishing, but I was too busy to take her call.

Less than an hour later, the Press Briefing Room was crowded with wall-to-wall reporters who couldn't wait to hear what I had to say. They didn't care how late it was—none would miss the opportunity to show glee in their eyes in hopes that I would deliver an announcement about stepping down. But showing all of the confidence that I could, I stepped to the podium, addressing all that had happened in one day.

"Good evening and thanks to everyone for being here. It has been a very sad day for this country, and I offer my sincere condolences and prayers to the families of every brave soldier who lost their lives due to gun violence, to the families of another innocent black man who was killed by cops who continue to believe they are above the law, and to the families of the police officers whose lives ended tragically due to cowards. I can't stress enough that our country has to do better. Terrorism exists right here at home, and blood from our brothers and sisters are on the hands of every member of Congress, including myself. Every time we choose to ignore the serious racism problems in this country, hatred grows, people take sides, and we continue to be divided. Hardworking police officers who are determined to do a good job are targeted, and the end result is exactly what happened today.

"There are plenty of things that Congress can do to assist with some of these unfortunate matters, and as your president, I will fight to make sure we get the ball rolling. Meanwhile, there are also things that the American people can do to help us change course and put an end to some of these very tragic incidents. One, if you notice someone spewing hate and threatening lives on social media, report it. Two, if you know of anyone with a mental illness who seems unstable and has possession of a firearm, don't be afraid to reach out and get help. If you work for a police department and you see or notice people within the same department who have hatred for other races, especially for black men and women who continue to be the main targets, go to your supervisors. If your supervisors share the same hate, don't hesitate to call the Department of Justice. My administration created a call center that is able to handle concerns about all of these issues. We will thoroughly review each report and follow up on it. Your name will remain anonymous.

"As Americans, we have to be brave. We have to stand for others, even when they don't look like us or share the same views as we do. We have to speak up when we know things are not right, and hold those who are wrong accountable. We also have to demand that our government do whatever is possible to prevent people who should not have guns, from having them. With an all-hands-on-deck effort, we can, and will, begin to create a new America.

"Finally, I know some of you have concerns about photos that were seen today on many of your televisions, computers . . . what have you. The man in those photos is undeniably me, and the woman in the photos was the one who decided to put our personal business out there on her nightly show. The photos were doctored to hide her identity, but since it's out there in the open now, then we must tell the full truth. For many reasons that revolve around very unfortunate situations with my wife, I have been unfaithful to her. Not once, however, have I ever had sexual relations with a prostitute or stripper.

"My wife is well aware of the individuals I've been with, and I ask no one to define me based on the flaws in my marriage, but rather on what I can, and will, do for our nation. Judge me on that alone, or judge me not. I will not elaborate further on this private matter, but I will conclude with this. Anyone looking or hoping for me to step down, go ahead and wipe your tears because that will not happen today." I looked into the audience at the reporters who all looked to be frozen. "You all can breathe now. And two questions are all I will take."

I called on one reporter who was sitting up close.

"Mr. President, many people probably feel that you owe a better explanation and an apology to the American people for what our eyes witnessed today. If you're not committed to your wife, how can you be committed to getting things done for the American people?"

I just stared at the fool for a few seconds. "I guess you didn't hear me when I said I wasn't going to elaborate more on that subject. But just so you know, the only person who will get an apology from me is my wife."

I looked past Michelle Peoples who had been staring at me ever since I stepped up to the podium. Called on a reporter who sat directly behind her.

"Mr. President, I like the idea of having a call center for people to reach out to, and there really isn't much else for us to say on that subject. What I would like to know is how the first lady feels about all of this. Also, there are plenty of women with shows on the nightly news. Can you tell us the woman's name in the photos?"

I didn't have time for this—really, I didn't. The media didn't understand what was really important and what wasn't. But just for the hell of it, I removed from my pocket one of the most salacious photos there were of me and Chanel . . . held it in my hand, then flicked it into the audience.

"Any more questions on that subject matter, ask *her*."

Many reporters scrambled to get the photo. And as they examined it, I walked out.

17

President of the United States,
Stephen C. Jefferson

As expected, the news spun for the next forty-eight hours, and then everyone was on to the next big stories, which were Speaker Robinson's death and Chanel Hamilton being fired. I too had lost some support, but I knew what I had to do to gain it back. I sat with Andrew, discussing ways that I could do just that.

"You need to work harder on gun control," he said. "And as you mentioned before, now is the time for you to go out there and walk the streets with people of color who feel as if this country is against them. There will be time for us to meet with leaders from other countries, but we must take care of America first. We're losing right now, and you have an opportunity to use all of that energy inside of you in a positive way."

I nodded with my hands clenched behind my head. "I feel the same way. Senator Bass and I are scheduled to meet, again, tomorrow. And from what I've heard, she's got some good news for me."

"I'm hearing the same. Maybe people are feeling some kind of way after Roy's death—I'm not sure. But his funeral is tomorrow. We'll all be in attendance. I guess I don't have to ask if you will be there."

"Don't ask, because you already know. Thanks for everything and let me know if you hear anything from

Tyler. I know he's been busy trying to console people who are grieving the Speaker's death, and he mentioned something about going to see his father. We haven't spoken much lately, and I'm starting to feel, even more, that there is something wrong with him."

"I've had that feeling for a long time, but we'll discuss it later. Meanwhile, why don't you get out of this office and go get some fresh air? I don't think you've left this office in two days, have you?"

"I have, but not for long. Just working on some things; things that are very important. But getting some fresh air sounds good. I just may do that later."

"Good. And stay away from Chanel Hamilton. She's very upset about losing her job. She's been trying to reach you, but I figured that you didn't have much to say to her."

"I don't, but the next time she calls or wants to stop by, please allow her to. The harm has been done, and the only person she hurt was herself."

Andrew nodded, then left my office a few minutes later. I started to review some classified information that was given to me earlier from the director of National Intelligence. Terror attacks were on the rise, but we now had major capabilities to shut down many of those attacks. That was a good thing. The bad thing was a possible war brewing. Countries that used to be our allies were now our enemies. The backlash happened before I became president, and many felt that I wasn't the kind of president who was capable of mending fences. That was false. I was more than willing to meet with anyone. My tone would remain as is, and any leader who disrespected the United States would be cussed the fuck out and never allowed to step on American soil again.

I was in deep thought, wondering if I should reach out to Michelle. She had left me numerous messages since the other day. The real reason I hadn't reached out to her was not because of Raynetta. She was still acting nasty toward me, and we were barely speaking to each other. I hadn't called because I had been extremely busy. I also knew that many people were watching my every move, and Michelle was the kind of woman that I didn't want involved in any scandals. There were already people who knew too much, and she definitely had her plate full with her husband. We hadn't talked that much about him, but in her last message, she sounded tearful. She expressed that she was going to finally call it quits with him. All she wanted to do was talk to someone who could make her feel better about her decision. I wasn't sure if I was the one who could do it, but I decided to finally return her call. She answered immediately.

"I guess you've grown tired of my long messages about what I'm going through over here," she said. "And shame on me because my problems could never amount to the ones you have at your doorstep every day. I hope you don't think I'm selfish, but in a way, I guess I really am because I enjoy our conversations and miss them."

"I enjoy our conversations as well, but I don't want you to take my delays with getting back to you personal. I am, however, glad that you're taking steps to finalize your situation with your husband, and I hope that you don't backtrack."

"I won't. I'm planning to have the divorce papers served tomorrow. I'm a little sad, but I know that what I'm doing is best for myself and the kids."

"I'm sure it will be too. A year from now, you're going to wish that you had done it sooner."

She laughed, then paused for a few seconds, as if she was in deep thought. "I'm sure I will, but you know what? Enough about me. What's been up with you ever since you bravely stood up and told America about you and Chanel? I had no idea that you were involved with her. That totally shocked me. So did those photos."

"What can I say? Everyone was shocked, but no more secrets, huh?"

"Well, one little secret. One that will stay between me, you, and I guess your wife who seems to somehow know about our meeting in the park. Did you tell her about us?"

"No, someone else did. Someone is always watching, and when I mentioned no more secrets, I was only kidding. Around here, there are no secrets. Everybody knows something. It's just a matter of time when people will spill what they know."

"That's not good. But the question is, do you care?"

"Sometimes I do, many times I don't."

"Well, I don't care. It would be nice if you would meet me at the park again. Please. And this time, I'll bring a blanket and pillows."

I tapped my fingers on my desk, thinking that I was more than ready to go get the fresh air I needed. "All you really need to do is bring yourself. I'll see you in about an hour or so."

I hit the button to end the call. Definitely needed some time to relax and chill, as well as to indulge in "other" things. I finished reviewing the information before me, and then I reached out to Levi Jamieson who was not only a friend of mine, but now my new senior Secret Service agent. Maybe more like a bodyguard, because he was one big dude. He came right in, closing the door behind him.

"I need to go make a run," I said. "Can you take me somewhere?"

"Man, anywhere you want to go. And before you get in my shit, I have to let you know that it may take awhile for me to start referring to you as Mr. President and all those other elite names around here. All I know is you my boy, and you don't have to worry about me having your back."

I reached out to give him dap. "You'd better have my back, and then some. As for referring to me as Mr. President, all I can say about that is practice."

We laughed, then made our way to Levi's black SUV without many people seeing us leave. But no sooner than I sat on the backseat, my cell phone rang. My mother's number flashed on the screen, and since I didn't want to keep ignoring her calls, I answered.

"You were about to get your feelings hurt so badly," she said. "I've been calling and calling and calling you like crazy. If I could have come over there, I would have. But since I checked into rehab the other day, they recommended that I not leave until I get my mess together."

"I recommend that as well, and I told you that if you needed me—"

"Yeah yeah yeah . . . That's what people always say. If you need me, call me. Then when you need them, they don't ever answer their damn phones. I know you're busy, so I didn't want to bother you. But after seeing those pictures of myself in the newspaper and on TV, I said no no no. I can't let anything like that happen again, and I've got to get this drinking under control."

"I couldn't agree with you more. I'm glad you recognize what you need to do, and I have all the faith in the world that you will beat this."

"I will. You know I will."

I swallowed the lump in my throat while gazing out of the window. "I love you, Mama, and I will stop by there tomorrow to check on you. Do you need anything?"

"Nope. Just want to see you so I can hug you, that's all. And I love you too. I would love you even more if you would get that wife of yours together. I'm still up in arms about that purple dress she had on that night. How could you allow her to leave the bedroom like that? The first lady shouldn't show her breasts like that, and she had no problem putting them out there for the world to see."

I had to shake my head. "Good-bye, Mama. See you tomorrow."

I tucked my phone in my pocket, then lay back on the seat with my eyes closed until Levi reached the park. I directed him to pull over in front of the bench where I saw Michelle sitting. A blanket was next to her, along with two pillows. I opened the back door wide, inviting her to come inside the SUV.

"But I thought that we—"

"Yeah, I know. Just come inside. Bring your stuff with you."

Michelle picked up the blanket and pillows, along with her purse. Showing a little skepticism, she peeked inside, before getting in.

"Don't you want to—"

I placed my finger over her lips. "Levi, if you don't mind, I need some privacy."

"No problem, man. I mean, Mr. President."

He raised the tinted window that separated the front seats from the back. The seat Michelle was in faced mine. Keeping her quiet, I removed my shirt, then got on my knees, positioning myself between her legs. She gazed into my eyes, and as I proceeded to lower her dress underneath her breasts, she reached out to rub the back of my head.

"I don't know how long this is going to last," she said softly, "but I wish I could look into the future to see if you will still be there."

"In this case, it's not wise to look into the future. And I don't know about you, but I'm more focused on what's before me right now."

Before me were her firm, healthy breasts that I cuffed in my hands to squeeze. My mouth latched on to her nipples, and my tongue turned circles around them, causing each to stiffen, like the last time the strawberry fragrance all over her sexy body drew me right in. I wasted no time leaning her back on the seat, spreading her legs real wide. I could feel her moist haven thumping against my rising steel that slipped into her. I was hungry for Michelle, and with every long stroke, with every sensual kiss, with every ounce of her juices that she fed me, she satisfied my appetite to the fullest. Even when she straddled my lap to ride me, I felt as if, just for those several minutes, all of my problems had washed away. The tip of my tongue traveled from the nape of her neck, down her spine, as I changed positions and served her well from behind. She was bent over on the seat, and the way she called out to me made my thrusts travel deeper—so deep that her mouth opened wider. Her moans went up a notch, and her pretty round cheeks clapped, more so applauded me for bringing her to her first orgasm of the night. A hotel wound up being our final destination, and before the night was over, there was nowhere else for us to explore and nothing else left for our bodies to give. We lay in bed holding each other, exhausted. For the first time, in a long time, I slept—well.

18

Vice President Tyler McNeil

It wasn't supposed to happen like this. Roy wasn't supposed to suffer from a massive heart attack and die, right when things were starting to swing in my favor. He was the only one who could get through to the Republican caucus, and now we weren't sure what would happen since Senator Bass had taken over. She was soft, and deep down, I could sense that she was fond of Stephen. I was worried about him being able to get through to her. My eyes and ears were wide open, and from talking to some of the other Republicans in the House and Senate, it seemed as if she was trying to convince them to listen to the president and to the American people. Many of them were in line with the president's new agenda.

I truly thought that he would lose a substantial amount of support after those photos were released. But thus far, it didn't seem as if he'd lost enough support to really make a difference. Several members of Congress made a big deal about it, as well as the media. But as with any news, the conversations only lasted for a few days. Roy's death was now the big topic, and everyone wondered what the Republican Party was going to do. They had already started to pose those questions after Roy resigned. It was one big mess, and my grandfather, along with many of his close friends, were not happy campers.

They demanded more action from me. I was getting pulled in many directions, and often being chewed out because I was the closest to Stephen. What they didn't know was, Stephen had distanced himself from me. He went to Andrew for answers, and he rarely listened to anything I had to say. I wasn't sure if he suspected what I had been up to, but I was sure of one thing. He didn't trust me. He didn't want me around, and that was definitely bad news for me. I explained the lack of trust Stephen had for me to my grandfather. We were riding in a limousine and had just left Roy's funeral, where there was standing room only.

"My question to you, Grandfather, is, where do we go from here? We tried to get Secret Service to handle things, and that didn't work. We thought that this thing with Chanel Hamilton would do major harm, but it didn't. Roy was our only hope, but now, he's dead. I don't know how to get Stephen where it hurts. What else would cause him to step down so that I can take over?"

My grandfather grabbed my neck, squeezing it lightly. "There is only one way. Out of all of us, you're the only one who has clearance to get into the White House whenever you want to. You can get close to him, and there is only one thing left that we can do. Assassinate him. There is no other way, but you can't let anyone see you. You have to be brave and understand that you're doing this to save the Republican Party. This is our last chance. If we do not gain control soon, we will never get control again."

I wholeheartedly agreed with my grandfather, but I had never, personally, killed anyone. I guess it wouldn't be that hard to wipe the face of a black man off of this earth, and how many people would really miss him? Sure, some people would be devastated—mostly blacks who viewed him as their king. They'd get over it, though, and when I became president, I would make sure that they did.

"Sneaking up on him and catching him off guard is something that I could do. And it may even be better if I claim self-defense and say that he drew his weapon first and came after me. The reason could be because I disagreed with him regarding the issue with the black man being killed by cops. Many would see the president as just an angry black man, and they would take my side in a heartbeat."

"You're damn right they will take your side, so you go-ahead and do what you need to do. Be careful and watch out for the president's new *homeboy*, Levi. I've noticed that fat slob hanging around the president more often, so you may need to get the chef to fix some soul food in order to lure him away from that door."

"I just may do that, but before I do anything, I want to make sure you're okay. Roy was a good friend of yours. I know you're going to miss him."

My grandfather sat in silence as he looked out the window. A few minutes later, he spoke up. "Hell, yeah, I'm going to miss him. We're all going to miss him. He was good to us, and I hope the others get on board and do the right thing. If not, we're going to vote their asses out of there so fast their heads will spin. Especially Senator Bass. Keep an eye on that bitch and make sure she doesn't do anything that she's not supposed to do."

"I'll take care of her once I'm done taking care of Stephen."

That was like music to my grandfather's ears. When we arrived at his mansion, I hung around for fifteen measly minutes. I couldn't get Stephen off my mind, and I wasn't sure if this was going to be the night I decided to take him down or not. The more I thought about it, maybe so.

19

President of the United States, Stephen C. Jefferson

After my productive conversation with Senator Bass today, things were looking up. She had a meeting with the Republican caucus, and she informed me that there was movement on that end. Many Democrats were already on board; all we needed were several Republicans to do the same. Senator Bass insisted things were about to change, and they had already started working on a bill that could be suitable enough for me to sign. I informed her that I didn't want any tricky shit. Didn't want any pork-barrel projects added to the bill, and when it came across my desk, it had to be clean and address one thing. Gun Control.

While thinking about my first piece of important legislation, I sat on the Truman Balcony wearing a deep-blue vest and slacks. A crisp and clean white shirt that tightened on my muscles was underneath the vest, and since business had been completed for the day, a few buttons on my shirt were undone. I inhaled deeply, sucking in fresh air while gazing at the beautiful scenery from the South Lawn. On a few occasions, I relaxed in one of the lounging chairs outside and wound up falling asleep at night. It looked as if I would do the same tonight, especially since I had gotten comfortable in the chair and propped my feet on the table. My hands were behind my head, and my thoughts were on everything from the ill treatment of blacks in this country, to a potential war brewing with some of our longtime allies. I also thought about Michelle. Wondered how things had turned out when she served her husband those divorce papers. I also thought about her children. It was a messed up situation; I prayed that they all would be okay. My thoughts of Michelle led to my thoughts of Raynetta. I couldn't believe that she was still upset with me, but at times, she was just as stubborn as I was. I was sure that she would come around soon, or, at least, I hoped she would. As I started to think about my mother, I heard someone call my name. It was Andrew, and right behind him was Chanel Hamilton.

"I'm sorry to interrupt you, Mr. President," he said. "But you told me that if she called again, that you wouldn't mind speaking to her."

"Yes, I did, and no problem at all." I removed my feet from the table, then sat up straight. My eyes shifted to Chanel who stood with a tight look on her face.

"I'll leave the two of you alone." Andrew turned to leave.

Chanel came over to where I was and stood with her arms folded. I pointed to the lounging chair across from me.

"Before you start going off and displaying more ugly faces," I said, "why don't you have a seat?"

She plopped in the chair, then crossed her legs. While sitting with good posture, she wasted no time telling me what was on her mind.

"I don't know where to start with you. And while I take full responsibility for what I did, I want you to understand how you left me with no choice. I had been very nice to you, Mr. President. There was no reason for you to treat me as you did and just throw me away like I was some kind of two-dollar whore who wasn't worth a penny. It's like you wanted me to kiss your tail, and after our encounter on Air Force One, I thought we were good. I wasn't trying to replace your wife or be your side chick. I figured we could have a little fun and get together every now and then. But you made me feel as if I was wrong for wanting that. I don't get it, and that's why I showed those photos. I wanted to wake you up and let you know that how you treated me was wrong."

I touched my chin, nodding the whole time she spoke. It seemed as if it was my turn to respond, so I did so without trying to hurt her feelings.

"The truth of the matter is, you showed those photos because you wanted to do me harm. It backfired on you, and as much as you have studied me during my run for the presidency, up until now, you should've known one thing. That is, I really don't give a fuck about much. I don't care how you felt after we had sex, and it's not like I have much time around here to think about it. It wasn't my intentions to treat you ill; doing so never crossed my mind. I assumed that you, of all people, understood how important this job I've been gifted with is to me. When I first laid eyes on you, I didn't expect for you to demand sex and seek revenge when you couldn't get it. And I never thought that you would look my wife in the eyes and give her details about what happened between us. That's messy, and I don't do mess. Because when the juices stop flowing, the orgasms are all done, and the come has dried up, I'm always coming home to the woman I truly love. You and I . . . We had our fun. It may not have lasted as long as you wanted it to, but what you wanted never really mattered to me."

I could see fire burning in Chanel's eyes. It was apparent that some women didn't appreciate the truth. She gritted her teeth, and when she reached out, I knew a slap was coming my way. I caught her hand in midair.

"Don't let my title fool you," I threatened. "If you did your homework, you know where I come from."

She snatched her arm away from me, now standing in anger. "You're darn right I know where you come from. The gutter! You're a gutter Negro, all dressed up in your fine suits, fancy ties, expensive shoes, and cheap jewelry. Your day is coming, Mr. So-called President, and I'm going to sit back and laugh when these white men around here, who are some of your closest confidants, strip you of everything and drag your ass back to the cotton fields where you truly belong."

Some black people just didn't know better. "And I'm going to sit back and laugh when my Secret Service agent arrives and drags your ass back to a sleazy, cheap strip club where you belong. Finally, if you refer to me as good ole Mr. President during sex, I can't be your so-called president now."

I turned my head and saw Levi standing to my left near the doorway.

"Please escort this . . ." I paused to catch myself. Had to remember for a second where I was at. "Get her out of here and never allow her to clear the gates of *my* house again."

Chanel fired every name in the book at me that she could as Levi dragged her away. I got a headache listening to her madness, so I leaned back on the lounging chair, closing my eyes again. Somewhere within the next several minutes, I started to fade. But when I heard someone step on the balcony, I opened my eyes without turning my head.

"Did you get rid of her?" I said, thinking that the person was Levi.

"No, I didn't. But I am going to get rid of you."

I snapped my head to the side; the only thing I saw was a nine millimeter in his hand. After that, I charged out of the chair, preparing myself to hurdle over the the balcony, while hearing whistling bullets whiz by. The balcony was a long way up from the ground. All I could pray for was a safe landing, if I had to jump.

20

First Lady Raynetta Jefferson

Stephen was in bed, bruised and shaken up from some-one trying to assassinate him. Thank God Levi was there to chase away the person who shot at Stephen. More so, I was thankful to Levi for stopping Stephen, before he jumped over the Truman Balcony. He got banged up from running into the steel rails that surrounded the balcony. We were all on pins and needles, trying to keep this incident a secret. But as with any and everything that transpired in the White House, the murder attempt on Stephen's life leaked. Reporters were everywhere. Secret Service had been running around like madmen too. Everyone wanted to see Stephen, talk to him, find out the specificities of what had happened, but he made it clear that no one was to enter our bedroom, with the exception of his doctor, his mother, Levi, and me.

The doctor had just got done examining Stephen. His badly bruised midsection was wrapped in bandages, face was a little scratched on the left side, and hands were swollen.

"You're going to be just fine," Dr. Fields said to Stephen, as he sat shirtless on the bed with his back against the headboard. I stood next to him, Levi was by the window looking out, and Stephen's crazy mother, Teresa, had stepped away to go to the bathroom. Lord knows I didn't want to deal with her tonight. But Levi had left, immediately following the incident, to go pick her up from rehab—per Stephen's request. He didn't know if there had been a hit put out on any of us, so he wanted us all there, under one roof.

"Be sure to take your pain medication," Dr. Fields ordered. "And please, Mr. President, get some rest. Stay in bed for, at least, another two or three days to allow your body to heal. The soreness will not subside if you do not rest your body."

"I will get as much rest as I can. Thank you, Dr. Fields. Levi will now escort you out."

Dr. Fields gathered his belongings, and right after he and Levi left the room, Teresa came out from the bathroom. She looked at me, and then the direction of her eyes traveled to Stephen.

"I don't know what to say about this." Her hand was on her hip. "Who in the hell would want to kill you, and how in the world did they get in here? I told you before to let me handle that damn Secret Service. Since they have failed you, I'm going to do exactly what I planned to do all along."

Stephen quickly spoke up. "That won't be necessary." He reached over to the nightstand for his pain medicine. "I have this under control, and the reason why you're here is so I can keep a close eye on you. I don't, however, want you to get involved in this."

"Tuh. I'm already involved. And in case you haven't noticed, this place, the White House, is no safer than where I was at. Please explain how in the heck can somebody just come up in here and shoot at you? I don't know about that. Something is very fishy, if you ask me."

Stephen hit us both with breaking news. "It was an inside job, Mama. The person who attempted to kill me was my vice president, Tyler McNeil."

My eyes grew wide; I was shocked by what he'd said. "Tyler? Are you kidding me? Why would Tyler want to kill you, and—"

Teresa quickly cut me off. "Stop asking dumb questions, Ne-ne, and don't interrupt me while I'm trying to converse with my son. None of this would have happened, if it wasn't for you. This is what can go down when you don't keep an eye on your husband."

This was the wrong time for Teresa to talk mess to me. Not today. I wasn't having it. "No. Don't you dare interrupt me while I'm speaking to *my* husband. And who in the hell are you, blaming me for this? Go sit your ass down somewhere and shut up!"

"What?" she shouted. "Bitch, I will—"

"Enough, damn!" Stephen shouted with a scrunched face. "If the two of you can't stay in this room for five minutes without tearing each other apart, then leave. I don't have time for this tonight. Tyler just tried to murder me, and all the two of you can do is stand there arguing with each other."

Teresa crossed her arms, then rolled her eyes at me. "She's the one who started it. All I wanted to know was who and why. She act like Tyler needed a reason to do what he did. You may want to check her pockets to see what *she's* hiding. It wouldn't surprise me if she has a bullet or two in her pockets for you too."

"Oh, please," I snapped. "The only person I have a bullet for is you. And you're going to catch one in your face, if you don't stop running your mouth."

"Right back at you, tramp."

I bit my tongue to prevent myself from going ham on Teresa. Stephen growled loudly, then sighed. He tossed the sheets back, slowly moving away from the headboard. Wanting him to follow the doctor's orders, I reached for the sheets to cover him again.

"No, you're not going anywhere tonight. Dr. Fields wants you to stay put for, at least, the next two days. Did you not hear what he told you?"

"To hell with Dr. Fields. I have work to do, and besides that, Dr. Fields doesn't have you for a wife and her as a mother."

He nudged his head toward Teresa.

"What is that supposed to mean?" she said. "You're darn right he doesn't have me as a mother. You do, so therefore, you need to get some control over your foul-mouthed wife, and you need to tell me where I can find Tyler. He won't live past midnight, if it's left up to me."

"Thank God it's not," Stephen said, moving the sheets away from him again. He turned sideways on the bed, struggling to get up. He looked at me before pointing at the chair. "Go get my robe."

"No," I replied. "Where are you trying to go? You're not leaving this room, and if you attempt to, you'll have to go through me first."

"That should be easy," Teresa said. "You're fake, so no challenge for him there."

"Mama!" Stephen barked again. "Get out. Go sit in the Yellow Oval Room for a while and chill. I got too much on my plate right now. The last thing I want to deal with is the two of you."

Just then, Levi came back into the room. Teresa walked to the door, side-eyeing me as if she had so much more to say. I was sure she did, because I did too, even though Stephen didn't approve.

"Stay away from the liquor bottles out there," I said, unable to control myself. "If you can't, I'll call downstairs to make sure they bring you a bunch of red plastic cups."

"And I'll call your beautician to make sure she never fucks your hair up like that again. You look terrible."

This time, Levi intervened, displaying a scrunched face. "Ladies, ladies, really?"

Teresa walked out, slamming the door behind her. Levi looked at Stephen with his face still twisted.

"What is going on in here?" Levi questioned. "Exactly what did I miss?"

"Nothing." Stephen carefully eased off the bed. He looked at his robe hanging over the chair that I refused to get. "Man, hand that to me," he said to Levi.

"I was going to get it for you," I said. "But please listen to me. You can't—"

"If you were going to get it, Raynetta, you damn well would have gotten it, instead of standing there like a damn fool, arguing with my mother! Now, move out of my way and go find something constructive to do, while I go confront my shooter!"

My body quivered from the sound of his shrill voice. How dare he speak to me like that, especially when I was only trying to help! If he wanted to be a bully and not listen to me, fine. I stormed toward the door, but when I placed my hand on the knob, he yelled at me again.

"Do not go far! I can't protect you if you leave this house, so whatever you do, stay right here where Levi or one of the other Secret Service agents can cover you."

I didn't bother to respond. The truth was, we weren't safe no damn where. There were people plotting to bring us down from Iraq to China, to right here in the good ol' United States. Stephen couldn't keep me safe if he tried, and if he depended on Secret Service to do it, he was kidding himself.

Needing some alone time, I made my way down the hallway where I had to, unfortunately, pass by the Yellow Oval Room. Teresa was inside, sitting on a yellow, velvety sofa that was in front of a fireplace. The room was dim, but the crystal chandelier hanging from above gave off some light. A peach, green, and white flower arrangement was on the glass table, exactly where she had placed a glass filled with brown liquid. Her legs were crossed, and when she spotted me, she lifted the glass from the table, tilting it toward me.

"Here's to you for making my son hate me," she said. "He will be so much better off without you, and I'm looking forward to the day you are no longer Mrs. Stephen C. Jefferson."

"Don't hold your breath, then again, please do so because it stinks. And for the record, I *will* remain Mrs. Stephen C. Jefferson until the day you die."

I cut my eyes at her before pivoting and making my way to the main level of the White House where it was busy as ever.

21

President of the United States, Stephen C. Jefferson

The second Raynetta exited the room, I got dressed. I didn't have time to sit in bed and do nothing—too much was at stake. If Tyler had put forth this much effort to kill me, there was no telling what other plans were in place. I had to meet with Secret Service, wanted to sit down with Tyler's wife, Gena, and I also needed to speak with Tyler himself. I also had to address the American people who, I was positive, had some concerns. It was a very chaotic night; surely, it would be a long one.

Suited up and pretending as if my body wasn't hurting all over, I made my way down the corridor with Levi next to me. So many people had questions, but I didn't say a word as we passed by them.

"Mr. President, are you okay?" one of my staff members asked.

"Is it true, Mr. President? Did someone try to kill you?"

"Have you seen the vice president? Where is he?"

I ignored all questions. My head was up high, strut was like it had always been. The only time I halted my steps was when Andrew jumped out in front of me. Levi grabbed his shoulder, adding pressure to it.

"Ooouch! Uh, Mr. President, I really need to speak to you," Andrew said, then shifted his eyes to Levi. "Can you please not do that? All I want to do is speak to him."

I tossed my head back, causing Levi to let go.

"Thank you," Andrew said, straightening his suit jacket. He was real panicky—sweat was visible on his forehead. "What is going on here? I've been provided very minimal information, and as your chief of staff, I demand to know what is going on. Do not leave me in the dark, please."

"We will have a discussion as soon as I get finished taking care of a few important matters. Meet me in the Oval Office in about an hour. Call Gena and tell her to come here. It's imperative that I speak to her. Also, find Sam. Tell him to prep the Press Briefing Room. I'll need to speak to the American people after I meet with you and Gena."

"Will do, sir. See you in one hour."

Levi and I walked off to journey to our destination. But as soon as we entered the private staircase that led to the lower level of the White House, I dropped to one knee, yelping out in pain. It was in my side; I was forced to grab it. I tightened my eyes, sucking in several deep breaths to calm myself.

"Are you all right?" Levi said, standing over me. His hand was on my back as I remained on one knee, trying to recuperate for a few minutes.

"Yeah, I . . . I'm fine," I strained to say. The truth was, the severe pain in my side was kicking my ass. Not to mention what I felt in my achy legs. I massaged my muscles, then made an attempt to stand. Stumbled when I tried.

"Man, you don't look so good. You want me to contact the doctor and ask him to come back?"

"No. What I want you to do is get me to that motherfucker who tried to kill me. After I see him, I'll be just fine."

Levi nodded. "Okay, but just so you know, you may not recognize him. I had to straighten him up a bit, just to get him to keep his mouth shut and stop calling me a nigger."

Hearing that nonsense gave me a little more strength. I followed Levi down to the lower level and into a heavily secured tunnel system that was supposed to be used for emergency shelter or an escape route. Several rooms were off the tunnel, and we entered the one where Tyler was at. It was dark and muggy. Had concrete walls and cameras that monitored him. His hands were cuffed behind him, and the first thing I thought while looking at him was that Levi had done quite a number on him. His wet, sweaty hair was spiked all over, as if it had been pulled. His shirt was ripped—bruises could be seen all over his thin body. Blood stained his face that had cuts and lumps on it. Slacks had holes at the knees, and his feet were black as tar. I stood near the door with my arms folded. Levi walked over to Tyler, snatching his head up so he could look at me.

"Stand your ass up and address the president when he comes into the room."

Tyler remained slumped, looking weak as ever. To help him stand, Levi pulled him up by his hair.

"Ahhhhh," Tyler whined while squeezing his eyes together. "I'm standing, okay?"

Levi didn't appreciate his attitude. He punched him in the gut, causing him to double over and fall back on the steel bench.

"Fuck!" Tyler shouted, then looked at me. "Tell this big-ass sloppy gorilla to back off of me!"

Levi laughed, then hit him again. This time, he back-handed Tyler with a clenched fist, causing more blood to gush from his mouth.

"Is . . . Is that all you got?" Tyler spit a gob of blood on the ground. He then sucked in his bottom lip, trying to prevent more blood from dripping down his chin.

"I got more of that coming your way," Levi said. "But I'm trying to be generous and save some for my friend."

Levi looked at me, but I glared at Tyler. "You're a mess," I said. "And I guess I'm wasting my time by coming down here to find out who put you up to killing me, right? From the way you're speaking to my friend, I take it that you really don't have much to say."

"I have plenty to say. That would be—go to hell, you fucking low-life nigger. I don't give a shit what you or your homeboy do to me. You won't get away with it. I have a whole lot of people out there waiting for something to happen to me, just so they can cut your freaking balls off and shove them in your mouth until you choke and die."

I reached down to cuff my package. "Sounds painful. I had a major reaction to that—what about you, Levi?"

"Yeah, I did too. Triggered my reflexes."

Levi backhanded Tyler again. He fell back, hard, hitting his head on the concrete wall. He hollered out in pain, then rolled on the floor with his hands still cuffed behind him.

"Yo . . . You're guuuud," Tyler said, then laughed. He played tough, which was fine by me. "Mr. President, I see why you want this big ol' cotton-pickin' nigger around. He's a good boy who will serve you just fine."

I hurried to speak up. "Trust me, you haven't seen nothing yet. Now who and why, Tyler? You have one opportunity to tell me. If you fail to speak up, I will offer your wife, as well as your daughter, my sincerest condolences for their loss."

Tyler looked me straight in the eyes, refusing to back down. "Fuuuuck you!" he spat. "If I die, you die. That I can promise you."

"See you on the other side . . . whenever I get there."

Always keeping my hands clean, I turned toward the door, opened it, then walked out. As I strutted down the hallway, I heard several loud shots that sounded like firecrackers. My thoughts . . . *Done deal.* Now it was time for me to go break the news to Tyler's wife and to the American people.

I entered the Oval Office, seeing that Gena and Andrew were already there. Almost immediately, Gena jumped to her feet. Her pale face was beet red. Eyes were filled with tears and dirty-blond, stringy hair was tucked behind her ears.

"Where is he?" she asked, then rushed up to me. "Have you seen him, Mr. President? Where is my husband?"

Not wanting to do this, but knowing that I had to, I lied. "I'm so sorry, Gena. The men who charged in here to assassinate me took Tyler. We do know that they were Americans. They belong to a hate group that has been sending threatening letters to the White House ever since I've been here. Homeland Security and the FBI thought that they were on top of this, but as Tyler was in here speaking to me tonight, he just happened to be in the wrong place, at the wrong time. I was able to get away, but—" I paused, swallowed, and blinked my eyes, pretending as if I was too choked up to speak.

With her trembling hands, Gena wiped snot from her dripping wet nose. "But what?" she cried out. "They took him and did what?"

I squeezed my forehead, then turned around so I didn't have to face her. "We have solid evidence that they killed him. I will be working closely with the FBI—"

"No, no, noooo!" she said, pounding my back. "Don't you dare stand there and tell me my husband is dead! He's not dead, and why would anyone want to hurt him?"

Andrew attempted to pull Gena away from me. "Ca . . . Calm down and let's go back over to the sofa and have a seat."

I turned around, and seeing how devastated she was, I could only think that if her husband had been successful at taking my life tonight, Raynetta could very well be in Gena's place instead.

She snatched away from Andrew who was trying to console her. "I don't want to sit down! Something isn't adding up, and if those men came here to kill you, why didn't they do it? How are you still alive, yet my husband is dead? How were they able to get by Secret Service? This is bull, Mr. President, and I want the truth—now!"

I remained calm as ever. The look of sadness stayed locked on my face. I did my best to convince Gena that what I had told her was the truth. She stared at me with evil eyes, so I unbuttoned my shirt so she could see the tight bandages wrapped at my midsection.

"I managed to get away. . Tyler didn't, so they took him away. One of the Secret Service agents assisted me, but many of us are aware that Secret Service has failed us around here and have put our lives in danger. I'm sorry that they allowed this to happen, and all I can do, going forward, is make sure nothing like this ever happens again. In the interim, we will hunt down and find who did this. Currently, we don't have Tyler's body, but we do have photos that confirm he is deceased. I am deeply sorry, and if there is anything . . . Anything that I can do to help your family during this difficult time, I will be more than willing to do it."

Gena released staggering cries. I stepped forward to secure her in my arms. She pounded my chest, crying harder as she slid from my arms, falling to her knees.

"I . . . I want you to find out who those animals are and kill them! I want them dead, and I want to see, see what they did to my husband's body! This can't be real, Mr. President. They can't get away with anything like this, you hear me! They just can't!"

"And they won't," I rushed to say, kneeling down next to her. "We will find them. You have my word that we will, but I need for you to be strong and stand with me tonight as I address the American people. Let's stand against all of this violence that has now made its way into the White House and caused irreparable damage. Racism has no place in this country, and tonight, you and I can stand against gun violence and hate groups who attempt to divide us. Tyler would want that. I know he would, and I will demand that his body be returned to us or else."

Gena lowered her head, continuing to sob. My eyes shifted to Andrew who stood as if he was a mannequin. A puzzled expression covered his face; he stared at me as if he could see straight through my lies. I turned my attention back to Gena who was rocking back and forth while still on her knees.

"Let me help you," I said, helping her off the floor. "I need you, Gena, but it's up to you, if you want to stand with me tonight. I'll be in the Press Briefing Room in about forty-five minutes. Call whomever you need to call and let them know about this. And please, offer everyone my condolences." I looked at Andrew who remained in awe. "Please go get Levi or another agent at the door. Tell them to take care of Gena, and make sure she is under tight security tonight."

Andrew and I helped Gena off the floor. She was barely able to stand; her skinny legs looked fragile. Andrew walked to the door, ordering a Secret Service agent, Kenny, to come inside. He escorted Gena out of the Oval Office, and once the door was shut, Andrew removed his glasses, releasing a deep sigh.

"If you don't mind, Mr. President, I now would like to hear the real truth. There were no threatening letters, and no one got by Secret Service and came in here with guns."

I walked over to my desk, taking a seat in the chair. "Are you calling me a liar?"

Andrew hesitated for a few seconds, before proceeding. "The truth, yes, I am, sir. I'm not buying that cockamamie story, and I demand the truth."

"I just told you and Gena the truth. If you don't believe me, too bad."

Andrew shook his head. "No, it's not too bad. I need to know what in the hell is going on, and I want to know right freaking now!"

His voice had gone up a few notches. It didn't move me, but it surprised me.

"For the last time, the truth went in one ear, and if you allowed it to exit the other, that's on you. Now, if you don't mind, I need to wrap up a few things before I speak to the American people. I also need for you to set up a meeting later with me, the FBI, and Homeland Security. I want every single agent who works here to join us, and if you can handle that little task for me, I would appreciate it."

"I can, but I won't. Not until you tell me the truth. For God's sake, tell me the damn truth! I'm not your enemy, okay? I don't know why you don't trust me, and if you can't fucking tell me what exactly happened here tonight, then maybe I don't need to be here!"

I slammed my hand on the desk. "Then get the fuck out, because I don't trust you. I will never trust you or no other motherfucker around here smiling in my face, yet waiting for me to fail! For all I know, you could have been plotting with Tyler. You could have given him the gun to kill me, and until I know every single detail about why the vice president of the United States attempted to kill me, my guard will stay up."

Andrew's mouth was wide open. "Ty . . . Tyler is the one who tried to kill you?"

"You look surprised."

"That's because I am. Why would he do something like that?"

"Take a look at my skin. It's black. But maybe you can tell me why, especially if you're one of those blind-ass people who don't think extreme racism exists."

"I swear to you, Mr. President, that I am not a racist, and I didn't know anything about his plans to kill you. I am completely shocked, and what . . ." he paused, then looked at the door. Seconds later, he turned to me again. "What about Gena? Why did you lie to her? If Tyler attempted to kill you, why didn't you just tell her?"

"You're asking too many questions, Andrew. Questions that I'm not prepared to answer just yet. Nonetheless, I will say this. Many Americans sympathize with white women, way more than they do with a black man, president or not. If I want gun control laws to be passed and hate crimes and racism against African American people to be dealt with, I know exactly who to put in front of the cameras. If you are just as concerned about those issues as I am, do whatever you can to make sure Gena is prepped, cleaned up, and ready to speak up tonight in the Press Briefing Room. Then again, if all you want to do is stand there and yell at me about not telling you the truth, then I damn well know whose side you're on."

"I'm always on your side, Mr. President. Don't you ever forget it."

"Then by all means, damn it, prove it."

Andrew walked away. My eyes followed him to the door, and after he left, I started jotting down a few notes that I wanted to speak about tonight. I prayed that Gena would be there with me too.

22

President of the United States, Stephen C Jefferson

Less than one hour later, I, along with Gena and
Sam, stood in the Press Briefing Room to speak to the
American people. We appeared torn. Broken. Devastated.
Tearful. Disgusted, as well as confused by a tragic loss
that shouldn't have happened . . . depending on who you
asked, of course. After my tearful speech about finding
the killers, pushing for gun control, and the need to
confront racism, the reporters started to weigh in. My
arms were around Gena's shoulders, comforting her as
she buried her head in my chest and cried.

"Mr. President," the male reporter said in a soft tone,
"we have never seen you quite this emotional before.
Do you worry that the killers will view you as a weak
president and attempt to come after you again?"

Stupid muthafucka, I thought. Any other time I wouldn't
have answered his question, but tonight, I needed to keep
my cool and make as many people as I could sympathize
with what had happened. I swallowed hard, then narrowed
my eyes, allowing another tear to fall.

"Even Jesus wept, and I assure you that He was not
a weak man. There has been a tragic loss in this house
tonight, and we all have to ask ourselves why. Why and
how could something like this happen? I'll tell you how.

Because we have allowed the NRA and people with guns to win. Sick people who have no business with them have them. Anybody who wants a gun can get it, and we defend this by referring to our Second Amendment rights, the right to keep and bear arms. And while no one wants to infringe upon those rights, we have to consider what is occurring in this country and be willing to make some changes. We should also be ashamed of ourselves for not standing up and saying enough is enough. We've told ourselves that a black man's life has no value, even when he is voted in to lead this country. The hate mail that I receive speaks volumes, and I am devastated, tonight, that my vice president had to ultimately pay the price in order for us to wake up and realize that racism is an extremely serious problem, not only in this country, but also around the world. If shedding tears for the loss of my dear friend and closest confidant makes me appear weak to anyone, then I'll be it."

"The president is right," Gena said, moving away from my hold and stepping closer to the podium. She wiped her tears, barely able to speak. "We . . . We can't allow this anymore. We can't sit back and not do anything. Tyler paid a huge price tonight for our lack of action, and even though gun control laws may or may not have prevented this, we do know that too many guns are getting into the hands of the wrong people. People who are killing others because of their religion or sexual preferences. And because of the color of their skin. No president should have to endure this kind of ill treatment, and who are we to sit quietly and allow it? For the sake of God, and in memory of my husband, I'm asking the American people to stand with us tonight. Pray that we find the killers, and to whoever they are, please send my husband's body back to meee!" she cried out uncontrollably.

There was a crisp silence in the room. Many eyes filled with tears. Every eye was upon us, and just as I had expected, *she* moved them. One reporter was brave enough to stand.

"Mrs. McNeil, I'm so sorry for your loss, and you too, Mr. President. Do you have any idea who the shooters were, and what are you planning to do about the makeup of your Secret Service detail? No one has ever been able to enter the White House with guns and do such a thing."

"Unfortunately, during the term of another president who happened to be African American, and unbeknownst to the American people, similar incidents occurred. Do your homework; I've done mine. Secret Service will be dealt with, but tonight, we ask for your prayers. Pray for peace, unity, resolutions, and that the killers are soon found. Thank you all for coming here, and may God continue to bless this beautiful country we live in."

We all stepped away, and after the door to the briefing room was closed, Gena thanked me. She then walked away with Andrew who was waiting to escort her to a car so she could join Tyler's family. I was just about ready to walk away too, but Sam stopped me. The door to the briefing room opened, and there stood Michelle Peoples.

"Mr. President, I know you're busy," Sam said. "But she wanted to know if she could have five minutes of your time."

The door to where we normally met was opened. I walked inside, Michelle followed me. She shut the door, then quickly rushed up to me, easing her arms around my waist. I deeply inhaled from the painful feeling of her squeezing my midsection.

"I'm so glad you're okay," she said, looking up at me. "This is such a scary situation, and I was so worried when I heard the news."

I removed her arms, backing away to ease the pain. "Thanks for your concern. I'll be fine, trust me. As for you, how did things go with your husband?"

"I gave him the divorce papers, and he thanked me for setting him free. Said he would be in touch, and then walked out. I'm just happy it's over."

I nodded, feeling glad for her. I also had many loose ends to tie up, so I had to make this quick. "That's good, and I hope that you get everything that is coming to you."

"Same to you. I know it's late, and I'm sure you have a lot of things to do. But I'll be up for a while. Want to celebrate my divorce, and you look like you could use a soothing body rub. My hands work wonders, you know."

"You don't have to convince me, but we'll see. I'll send you a text, if I can make it."

Michelle gazed at me as if she wanted to say something else. Whatever it was, she didn't say, but she reached out, again, to hug me. This time, she leaned in for a kiss. I could never deny the sweet taste of her lips, so we indulged ourselves for a few minutes. As I cuffed her pretty face with my hands, I brushed her soft cheeks with my thumbs. I backed my head away from her, looking into her eyes.

"My text may not come until two or three in the morning," I said.

"It doesn't matter. Whatever time you come, I'll be waiting."

I pressed my thick lips against hers, sampling them again before we parted ways. As we exited the room, Sam and Levi were by the door, and to my right, far down the hallway, was Raynetta. Her eyes were contracted, and an evil glare was visible in them. She rolled them at me, then walked away. So did Michelle who didn't see Raynetta. Levi did, and as he, Sam, and I, made our way down the corridor, Levi had several questions for me. Sam walked several feet in front of us; he couldn't hear much.

"What's next?" Levi said in a whisper. "We dumped him, photos were taken, and the fake video of two men coming in here has been created. When do you want it released, and how soon will it be before someone *discovers* his body?"

"Soon, but not yet. I'm working on a few more things, and get me some threatening photos and letters fast. I already have a few, nothing real violent though. I need something that will really shake up people when they see it. We'll release everything, including the video, to the FBI in a few. They're already prepared to review this stuff and speak to me. Kyle is leading the investigation, so we're good, if you know what I mean. There will be an intense meeting tomorrow, so be prepared. And do not go far tonight, because I may need you to do something else for me."

Levi saluted me. "I'm on it, man. I mean, Mr. President."

I released a light chuckle, even though it caused a hurtful jab to arise in my side.

It was already late, and things didn't wrap up in the Oval Office until the wee hours of the morning. The secretary of Homeland Security was there, Levi, FBI, my senior Secret Service agent, two more agents, and Andrew. Everyone had seen the tapes, even though a few of us knew they had been falsely constructed. The cut-up photos of me and violent letters worked well too. I used them as my exhibit while walking everyone through everything that had taken place tonight. Levi was there to fill them in on what transpired when he came into the room. There were plenty of questions and concerns, but the bottom line was, my secretary of Homeland Security, Phillip Bates, knew that he had failed me again.

"After watching that video," he said, "and hearing details of what happened here tonight, I have no other choice but to resign, sir. It was my duty to keep you safe, but I put together a team that seems unable to do it."

I didn't sympathize with him one bit. "I accept your resignation. Please have it on my desk by noon. I will search for your replacement; meanwhile, I have to revamp my entire Secret Service detail so that not only myself, but my family, are protected as well. I'm going to assign Levi as my senior agent, and he will be tasked with finding capable agents who are willing to put their lives on the line to save mine. I reject a meeting tomorrow—don't have much else to say. I do, however, want to meet every new agent, and I want specific details of what their duties will be." I looked at Kyle who was leading the FBI's efforts to quickly get to the bottom of this. "If there is anything else that you need from me, I will fully cooperate. I need speedy action to be taken, and I, along with the American people, will be relieved when those murderers are found."

"We're already on it," he said. "No rest tonight, and we will not sleep until they are caught."

The meeting was a wrap. We all shook hands, and right after everyone left, I eased into my chair. I carefully removed my suit jacket, and then unbuttoned the top buttons on my shirt. While rubbing my chest, I thought about all that had happened. I predicted that I would soon get numerous calls and visits, especially from Tyler's family. If I played my cards right, this could turn out to be one of the biggest accomplishments of any president in a long time.

After the meeting was done, I stood outside of Michelle's loft with my jacket thrown over my shoulder. Levi stood by the elevator, making sure the coast was clear. Michelle opened the door wearing a gold-colored silk robe that revealed her smooth chocolate legs that looked dipped in baby oil. Her thick, natural hair was pulled away from her face and secured with a band. A light gloss was on her lips, and the peachy smell of her fragrance reeled me inside. I had never been to her loft before. It was simple, neat, and nice. Black-and-white photos of her children were on the walls, a microfabric sectional was in the opened living room, and many books were stacked on bookshelves in the corners. A furry rug covered the hardwood floors, and a long kitchen island separated the living room from the kitchen.

"Where are your children?" I asked while standing near the living room.

She placed her finger over her lips. "They're sleeping. Been asleep since ten o'clock, according to the sitter."

"Is she here too?"

"No. She left after I got home."

Michelle took my hand, leading me down a wide hallway to the right. She pointed to pictures on the wall of her children.

"This is Brea, that's Que, and she's my youngest, Corrine. I named her after my grandmother."

I looked at the pictures, admiring how beautiful her children were. Michelle seemed to be a good mother—a decent person in general. I didn't want to cloud anyone's perception of her in any way, but there was something about her that I was drawn to.

"Your children are beautiful, as you are. I'm looking forward to having some children one day too."

She smiled, then directed me to the other side of the loft where there was a spacious bathroom. A Jacuzzi tub was in the middle of the floor, shower to the right. Countertops were topped with black-and-white swirling marble, as was the floor. The tub was filled with water and bubbles with steam coming from it. A bath sponge sat on the edge, along with numerous bottles of soaps and oils.

"I know I hurt you earlier when I squeezed your waist, and as you stood at the podium tonight, I could tell you were in pain from the way you kept touching your side. I suspect you've already seen a doctor, but allow me to take care of you tonight. Relax, and I promise to save the questions I have about what really happened at the White House for another day."

Michelle took my jacket from my hand, tossing it on the counter. She stood in front of me, unbuttoning my shirt, then peeling it away from my chest and shoulders. The bandages around my midsection were visible; she carefully removed them, then assisted me in removing my slacks. I stood naked, watching as she studied every inch of me.

"Those bruises look painful. Are you sure nothing is broken?"

"Positive. But now that you have me naked, what else do you need me to do?"

"I need you to come over here." She made her way to the tub, sitting on the edge of it. "Get in the water and relax. I hope it's not cold, and if it is, let me know and I'll warm it up for you again."

I stepped into the water; one word came to mind— Perfect.

"This feels fine," I said before sinking my body in the water and resting my head back on a contoured pillow. "Real good. Thank you."

"You're welcome."

Michelle reached for the sponge, lathering it with soap. She positioned herself on her knees, and while outside of the tub, she thoroughly washed and massaged me. I felt as if I had died and gone to heaven. My eyes couldn't stay open, and with every gentle touch, every massage that just happened to be in all the right places, and every kiss that she placed on my lips, I was sucked right in.

"Thank you, again, for this," I mumbled with my eyes nearly shut. "You are an incredible woman."

She didn't reply. And through my blurred vision, I saw her stand and remove her robe. She climbed in the tub with me, but instead of sitting behind me like she wanted to, I requested that she sit in front of me.

"I just didn't want to put any pressure on you from lying against your body," she said.

I wrapped my arms around her waist, pulling her body as close to me as I could, with her back against my chest.

"I can handle your body against mine. Any day and any time."

Michelle clenched her hands together with mine. We lay silently in the warm tub, taking it all in. Her eyes were closed too, and as my eyelids started to get heavier, I felt myself fading. Michelle lifted her head, turning it slightly to the side.

"I don't know if you can hear me," she whispered in a soft tone, "but I wanted you to know something. I'm falling in love with you. Trying so hard not to, but I can't help myself."

I had heard her. And I responded by leaning in and planting a gentle, passionate kiss on her lips. After that, I was out.

23

Real Estate Tycoon and Billionaire, Christopher J. McNeil

I cringed while watching the president and Gena on TV. Was she fucking stupid? My heart ached for my grandson, Tyler. Couldn't believe none of this had happened, but I didn't believe, for one measly second, that he was dead. This was a fucking game Mr. President was playing. He didn't have enough balls to kill Tyler, and he knew if he damn well did, he would wage a war that he wasn't ready for.

Unable to sleep, I paced the floor in my burgundy silk robe and house shoes. A pipe dangled from the corner of my mouth, and I kept turning my head toward the TV every time I heard a reporter mention Tyler's name. I always tuned in to watch Johnny Baton, but he was way off base tonight.

This is a tragic day for our country. No one could have ever predicted that our vice president, or possibly our president, for that matter, would ever be gunned down on the premises of the White House. Tyler McNeil served our country with great pride. At the president's request, Tyler boldly took on his new position, determined to assist in bringing both parties together. It is with a heavy heart that I say he will be missed dearly. As I watched his wife, Gena, and the president tonight,

I felt a deep desire to stand with them. We're all in this together. It is time that we put aside our differences and do what is right for this country as a whole.

Another female commentator spoke up. *I wholeheartedly agree. Our president has been through a lot, and he hasn't even been in office for one year. I witnessed the pain in his eyes, and I cried the whole time I watched him speak. This is terrible, and this is not who we are as a country.*

My eye twitched as I watched those two idiots speak about Tyler and give their take on watching the press conference tonight. I was sure many others empathized with Stephen, and it angered me so much that I picked up a glass, throwing it at the TV. The only thing that cracked was the glass. Shards hit the floor, as did one of my wife's porcelain statues. She came into the room, tightening her robe. Her eyes were red from bawling so much after receiving the news that Tyler was dead. Unfortunately, she believed it, even though I told her it was a bunch of bull.

"Christopher McNeil, why don't you turn that TV off and come lie with me in bed? I've been trying to reach Margie and Gena, but no one is answering their phones. We should go there by noon, that's if you ain't done spoken to them already."

"I have spoken to them. They're coming here tomorrow, so hush and go lay your head on a pillow. I'll join you shortly."

"You need to join me now. Breaking things in here won't help you one single bit. And if you're convinced that Tyler ain't dead, then why are you in here fussing with yourself?"

Sometimes my wife irritated the heck out of me. "Shut your fat mouth, woman, and go to bed! Let me be and stop talking to me while I'm thinking."

She mumbled something underneath her breath before leaving the room. I fell back in the chair, thinking of ways to get ahead of Mr. President. I knew what he was aiming for, and I would do everything within my power to make sure he didn't get it. First, I had to find my grandson. I needed to know where Tyler was. If he was, indeed, dead, I would personally go to the White House and burn that sucker down—with Mr. President and his family in it.

Later that morning, I sat with numerous family members including Gena, Tyler's mother, Margie, and his father, Gerald, was expected to join us this afternoon. Also in the room was Senator Bass and six other Republicans in the House of Representatives who owed me dearly due to my numerous contributions to their campaigns. I stressed, immediately, that I thought the president was being untruthful about what had happened to Tyler. Some agreed; some did not.

"What do you suppose happened then?" Senator Bass questioned. "The president provided proof. He released the threatening letters he received, and there were photos of him and his family with their heads cut off. You may not like the president, sir, but I don't think he would fabricate a story quite like that one."

"Neither do I," Gena said tearfully. "All I want to know is, where is Tyler? Nothing else matters, and I'm holding on to hope that he's still alive."

"Me too," Margie said, hugging Gena.

I gazed at the three foolish women. Didn't want to tell them what was on my mind—I would hurt some feelings.

"I'm willing to make a bet with any person in this room who believes Tyler is dead. I have a million dollars that says he's alive—I feel it in my heart. That grimy nigger is playing games with us and with the American people. Why can't you idiots see through his bag of lies? He's using us to get what he wants, and Senator Bass, your ass better be ready to shut him down! Our party is on the brink of losing everything. We will lose our majority in the Supreme Court, and the Democrats will continue to have their way. I keep hearing about movement on gun control, and if any of you vote for a bill that is in line with what Stephen C. Jefferson wants, I will have your heads on a silver platter. My partners and I will no longer fund your campaigns, and you all will be left with a bag of bones to feed your families."

"I don't want to hear this right now, Father," Margie said, snapping at me. "Tyler could very well be dead! The focus should be on finding out what happened to him, not on the goddamn Republican Party. Why must everything be so political to you? Don't you even care about your grandson?"

I lifted my finger, pointing at her with raised brows. "Margie, you lower your voice or leave this room right now! You will not speak to me that way in my house! Of course I care about my grandson. But I'm not going to stand by and allow a nigger to tell me he's dead, when I think otherwise. How in the hell can you trust a nigger, and you know how much they lie. I won't stand—"

"No, Christopher," Senator Bass said, interrupting me. She stood, then tucked her purse underneath her arm. "I won't stand by and listen to you use that kind of language when referring to our president, and I don't care how much money you've contributed to my campaign over the years. Enough is enough, and using racial slurs like that is very upsetting to me. I won't be a part of this anymore, so ladies and gentlemen, please excuse me. I do have work to do."

Senator Bass started toward the door, but I yelled after her. "You can walk out that door all you want, but if your fat ass does not fall in line, you are done! You will *never* hold public office again, and I will make sure that when history is written, it will recognize you as the nigger-loving cunt responsible for the demise of our party!"

"No, Christopher. When history is written, my dear, it will recognize me as a courageous woman who stood against racist fools like you and saved our party's reputation. It will show that I respected others, all while protecting our conservative values. This won't be over until the fat lady sings, and trust me when I say, you haven't heard me sing yet."

I sucked my teeth, then spit tobacco in a cup. "Hush your mouth, woman. I've heard you sing, moan, groan, and weep in my bedroom, and it still didn't do the job. The only reason you're Speaker of the House is because *I* put you there. And at the snap of my little ol' finger, I can make you disappear."

"You mean, like I'm about to do when I walk out of here? Good-bye, Christopher, and please beware . . . When I do sing, my voice is going to be loud and clear. You're not going to like it, but that's too bad. You'll get over it, as you did when I walked out on you years ago, because, quite frankly, my dear, your sex was horrible. Those moans and groans you still remember were fake."

Senator Bass left the room. Margie stood too.

"I've heard enough of this God awful mess. Do whatever you plan to do to fix this, Father. In the meantime, my concern is for my child."

Without saying a word, Margie and Gena left the room. I looked at the others, waiting for them to speak up. No one dared to.

"Eyes and ears open," I said. "There will be a big reward for anyone who can tell me where my grandson is or find out what really happened to him. Until then, can I count on everyone here to stick together? Let me know now; I don't want any surprises. If there are cowards in the room, please come forth."

All eyes shifted around the room. We exchanged handshakes, and I assumed we were all in agreement about what needed to be done.

24

First Lady Raynetta Jefferson

I was starting to lose my mind up in here. Stephen had his mother and me on lock; I was barely able to take a piss without Secret Service lurking over my shoulders. I was, however, able to listen to Stephen while in the Press Briefing Room. And when he left, I saw him enter one of the meeting rooms with Michelle Peoples. I wondered what they discussed, but since he didn't even come back to the bedroom last night, I could only assume where he was. Bastard—it was time for me to make a move. I only had two hours of sleep. Got up, checked my schedule for the day, and talked to my assistant, Claire. She was always ten steps ahead of everyone around here. She confirmed that Stephen had left the White House hours ago and had not yet returned.

"Any idea where he went?" I asked while sitting on the sofa in my office. My legs were crossed, and I bit my nail, looking at it and thinking how badly I needed a manicure.

"No idea, because the Secret Service agent I usually get my information from was released of his duties. There are other ways to find out, if you want me to."

"No, that's okay. I'll find out, and in the meantime, give me a rundown of my schedule today."

"Late last night, the president requested that your schedule be revised. He cleared the entire thing and is demanding that you stay here. I can, however, tell you what your prior engagements were. If you'd like to keep those appointments, please let me know."

"I don't care about the president's demands. Keep my schedule as is, and after I eat breakfast, I'll meet you right back here so we can go. Will you be joining me for breakfast or not?"

"I already ate, but thanks. I'll see you within the hour, and I'll let Secret Service know when you're ready to go."

"Thank you, Claire. I appreciate you."

In an effort to get some privacy, I headed to the President's Dining Room on the second floor, near the North Lawn. I had hoped Stephen would be there, but he wasn't. A Secret Service agent was close by, one I hadn't seen before. He had been following me, ever since I was on the lower level. I was annoyed, especially when I sat at the round table that already had an array of fruits and breads on it. The agent came inside of the room, standing by the door.

"Really?" I said, turning to face him. "Is this necessary?"

"Per the president's request, I am not to let you out of my sight. So, yes, it is very necessary."

"Do you have to be so close? I mean, if I pass gas, you can probably smell it. Can't you go somewhere and watch me from afar?"

He chuckled, showing his pearly white teeth. I couldn't help but to think that he was kind of cute, but almost a little too short for my taste. Bald head had a shine, goatee suited his chin well. His build was impressive too, and in addition to that, he was a sexy chocolate, like Stephen, but definitely not as handsome as Stephen was.

"Please don't do that," he said, referring to me passing gas. "Especially not while you're having breakfast."

"I promise not to, as long as you go stand somewhere else. I don't like people to watch me eat."

Without saying a word, he moved outside of the door so I wouldn't see him. I reached for a roll to put butter on it. As I spread butter on the roll with a knife, I heard a loud voice coming my way. I looked up and saw Teresa, fussing at an agent who was behind her.

"I'm not having this," she said. "Where is Stephen? I need to talk to him right now."

I was blunt, as usual. "He's having breakfast with one of his whores. I'll be sure to let him know you're looking for him . . . whenever he gets here."

Just to annoy me, Teresa pulled back one of the chairs, sitting at the table with me. This early in the morning, she was all dolled up in a tan linen suit with pearls draped around her neck. Her salt-and-pepper hair was styled in a neat layered cut with bangs covering her forehead. Her manicure looked freshly done, and her makeup looked done by a professional. Diamond rings were on her fingers, and I surely wondered where she was headed today looking rather jazzy.

"You don't need to tell him nothing for me. I will probably see him before you do, and if he's with one of his whores, that's your problem, not mine."

She reached for a plate and started scooping mixed fruit from the bowl. Minutes later, one of the White House servers asked if we wanted anything else to eat.

"I only put fruit and bread on the table because that's what the president normally eats. If either of you would like something else, I'll be happy to prepare it. I know how much you like my pancakes," Joe said, smiling at me. "It will only take me ten or twenty minutes to make them for you."

"No, thank you, Joe. The fruit is fine, and so is the bread. I would, however, like some apple juice. Can you get some for me?"

"Of course. I'll be happy to."

"And while you're getting her apple juice," Teresa said, pulling him closer and whispering, "would you get me a glass of wine and two aspirin? My back is killing me from sleeping in that bed, and how in the world do they have uncomfortable mattresses like that in the White House? I can't wait to get out of here."

"I'm sorry to hear about your back, but any particular kind of wine? And I'll be sure to get your aspirin too."

Teresa looked to be in deep thought before snapping her fingers. "What about a bottle of Petrus Pomerol from Bordeaux, France. They make some of the most exquisite wines, and if there are any bottles around here, I would love to have them."

"I don't know if we have that one in particular around here, but I'm sure I can find you something else very tasty."

Just that fast, she snapped. "If it's not that one, I don't want it. Thank you very much, though."

Joe smiled, then walked away. I just shook my head at Teresa. Who in the hell drank an expensive bottle of wine like that this early in the morning? I hated to sit at the table with her; it was difficult to ignore her.

"Ne-ne, pass me the butter over there. These rolls are a little hard. I need something to soften them up a bit."

Without looking in her direction, I passed the butter to her. She didn't bother to say thanks, and as soon as we heard Stephen's voice, both of our heads snapped to the side. He walked into the room with Levi on his right, and two other men to his left. The other two Secret Service agents who were outside of the room came inside with Stephen.

"Well, well, well," Teresa said, putting her hand on her hip. "Nice of you to finally show up. Now that you're here, we need to talk about all of these men following me around. I don't like it one bit, and after I get finished fighting to put butter on these hard rolls, I'm going to need one of them to take me home."

"Sorry, Mama, but you're going to have to make yourself at home right here. At least for another week or so, and I'm not going to argue with you about this."

She cocked her head back, as if she was in awe. "Like *hell* we won't argue. Yes, we will, because I'm ready to go home *now*."

Stephen turned to the men standing by him. "Levi is going to show everyone around. We'll meet in my office in a few, all right?"

They all nodded, then left the room. Stephen hadn't even looked at me. He stood next to his mother, continuing his conversation with her.

"One to two weeks, Mama, that's all I ask of you. If you go home, there is a good chance that someone will attempt to hurt you. What happened here last night was serious. And I won't feel safe until we find out who, exactly, is behind this. Trust me when I say the VP wasn't working alone."

Teresa released a deep sigh. "I guess I don't have a choice, but tell me this. What's the deal with all of these black men running around here? You know I don't have anything against our people, but you need to do a thorough background check on each and every one of them. Some people like to steal shit, and I'm not going to be responsible for anything historic, with a high price tag on it, walking up out of here."

"Background checks have already been done, and they are cleared. And just so you know, you sound ridiculous. If you don't have anything nice to say, then don't say it at all."

Stephen finally sat at the table. He looked over at me, as if he were studying me. I tried, but I just couldn't bite my tongue.

"Good morning to you too, honey. Is your private part still wet or have you already taken a shower to cleanse the filth from your body? Didn't mean to pry, but I had to inquire."

"Whew, chile," Teresa said, fanning herself. "This is too much for me, and this conversation should be between a man and his jealous wife. I'm going to step away from the table and allow the rumbling to continue."

Teresa got up from the table and left. Stephen picked up the pitcher of orange juice, pouring himself a glass.

"Did you sleep well?" he asked, ignoring my comment as usual.

"I didn't, but I'm sure you did."

"As a matter of fact, I did. Better than I've slept in a long time, considering all that happened last night."

"Oh, yeah . . . about last night. Are you planning to tell me more about this thing with Tyler attempting to kill you, or is that none of my business too?"

"What you know is what you heard. I tried to provide details, but you thought it was more important to argue with my mother. Now it's too late, and all we can do is move on."

"Move on or move out. I'm seriously considering both, and I'll let you know what I ultimately decide."

I got up from the table, leaving Stephen alone to dine with himself. But when I returned to my office where Claire was, she was in a heated argument with the same Secret Service agent who had been following me around. I assumed the tour he was on was already over.

"The first lady wants to leave, and you can't stop her," Claire said. "She has an important luncheon scheduled at eleven o'clock, and the hospital staff is counting on her to be there."

"Yes, they are," I said, interrupting. "And I *will* be there."

He walked up to me, standing real close. "I have an important job to do. That's to protect you, per the president's order. I don't want to fight with you for the next few weeks, and keep in mind that all I'm here to do is help."

I glared at him without saying a word. Didn't dare to say what I was thinking to myself, and instead of arguing with him, I tossed out a question.

"If I'm not allowed to go anywhere, then what else am I supposed to do? Stay in here, twiddling my thumbs, eat until I can't eat anymore, or go to the bedroom where my mother-in-law is and toss back drinks with her?"

"You can do whatever you wish inside of this house. As spacious as it is, I'm sure you can think of something."

Maybe so, I thought, as I envisioned him naked.

Later that day, I found myself in the bowling alley with my mother-in-law and Secret Service. We were told that the president wanted to keep us busy and give us an opportunity to interact with each other. I wanted out of here, but as I attempted to leave the house, I was snatched up by the agent who warned me against doing such a thing. So, for now, I did as I was told.

"If you want to knock down those bowling pins," Teresa said with a bowling ball in her hand, "this is how you do it."

She was still jazzed up in her linen suit with stockings on. Her shoes were off, jewelry still on. Her idea of rolling the ball down the lane was to spread her legs, bend over, and push the ball hard. That was what she did, and glee was in her eyes when she knocked over most of the pins, leaving one standing. On the next try, she knocked that one down. She turned, swiping her hands together.

"I told you. You can learn a lot by watching me, but you just won't listen. Your turn, now, let me see what you got."

I was still dressed up as well. Had on a black-and-white striped skirt and canary yellow blouse. My hair was parted through the middle with loose curls hanging past my shoulders. I removed my heels while sitting next to the agent who couldn't keep his eyes off of me.

"Here," I said, removing the gold necklaces hanging from my neck. "Hold these for me and don't lose them."

"I won't, and don't hurt yourself, all right?"

"Hurt myself? How in the heck am I going to hurt myself by bowling? I know how to bowl. I do it all the time."

"Well, shut your mouth and go show us what you got," Teresa said. "Besides, I'm not going to be in here much longer."

She looked at the agent who was there to keep his eyes on her. He was cute too, but his personality sucked. It was nothing like the one who was watching over me. At least he smiled from time to time.

I reached for a ball, and when I tell you that sucker was heavy, it was *real* heavy. I struggled to carry it onto the slippery platform where I needed to stand in order to roll the ball down the lane. I took a deep breath, and when I reached back with the ball to give it a little extra push down the lane, the ball slipped from my hand. It flew backward, almost hitting one of the agents and my mother-in-law. Thankfully, they ducked.

"Hell, naw," she said. "My poor handsome son. What kind of man stays married to a woman who can't even bowl? Girl, you need to get some skills—fast."

"An intelligent, wise, attractive, motivated, and go-getting man with good sense stays married to me. That would be your son, so get over it."

"I didn't hear you say faithful. Is that not one of your requirements?"

Teresa was just trying to get underneath my skin. I ignored her, especially when *my* secret service agent got up to get the ball that had rolled on the floor behind us.

"First of all," he said, easily carrying the ball in his hand, "this ball is too heavy for you. You need something much lighter like . . ." He took a few seconds to sample some other balls. "Like this one here. Hold this one and see how it feels."

I reached for the ball; it *was* much lighter. "Better. So much better, and it's not weighing my arm down."

"Good. Now step up here and stand in front of me. I want to show you how to carefully lift the ball and glide it down the center of the lane."

I liked his style, for sure. Did as I was told and stood right in front of him. We held the ball together, and as I bent slightly over, so did he. He assisted me in rolling the ball down the lane, and sure enough, we knocked down every single pin. I threw my arms in the air, waving my hands.

"Yippee! Look what I did! What do you have to say about that now, Mrs. Know-It-All over there?"

Teresa sat with her lips pursed, arms folded. "What I have to say is, a woman who needs help doing every little thing that she does is no woman at all. He knocked those pins down, *not* you."

I threw my hand back at her. "Stop being so jealous. Your turn, again, and you may want to take that suit jacket off because it's about to get real up in here. Besides, I don't know why you're so dressed up anyway. You're always dressed up, and was it necessary to sit at the breakfast table like that?"

"Yes, because I do care about my appearance. And whenever I croak, I will not be caught with dirty clothes on, particularly with dirty panties on like you. Now hush so I can show you—again—how to do this *all by yourself.*"

Teresa did the same thing she did last time. This time, however, the ball went into the gutter. I laughed, causing her to quickly turn around. Instead of looking at me, she looked at the agent who was assigned to protect her.

"Is there any way I can get you to come up here and show me how to do this like he just showed her? Or are you just going to sit there pretending you're taking your job serious?"

He was straightforward. "I *am* taking my job serious, so please proceed without my assistance, ma'am."

Teresa mocked him. "*Please proceed without my assistance, ma'am.* I will, thank you very much."

She attempted to roll the ball down the lane again. Back to the gutter it went. "I'm done. Besides, all you're going to do is play unfairly," she said to me.

"Are you quitting? I know you're not a quitter, are you?"

"Never a quitter, but a go-getter . . . like my son." She looked at the Secret Service agent. "Follow me outside so I can go pick some flowers or something. Or better yet, take me to the kitchen so I can help with dinner. Somebody down there is fucking up those rolls. I need to show them how to cook."

The agent stood, following Teresa as she made her way to the door. She stopped in her tracks to say something else to me.

"If I were you," she said, looking from me to the agent standing next to me, "I would seek all of the help I could get from Junebug, if you know what I mean."

She winked, and knowing exactly what she meant, all I did was smile. So did the agent. He walked over to the bench to take a seat.

"You may as well get right back up, because I'm not about to bowl by myself," I said. "Let's play against each other."

He leaned forward, placed his elbows on his knees, and clenched his hands together. "If I win, what's in it for me?" he said bluntly.

I didn't hesitate to reply. "Not a damn thing."

"Good. Then I'll just watch. I love to watch you, and my job gets better and better by the minute."

"I'm glad it does, but are you trying to flirt with the president's wife? You know he's not going to like that, especially when I tell him. You should stop while you're ahead."

"I'm here to protect the president's wife. Nothing more, nothing less. And if you want to tell him that I'm flirting with you, that's totally up to you."

I cut my eyes at him before grabbing a ball to continue the game. As I stood with the ball gripped in my hand, I narrowed my eyes to focus on the lane, as well as on the pins before me. I nearly jumped out of my skin when I felt the agent behind me again. There was no breathing room between us. He reached for my hand, lifting it with his.

"You're still not holding the ball right," he said. "But after a little more practice with these balls, you should be proficient."

I hurried to turn around and face him. "Look, Junebug, or whatever your name is, I don't play games like this. Back up and watch like you said you were going to do or go help my mother-in-law pick flowers."

"Landris," he said. "That's my name, but most people call me Big L."

"I don't know why, especially when you're so short."

"If you weren't the president's wife, I would show you why they call me Big L. Then again, the president doesn't really matter. My height doesn't either, and the last time I checked, five-eleven wasn't all that bad. I'm sure you can work with that, can't you?"

"No, but thanks. Game over, and if you must follow me, please learn to show me some respect. After all, I *am* the first lady, and I should be treated like one."

He lifted my hand, planting a soft kiss on the back of it. "You're absolutely right. And you should be. Forgive me if I offended you. Just couldn't help myself, because it's not often that I'm in the presence of such a beautiful, fun, and very interesting woman."

Flattered I was. A fool I was not. I walked away thinking, again, how sexy he probably looked naked.

25

President of the United States, Stephen C. Jefferson

I sat in the Oval Office with so much on my mind. Everything pertaining to Tyler was going according to plan, but I predicted things were about to heat up. I was awaiting a call from the pope. He wanted to pray with me and offer his condolences, as did many of our allies whose leaders I had already heard from. I rubbed the minimal hair on my chin, while also thinking about Michelle. I was impressed by the way she made love to my mind without using her body. She was sexy in every way, and she knew exactly what I needed, in the moment, which was not sex. It had been years since Raynetta did something like that, but after many years of marriage, I guessed we were to the point where taking advantage of each other seemed to work best. My thoughts shifted back to the situation with Tyler, but they were interrupted when one of the Secret Service agents came in, announcing that my mother was there to see me.

"Let her in, please. Thank you."

My mother came in with flowers in her hand. She laid them on my desk, standing in front of it.

"Those are for you, and be sure to put them in water. I didn't get a chance to ask how you were feeling this morning. I hope better."

"Thanks for the flowers, and I'm okay. Still sore, but that's to be expected."

"I would think so. I know you can't share everything with me, but what's going on, for real? I'm starting to feel like I'm in prison around here, and I don't like it when I'm not allowed to go take care of things that I need to do."

"It's for your own safety, Mama, and I need you to bear with me. If you can do that for me, I'll be forever grateful."

"I'm trying, so bear with me. Also, what are you thinking by having all of these good-looking black men running around here? My hormones are starting to work overtime, and Lord only knows what that wife of yours got swarming around in her thick head. That agent you have watching her is *really* watching her. She may have her eyes on him too—and don't say I didn't warn you."

"Thanks for the warning. Now, is there anything else? I'm waiting on an important call from the pope. Kind of want to prepare myself for it."

"No, you go right ahead. I'm going back to the kitchen to help those cooks in there. They all looking at me like I'm crazy, but I'm in the mood for some smothered pork chops, garlic potatoes, and corn on the cob. Will you be able to join me for dinner or not?"

"I plan to, but you just never know."

"Okay. See you later, and don't forget what I told you about the Secret Service."

I laughed at my mother's humor. But the more I thought about it, it wasn't exactly, a laughing matter.

Right after I ended my call with the pope, I received another interesting call. I was in the midst of trying to gather my Secret Service detail so I could speak to them and got sidetracked by a call from Chanel Hamilton. Andrew forwarded the call to me, but I let him know that this was the last time I intended to speak to her.

"Please, don't hang up on me," she said. "I feel horrible about some of the things that I said to you, and I just wanted to apologize. Forgive me for acting the way I did, and I'm so sorry about what happened after I left. I'm glad you're okay, though. My prayers are with you, your staff, and Tyler's family."

"Thank you, and just so you know, what I said to you still stands."

"I didn't expect you to renege on anything you said, hurtful or not. But in response to that, I will say that I'm highly disappointed about your relationship with Michelle Peoples. I never thought you would be interested in a married woman with three kids, nor in a woman who hasn't had nearly as much success as I have in our field. After six years, she's still trying to find her way."

"Again, I thank you for calling. Take care."

I didn't have time for Chanel. Many of the Secret Service agents started to enter the Oval Office, and by the time I had poured some water and went to the bathroom, they were all there. Levi gave a quick overview, telling me who they were, elaborating on their credentials, and sharing what positions they would take at the White House. There were twenty-seven men; twenty African American, seven Caucasian. I shook all of their hands, thanking them for being there and making them aware of my needs.

"By any means necessary, protect me, my family, and my staff. For the next several weeks, no one is to enter the White House without clearance or approval. All tours have been cancelled, and there will be no guests allowed, unless I invite them. At all times, two agents should be outside of my door. The North and South Lawns should be under tight surveillance, particularly where the Truman Balcony is. Lastly, I would like for someone to keep an eye on every single person in the kitchen, preparing my food. I have to be cautious, and I sure as hell don't want anyone in there trying to poison me."

They all stood professional and attentive while listening to me speak. When I asked if there were any questions, no one had any.

"Good," I said with my hands in my pockets, strolling across the room in my black leather shoes. "Which two have been tasked with keeping the first lady and my mother safe?"

Two agents stepped forward. I looked at both of them, thinking about what my mother had said.

"Which one of you is handling my mother?"

The agent raised his hand. I stepped up, standing face-to-face with him. "Let me see if I remember." I paused to think of the name Levi said, during the introduction. "Charles, right?"

He nodded. "Correct, Mr. President. Charles Keith Johnson. Nice to meet you."

I extended my hand to his. "Same here. Has my mother been giving you any trouble?"

"No, sir. She's been just fine."

"I doubt that, but please, please, please, do not allow anything to happen to her. She means a lot to me; I'm sure you understand."

"I do, Mr. President. I feel the same way about my mother, so I do understand well."

I patted his shoulder, then moved over to the other agent who had been assigned to protect Raynetta. Fairly nice-looking young man. Bright smile, worked out a lot, and had light brown eyes, similar to mine.

"And you are, Landris," I said without pausing to think. "You've been tasked with protecting one of the most precious things to me. My wife, right?"

His smile was wide. "Yes, Mr. President. And, thus far, everything has been all good. I think she and I will get along fine."

"That's what I was afraid of, so if you don't mind, I'm going to replace you with, uh . . ."

My eyes shifted from one agent to the next. I pointed out the nerdiest one I could find. He just happened to be Caucasian, and with a tight, stern look on his face, I predicted that Raynetta and he wouldn't get along at all.

"Alex Fischer," I said, stepping up to him. "Correct?"

"Yes. Yes, Mr. President, Alex Fischer."

"I'm impressed by your credentials, and your years of service to this country are commendable. I'm personally assigning you to take care of the first lady, and if she gives you a hard time, be sure to let me know."

"Will do. And thank you so much for trusting me, sir. I'm honored to serve you."

I turned back to Landris who looked as if he wasn't standing as straight as he was before. He didn't even make eye contact with me—not even when I looked him straight in the eyes.

"You're dismissed," I said, then looked at Levi. "Cut him a check and make sure he gets it."

After that, I left the Oval Office, on my way to see my chief of staff. But just as I was making my way down the corridor, he was walking with great speed toward me.

"Mr. President," he said in a panic, like always. "The FBI is in the process of making an arrest. Kyle wants to speak to you. From what I gather, these guys are racist pigs, definitely out to get you, as well as your family."

We hurried to the Situation Room, located in the West Wing. I went inside, but gave Andrew an order to assemble other staff members so they could join us and hear most of what Kyle had to say. That way, we all could discuss the best way forward. Andrew hurried away to get the others, and I picked up the phone to take Kyle's call.

"Is anyone near you?" he said in a whisper.

"No. Go-ahead and speak."

"These idiots fit the bill, and we're only going to grab the top two leaders. They're perfect, and our national intelligence workforce has already been watching this hate group brew for quite some time. They have very disturbing photos of you, and we've collected detailed plans where they intended to bomb more black churches, schools in mostly black neighborhoods, as well as concerts that included black artists. I mean, their goal is to make some noise, and these are the kinds of criminals who would plot to come into the White House to kill you."

"Make the arrest. Make sure every detail gets leaked to the media, particularly the Associated Press. And do whatever you can to, you know, make it look good."

"Will do. The shit will hit the fan in about thirty or so minutes. Be prepared."

Kyle said thirty minutes, but it was less than that. We were all in the Situation Room, tuning into the festivities. Every news channel had breaking news, and they too were tuned in to the FBI's manhunt to capture the two individuals responsible for murdering the vice president. With bated breath, we watched the whole thing go down. The doors were kicked in, and within minutes, the two crazy-looking men were captured. As expected, the media started to spread information that wasn't true, but what the hell?

There were seven men total living in this house. All of them were arrested today.

Four men arrested, and the police think they may have discovered several bodies in the basement. More information to come.

These were some sick individuals. In the basement, the police found an effigy of the president, hanging from a noose.

There were more than 200 guns found in the home. These guys were out to cause some major damage.

The mastermind behind this is Brandon Walls, a mentally ill man with a very troubled past.

The media went on and on, telling some truth, but spewing a substantial amount of lies and spreading much false information that helped me, quite frankly, stir up the American people. I didn't mind, simply because of my purpose.

"This is crazy," Andrew said after we returned to the Oval Office. "Forgive me, sir, but I almost didn't believe you before. I am stunned, but I'm so delighted that those guys were caught."

"I am too, and I'm surprised that you didn't believe me. There are many hate groups out there like that, and one day at a time, we have to shut them down."

"Yes, we do. And, Mr. President, can I say this? I'm deeply sorry for what African Americans have endured. None of this should be. I think this will be a changing point, and sometimes, you have to lose something or someone to gain a lot."

"Thank you for sharing that, Andrew. Hopefully, many others will feel the same."

Even with phones ringing off the hook, Andrew and I were still able to discuss other important issues, including replacing the VP. Under the Presidential Succession Act, Speaker of the House was next in line to become VP. That, indeed, was Senator Bass.

"Are you good with that?" Andrew asked. "I know you've thought about it, but do you think you and she will be able to work together for the good of this country?"

I stood, looking outside. Hands were in my pockets, mind going a mile a minute. "Yes, we can. I do believe that she is my ticket to making some incredible things happen. Set up a meeting with her, and let's get the ball rolling. Meanwhile, I need to release a statement about those idiots being caught."

"Sam and I can work on preparing a statement for you, sir. Why don't you sit back for a few minutes and relax."

Just as those words left Andrew's mouth, his cell phone rang. He answered and listened to the caller with wide eyes. My phone started ringing off the hook again; I could sense something else had gone wrong.

"Ten suicide bombers went on a rampage, killing twelve Americans that we know of, and . . ."

As Andrew spoke, all I could do was sigh. Many people just didn't know what having a bad day really meant.

26

President of the United States, Stephen C. Jefferson

After about a week, things had settled down, but the terror alert remained high. Senator Bass and I had a productive meeting, and Congress was in the process of finding another person to replace her. She seemed thrilled about being vice president. Said that she would do whatever to assist me, but she also mentioned that her conservative values were very important. She wasn't going to encourage the Republican Caucus to waver on much, but we both were pleased that commonsense gun control legislation was in the works. We also discussed tougher punishments for people who committed hate crimes, including police officers who felt they were above the law. I was starting to feel good about the path we were on but got distracted when I was told Tyler's grandfather, Christopher J. McNeil, was eager to meet with me. Tyler's family had already had a small, private ceremony for him. I was invited to come and speak, so I did. His body hadn't been found yet, but I had a feeling that was about to change.

As Mr. McNeil came into my office, I stood to greet him with an extended hand. All he did was grunt before taking a seat on the sofa across from me. He rubbed his thin white hair before crossing his legs and looking at me with hatred in his eyes.

"You're a hard man to get a meeting with, Mr. President, and I tried to catch up with you after my grandson's ceremony. Your words were touching, but I didn't buy them one fucking bit. You may have the American people on your side right now, but I'm going to expose you as being one of the most cutthroat, deceptive, and danger- ous presidents we've ever had. Your reckless behavior is going to cause you to lose everything, including your beautiful wife, that bitchy mother of yours, as well as your mistress. By the way, have you spoken to her lately? You should check on her . . . whenever you get a chance."

I looked at the old man sitting across from me, feeling kind of sorry for him because his hatred for others caused him to lose much sleep at night. I could tell from the bags underneath his eyes, and with all of the money he had, he was still one very unhappy man who was deeply confused. I now knew where Tyler's hatred had come from. This generational curse of hatred for African Americans had affected many.

"I'm sorry you thought my words at the ceremony weren't sincere. I felt as if they came straight from the heart."

"From the heart, my ass. Where is my grandson at, you filthy nigger? I want to see him, *now!*"

His whole red face shook as he barked at me. I remained calm, pretending as if I didn't know a thing. "Look, I know the loss of your grandson is painful, but you must accept the fact that he's dead. His killers have been caught, and you should be delighted about that. Why you wouldn't be, I don't quite understand . . . unless you know something that I don't."

"I know more than what you will *ever* know. And one thing that I know for sure is, if you do not tell me where my grandson is, your mistress won't be the only one hurt. I'm warning you to do as you're told—or else."

I cracked a tiny smile, just to irritate him. "Warning, huh? I wish I could work miracles and bring Tyler back to life, but, unfortunately, I can't. But what I can do is escort you to the door, open it, and throw your ass out of here. Good day, sir. And please know that you will never be allowed to come into *my* office again."

I stood, and when I reached for Mr. McNeil's arm, he tried to pull it away from me. I wanted to take my fist and punch him in the face, but I had to keep my hands clean. Instead of taking action myself, I buzzed Levi. In a matter of minutes, he was dragging Mr. McNeil, by his collar, out of my office.

"Release me, you fat slob! You're good as dead too!"

Levi elbowed him in the face to quiet him. Just like Tyler, Mr. McNeil's threats and harsh words continued. But killing him would be too easy. We wanted him to stay around to witness all that would soon unfold.

As soon as they left my office, I hurried over to my phone to call Michelle. There was no answer, so I called again. I didn't leave a message, but when Levi returned, I asked him to find out where she was.

"I'll see what I can do. Do you think he really did something to her?"

"My gut tells me that he did. Hurry and find out what's up. Andrew is also good at finding out things, so stop by his office and tell him to look into it. The second either of you know something, please let me know."

"On it now."

"Thanks, and one more thing. Mr. McNeil wants to see his grandson. I think it's time to show him to McNeil."

"Been time. And like always, be sure to tune into the news."

Levi left my office, and almost twenty minutes later, Andrew rushed in as if the world was coming to an end. I was already nervous about Michelle's condition, and seeing him so frantic didn't help one bit.

"I really wish you wouldn't panic so damn much," I said with a frown on my face. "Did you find out anything for me?"

He released a deep breath, then nodded. "Yes, I did. Michelle Peoples is in the hospital. She's in critical but stable condition. Apparently, someone robbed her when she left work. Beat her up real bad, took her purse, and left her for dead. The hospital didn't say if she had been raped or not, but they are optimistic that she'll make it. The road to recovery, in their opinion, won't be easy."

I swallowed the lump in my throat that hurt like a motherfucker. My hands could get dirty for this, and all I wanted to do, right now, was slice Christopher J. McNeil's throat. I was a dangerous man under these conditions. He was so right about me. I should have killed that bastard when I had a chance, but first, I had to go see Michelle. She didn't deserve this. She was a beautiful person who did not need to be injected into any of this mess.

"Mr. President," Andrew said, shaking me from my vicious thoughts, "are you okay?"

"No, I'm not, but I will be. I need to go, now, to the hospital. Find Levi and tell him to go get the motorcade."

"If you go to the hospital, people are going to question why you're there and who you're there to see. You don't want—"

"Just do what I asked of you, please."

I was too sick to my stomach to go off on him about what people would think. I didn't give a damn, and when I entered the hospital with Secret Service in tow, there were many whispers, questions, and concerns. The entire fifth floor had to be cleared out, with the exception of patients who were already there, and two doctors who greeted me. Awe was in their eyes as they informed me of Michelle's condition.

"She's a fighter, I'll tell you that," one of the doctors said. "Her body was discovered in a Dumpster, where she was left to die. Both of her legs are broken, and there is a substantial amount of swelling all over her face and body. We have been keeping a close eye on her, simply because she seems incoherent at times. She doesn't know her name, and she can't remember why she's here."

This was sad news to me. I felt completely responsible; all I could think about was her children. I wondered where they were, and the thought of what would have happened, had she died, disturbed me on so many different levels. I thanked the doctors for the update, and then was escorted into the room to see her. I thought she was in the room by herself, and I was surprised to see a young lady sitting in a chair next to the bed Michelle was in. I almost didn't recognize Michelle. Her face was real swollen, eyes were shut, and lips were puffy. There was a small gash on her nose, and her hair sat wildly on her head. My heart went out to her. I walked farther into the room, and after seeing me, the young lady, who resembled Michelle, eased up from the chair. A perplexed look was on her face as she shifted her eyes from me to two Secret Service agents behind me.

"Are you Mr.—I mean, the president? President Jefferson?"

"Yes." I extended my hand to hers. "And you are?"

"I'm Mary Riverside. Michelle is my sister, but you must have the wrong room."

"No, I'm in the right place. Michelle is a good friend of mine. I just came to see how she was doing."

"Oh my God. Friend?" she questioned. "She never mentioned you as a friend, and we talk about you all the time."

"Hopefully, about good things."

"Yes, indeed. We're proud to have you as our president, and I offer my condolences to you, the VP, and his family. That situation at the White House was awful, but I'm glad the people involved were arrested. Now, we have to work on finding who did this to my sister. She doesn't bother anybody, and what happened to her was . . ." She started to get choked up, especially when she glanced at Michelle who hadn't moved. "This was unnecessary. She had less than fifty dollars on her. All they had to do was take the money and run."

If that was their only purpose, maybe they would have done that. But I knew better. Mr. McNeil had this done. He wanted to send a message—I totally got it. He did.

"Yes, this is unfortunate, and you have my word that whoever did this will be held accountable. Meanwhile, how has she been doing? Has she said anything, opened her eyes, what?"

"When my mother was here earlier, Michelle reached for her hand, smiled, and squeezed it. She also nodded her head and smiled at me, when I told her the kids were staying with me and my husband. We are a very tight-knit family. Our support will help her get through this. I know she's going to be shocked to find out you were here, and I hope you can stay, just in case she wakes up."

I definitely intended to stay for a while, but before taking a seat, I walked closer to the bed, getting a closer look at all the damage that was done. I rubbed the side of Michelle's face; it was cold and felt like stone. As I stared at her, her sister cleared her throat.

"Uh, Mr. President. Tell me, if you don't mind. How well do you know my sister?"

I didn't immediately respond, but I later told her that Michelle had done some impressive work for my press secretary, Sam. Mentioned that we'd gotten to know each other, and I was grateful to her for helping out around the White House when asked. What impressed me more was, that as close as Michelle and her sister seemed, Michelle hadn't shared anything about us being intimate. To me, that spoke volumes about her.

Nearly two hours later, the room was clear. Secret Service was outside of the door, and Mary had left to go check on Michelle's kids. I had just gotten off the phone with Andrew. Several people had been looking for me, including my mother and Raynetta. They were still being closely watched by Secret Service. And after what had happened to Michelle, I doubted that the security I put in place would lighten up. I didn't know what Mr. McNeil's future intentions were, and from this moment on, I had to do my best to stay ten steps ahead of him.

I was looking at a text message on my phone when I heard a soft moan, causing my head to snap up. Michelle's eyelids were fluttering a bit, but as I stood and walked over to the bed, her eyes got wider. She looked to be struggling hard to keep them open.

"Hello," I said with my hand on top of hers. "Can you hear me, Michelle?"

She closed her eyes; tears ran from the corners of them. When they opened, she slowly nodded.

"Good. That's good to know, and I just wanted to come by and let you know that you're in my thoughts, and I'm praying for you."

She slowly nodded again.

"Is there anything I can do for you? I'm going to find out who did this, but is there anything I can do for you now?"

All she did was lift her hand, lightly squeezing it with mine. Her eyes shut again, this time staying closed. I had to get back to the White House, so I planted a kiss on her forehead, then walked out. When I returned to the motorcade, I asked Levi to get Mr. McNeil on the phone.

"Who is this?" he said in a sharp tone.

"You made one mistake. You didn't kill her. Please allow me to show you how it's supposed to be done."

I left it right there. Hours later, the VP's body was found. It had washed up on the beach, where an elderly couple found it. Chaos ensued around the White House, and the media was in full force. I predicted that Mr. McNeil was watching.

27

First Lady Raynetta Jefferson

Stephen seemed stressed the hell out. I couldn't believe how crazy things were around here. Every day it was something. I had barely seen my own husband, and whenever I stopped by the Oval Office to chat with him, he was too busy. He had spent only one—*one* measly night in our bedroom. I didn't even know he was there until I rolled over and saw the back of his head. By morning, he was gone. He was back to being all that he could for everyone . . . with the exception of me.

In addition to that, I was still being forced to deal with my mother-in-law. I tried to be nice to that woman, but every morning during breakfast she always had something smart to say. At dinner, she criticized me for everything that she could. From my hair to the way I used my fork . . . She constantly had something to say. I just couldn't take it anymore; I was so on edge. The new Secret Service agent who trailed me had gotten on my nerves. I only wished that the other one, Landris, was still here. By now, I probably would have screwed his brains out and not had one single regret about it.

"Ne-ne," Teresa said, as we had just got finished with dinner, "is there a toothpick over there? Those meaty ribs *I* cooked got all in my teeth. They probably didn't get into yours, with all of those gaps you have."

"I don't have any gaps in my teeth, nor do I see any toothpicks. Ask one of the servers for one, and please stop bothering me."

Teresa cocked her head back as if *I* was the one who offended her. "*Bothering* you? How can I bother you by just asking for a toothpick? You're just in a crabby mood, like you always are. I don't think I've seen you smile one time this week—that is really an ugly thing. Then again, you did smile when Landris was behind you, trying to sample the goodies. Did you, or did you not, get you a piece after I left?"

She freaking annoyed me. I winced, then shot her a dirty look. "I'm not going to answer your ridiculous question, but what kind of woman do you think I am? While your son may be a whore, I was taught better than that by *my* parents who believe in the sanctity of marriage. They taught me that marriage is a sacred covenant between one man and one woman. That we must forsake all others, and if not, our marriage will become broken. So don't you dare sit there and accuse me of anything. The son *you* raised is the one at fault, so pat yourself on the back for not teaching him good morals and values."

She sucked her teeth and smacked her lips. "Yes, I did raise him. Raised him all by myself, and, bitch, I will tell you what a proud mother I am of the president of the United States. Don't go quoting Bible verses and talking to me about what your parents taught you. What they should have taught you was, if a man continuously cheats on you, you leave his ass. If he disrespects you, you diss him back. If he ignores you, find someone else who will give you the attention you deserve, and if he put his hands on you, beat his ass with a bat and send him to his grave. My motto, do unto others as they do unto you. If you believe my son isn't the man you need him to be, stop griping and walking around here frowning all the damn time. Pack your bags and march your wannabe happy ass out of here."

I jumped up from the table, leaned in close to her with gritted teeth, and said, "You would love that, wouldn't you? Just so I can wind up being lonely and miserable—like you. That will *never* happen. Stephen and I definitely have problems, but they are nothing we can't handle. Accept that and stay the hell out of our business."

I stormed away, feeling some kind of way about our heated conversation. Teresa took one last jab at me when she implied our marriage was broken. I had to admit that it truly was, and knowing that she was right hurt like hell.

Torturing myself even more, I sat in my office chit-chatting with Claire. We discussed everything from the discovery of Tyler's dead body to how chaotic the White House had been. Everyone was on edge, even Claire, who seemed to be keeping something from me.

"Spill it," I said. "You know you can talk to me about anything, and nothing really surprises me these days."

"I know, but it's like I hear all of this gossip around here, and I don't know what to pass on to you or when to keep my mouth shut. I have an enormous amount of respect for you, and you've been one of the coolest people I have ever worked for."

"That's good to know, and I enjoy working with you too. But if there is ever something that you think I should know, tell me."

Claire swung her hair over to one side, then crossed her legs. "There is a tiny rumor going around that the president is the one who killed the VP. Many are just speculating, and no one knows for sure, but he doesn't seem bothered much about Tyler's death. Also, a few days before Tyler's body was found, someone beat up Michelle Peoples really bad. She almost died, and some think it was payback for what the president did. I didn't know if you knew he'd been going to the hospital . . . quite often, to see her."

Breaking news was happening every day. I suspected that Stephen would do something vicious to Tyler, especially since he had already told me Tyler was the one who tried to kill him. But ever since then, we hadn't talked much about it. Everything was hush-hush. He told me he would reveal everything to me, but never did. I had very little information, but I was sure of one thing. I would never tell Claire or anyone else what Stephen had told me. They could keep on gossiping around here, but the rumors wouldn't get far. I was positive that Stephen had everything under control, but this mess with Michelle Peoples continued to be a slap in my face. Stephen was still holding on to her, and that was a huge problem for me.

"In no way is Stephen a killer, so you tell whoever is spreading that rumor to back off or they will be escorted out of here. He has been through hell these past several weeks, and we all need to be thankful that the killers were found and are now behind bars where they belong. It angers me that some people always try to make black men out to be murderers or criminals who can't help themselves from causing harm to others. He can never just be considered a decent man, trying to do the best for his country. As for Michelle Peoples, he and I will put that situation to rest soon."

Upset, I got up and walked out. Many more days like this, I would walk out for good.

28

President of the United States, Stephen C. Jefferson

Tyler was finally put to rest, and during his funeral service, I delivered a lengthy eulogy that was full of shit. Mr. McNeil was so distraught that he could barely walk. During my speech, he had to be carried out of the church. Afterward, he lunged out at me on the church steps, but wound up tumbling down when I nudged him away from me. Many people viewed this situation as an old, distraught man not being able to accept the loss of his grandson. I was the one to blame because the killing happened in the White House, my home. Some also felt as if there were a lot of holes in my story, but I had some very skilled, trustworthy individuals working for me. The truth would never be revealed; I was 110 percent sure about that.

After I left the funeral, I made a quick stop at the hospital. Michelle was doing better. She was sitting up and talking now. Her smile made me feel better. I couldn't tell her the truth about why this had happened to her, but the young men Mr. McNeil had paid to injure her were days away from being arrested. We knew who they were, and as president, I was privy to more information than most people thought I was. In the upcoming weeks, I was positive that Mr. McNeil would have to put up a lot of money, in court, to defend his actions. That would surely keep him busy for a while, and I predicted that he wouldn't be bothering me anytime soon.

I walked into Michelle's room, immediately seeing the flowers I had delivered to her the other day. She had other flowers as well—some from friends, as well as from her soon-to-be ex-husband. She mentioned that he had come to visit her, but I was glad that we hadn't crossed paths. I made sure my visits were short and sweet, but just enough to let Michelle know I cared.

"You're spoiling me," she said softly as I came through the door. Her eyes were real narrow, and the swelling remained. Someone had brushed her hair into a ponytail that had a huge puffball in the back. She was sitting up, and had just finished eating.

"I can't resist." I stood next to her, holding her hand. "How are you feeling today?"

"Better, day by day. My kids came to see me earlier so that really lifted my spirits. Seeing you also helps, especially when you come in here all cleaned up and polished with your suits on. You do wear them well."

"Thanks. Just came from Tyler's funeral. Sad, but it's time for us to move on. I have some good news for you too. We know who did this to you. They'll be arrested soon and off the streets. You don't have to worry about them ever coming after you again."

Michelle sat quiet. Her eyes filled with tears. As she started to cry, I sat on the bed next to her. I reached out to embrace her, holding her tightly in my arms.

"That day was so scary," she said. "I thought I was going to die. All I could think about was why they were doing that to me, and, of course, my kids. I prayed for God to spare my life. Asked him for one more chance. Said that I would be everything that He needed me to be, if He just gave me another chance."

"Shhhh," I said, holding her trembling body closer to mine. "He wasn't ready for you yet. And now you get to live on and continue to be the amazing woman that

you are. You also get to run my bathwater for me again.
You were truly on time that day."

She laughed. I wanted to lighten the mood because I
hated to witness women cry. Michelle pulled her head
back, just to look at me. We were face-to-face, staring
into each other's eyes. Simultaneously, we leaned in to
kiss. It was wetter. Juicer. More passionate than it had
ever been. Lasted for quite awhile, and so very sweet.
Once we were done, I pressed my forehead against hers,
gazing into her pretty eyes again.

"I'll be in touch. Go to therapy, work hard, and know
that I'm rooting for you. And if you need anything, please
let me know."

"I will. As for you, don't work at all, get some rest and
stop trying to do so much. You're only one man. One
incredible man who needs to utilize more of the talented
people you have working for you to accomplish your
goals."

Michelle smiled; I knew exactly where she was coming
from. I pecked her lips again before getting off the bed so
I could go. As I walked to the door, she called my name. I
turned to face her again.

"After a kiss like that," she said, "why do I get a feeling
as if this is good-bye?"

Sometimes, actions speak louder than words. I hated
myself for what I had done to her, and I could never let
something like that happen again. In an effort to make
this easier for both of us, I nodded, smiled, and then
walked out.

The following day, there was no time for hurt feelings,
regrets, or emotions to run high. Another extremist
terrorist group had struck again. This time setting off
bombs that killed almost a hundred innocent people in

another country. First and foremost, it was my duty to keep the American people safe. Then, everyone turned to me to keep the world safe as well. I had to make the call on deploying more of our troops, and making this decision couldn't be taken lightly. So many people offered their opinions, as did many of my advisors. When all was said and done, the terrorists needed to be stopped. Many of their organizations had grown over the years, and now we also had to deal with homegrown terrorism that kept the intelligence agency busy.

"You have to make the call, Mr. President," Andrew said while I pondered what to do in my chair. "We have the strongest military in the world, and we are capable of shutting down some of these organizations."

Many others agreed. I gave the order to deploy more troops, and then took my case to the American people. No country wanted to be at war, but in certain instances, we had to. I didn't feel good about it, and it turned out to be a discouraging day for me. The only positive thing was, Congress was expected to vote on gun control legislation later this week. There were enough votes in the Senate to pass the bill, but the House had stalled. Several more senators were needed; I was counting on my new VP to go on Capitol Hill and work her magic.

Later that night, I sat, alone, in the Oval Office, meditating and wondering what in the hell I had gotten myself into. Never imagined this job would bring about a multitude of so many challenges and an array of disappointments. It wasn't that I was clueless, but damn, this was unbelievable. All I wanted to do was help to make this world a better place. I made that decision years ago, trying to step up and do the right thing. I could only chuckle at how ambitious and determined I was. I had so much fire in me, and now, there was a lot of pain. I knew very well how to transform that pain into something better. But getting there wouldn't be easy.

My head was leaned back as I sat on the sofa. Shirt was unbuttoned, shoes were off. My thoughts were on the families that were affected because of their loved ones being deployed. But when the door to my office came open, I lifted my head. At the door stood Levi and Raynetta. She entered carrying two suitcases in her hands, and a heavy duffle bag hung from her shoulder. She dropped the load at the door immediately after Levi closed it.

"I just came to tell you that I'm leaving," she said with a straight face. She came closer, standing directly on the presidential seal. "I can't do this anymore. This is one lonely-ass place to be in, and I do not know how any of the first ladies coped with living here. I have never been so miserable in my life, and you have done nothing, not one damn thing, Stephen, to make me feel as if we're in this together."

I wiped down my face with my hand, feeling even more frustration coming on. "You chose me, Raynetta. And I chose this. For better or worse, you agreed to be here. The only difference between you and the other first ladies is they understood the demands and responsibilities their husbands' occupation brought about. They didn't run when things got tough. They didn't wait around for their husbands to give them orders; rather, they took it upon themselves to create the best life that they possibly could during their stay here. They knew it wasn't going to be easy, and they came up with programs and other beneficial things for the American people so that they could leave their own legacies. I'm not perfect, no. But if you want to leave, then go ahead and do it."

Raynetta blinked fast to fight back her tears. "I am, because I assure you that many of the first ladies you're referring to, they didn't have to deal with crazy-ass mothers-in-law and arrogant husbands who ignored them.

Their husbands probably didn't go around killing people and lying to the American people. And while some of their husbands may have had affairs, they probably didn't fall in love with their mistresses and spend more time with them than they did their own wives."

Raynetta just didn't get it. "Are you fucking kidding me? It takes an arrogant, confident man to be here, and, sometimes, he has to ignore a whole lot of shit, as well as people, so he doesn't lose his cool. Every single president has lied to the American people, and as far as affairs go, allow me to share some names: Eisenhower, Wilson, Garfield, Harding, Johnson, Bush, Washington, Cleveland, Buchanan, Roosevelt, Kennedy, and we all know about the infamous dress associated with President Clinton. The little black presidential book that I have in my possession will shock the shit out of you. It exposes more of what some of our presidents did while living here. You don't know the half of it, and if you did, you would then know how ridiculous you sound, coming in here talking about leaving me. Based on what?"

"Based on the fact that I have never considered cheating on you until recently. That is a good sign that this is over for me. This is the last thing that I want, but—"

"Want? Okay. Let me tell you what *I* want. I want you to act like you love me and show me some damn support. Stand by me, stop complaining, stop whining, and just . . . just show me that you're proud of some of the things I do. I have flaws, no doubt, but must that be the only thing I hear about? I don't want to lose you, and it would crush me if you walked out that door. I also take issue with you thinking about making love to another man, but I accept that I haven't been one hundred with you. So my question to you is, what do you want? And what do I need to do to prevent you from walking out that door?"

I waited for Raynetta to respond. She replied with a hard stare.

29

First Lady Raynetta Jefferson

I was prepared to leave Stephen. Talked to myself about it all day. Came up with good reasons to leave, and then I had to face Stephen in all of his sexiness tonight, as he came up with the right things to say. Damn him. I was tongue-tied, so I stared at him, thinking about what I wanted. Earlier, I knew what it was. Now, I didn't. He had me looking at things from his perspective, and when it came to marriage, that was a requirement.

"Did you not hear what I just said?" he asked. "What do you want, Raynetta, and what must I do to stop you from leaving me? Tell me now, just so I'll know."

"If I tell you what I want, will you do as I ask?"

"Tell me, then I'll decide."

"I want you to stop loving Michelle Peoples and quit having sex with her. I want you to tell your mother that she cannot refer to me as bitches and hoes, and that you will not stand for it. I want you to show me that you love me more. Come have breakfast, lunch, and dinner with me, join me in our bedroom and tell me how your day is going. Inquire about mine and applaud me for some of the things I do to assist others. And one of the biggest things—stop ignoring me. As for tonight, I do have specific requests. I want you to get up, take off your clothes, and make love to me. Drink all of my juices, please me in every way, and tell me how much I mean to you. That, Mr. President, is what I really and truly want."

Stephen examined me from head to toe. He then stood and removed his shirt. Took off his slacks; briefs came next. Naked, he was. Sexy, without a doubt. Hard, yes, indeed. Ready for this moment, we both were.

"For the record," he said, moving to the center of the presidential seal where I was, "I never loved Michelle Peoples. The only woman I have ever loved is you. My mother is wrong. Forgive me for not correcting her sooner. We can have breakfast, lunch, and dinner anytime, but, sometimes, you'll have to excuse my tardiness from the bedroom because I can be very busy. Let's just stop ignoring each other, and in regards to your specific requests tonight, I can certainly handle all of the above."

Stephen started to undress me. He tossed my clothes on the sofa, and as I stood naked, so did he with his body pressed close to mine. Our eyes were connected, and as his fingers lightly touched my lips, he looked to be in deep thought.

"Who was the man you thought about making love to?"

I couldn't help but to laugh. He didn't. "I knew you were going to ask me that, but a good girl like me never tells."

"I figured you would say that, but a smart, very observant man like me already knows. Landris could never satisfy you like I'm about to do right now. So keep what you have; just learn to tell me what your wants are more often."

"Will do, Mr. President. Definitely will do."

I lowered myself on the circular rug, feeling horrible about the juices I would leave on the seal. But I couldn't help myself. My body temperature had risen, and as Stephen lay over me, my temperature ticked up a notch. My legs were spread wide—I wrapped them around his back, as he started to deliver delicate kisses along the side of my neck. I turned my head to the side, closing my eyes and savoring the feel of his thick lips that traveled from north to south. His tongue dipped into my belly button before sinking into my warm, dark cave that had become tight as a knot. With every light lick, every rotation of his tongue, and with a little bit of force, he loosened it. My insides started to rain—rain in his mouth, as well as on the rug. I squirmed from the intense feeling of him sucking me dry, but in no way did he allow my insides to stay dehydrated. This time he entered my dark cave again, filling it to capacity with nearly twelve inches of satisfying meat. I gasped from the feel of his rhythmic long strokes, and that's when he covered my mouth with his, so I could taste what I had fed to him. As we intensely kissed, he held my hands above my head, clenching them with his. His strokes were at a tranquillizing pace that had me on the brink of shouting his name and spewing words that couldn't be found in the *Urban Dictionary*. This . . . was . . . good. My husband felt so good inside of me, and with our hands still clenched together, I lifted my back, forming an arch in it. My firm breasts were now at attention, causing him to lower his head and tackle them one by one. I squirmed even more, grinded my hips, and secured my legs tighter around his back. Stephen was hungry for more, and when he positioned my legs close to my chest, I felt his steel tamper with my G-spot even more.

"Ohh, baby, you are almost therrrre!" I cried out. "Get in there and find it!"

"I'm digging, baby. Digging real hard, and I think I'm about to strike gold."

"Hell, yeah, you are. Find it and be sure to give me some. I want all of it. Every last ounce of it."

I was soaking wet . . . could feel Stephen's muscle throbbing inside of me. He quickly eased out of me, just to switch positions. And with both of us lying on our side, he was comfortably behind me. He separated my legs, placing one of them over his. Before entering me again, he took a few minutes to massage my thighs, caress my breasts, and give special attention to my perfect ass that he admired so much. He separated my healthy cheeks, before gliding his way back in. His fingers touched my precious pearl; it wasn't long before my insides started humming again. This time, I turned my head sideways to kiss him. Tried to muffle some of the excitement I felt, but couldn't.

"Wh . . . Why did we wait so long to do this?" I started to cry, simply because I loved my husband so very much and never, ever wanted to lose him.

He answered by kissing my tears away. I was so emotional, it took Stephen's words to calm me.

"I love you," he said repeatedly. "And I promise you that we will never wait this long again."

That was music to my ears. We made love in the Oval Office for what seemed like hours. From the Resolute desk, to right by the fireplace, we left our mark. I could only hope that other presidents brought this much pleasure to their wives, but then again, there was only one Stephen C. Jefferson.

Later that week, his biggest accomplishment had come. Many presidents had tried to pass sweeping gun control legislation but had failed. He did that, and I was so proud as he stood at the podium, dressed in a coal-black, crushed velvet jacket and tailored slacks. His face was shaved cleanly; minimal hair suited his chin. Caesar cut was lined sharp and polished to near perfection. Vice President Bass stood next to him. I couldn't help but to hear her whisper to Stephen what another vice president had said in 2010, when the Affordable Care Act had passed.

"This is a big fucking deal," she said, smiling. Those who had heard her laughed. So did Stephen as he gave her a hug, congratulating her as well. He also gave a shout-out to Andrew, who, all along, had Stephen's back. Then he addressed the crowd, as well as the American people.

"This is a big deal, a big fucking deal, yes, and this is what can happen when we keep our eyes on the prize and do what we must do for the betterment of our country. We still have a long way to go, but as long as I am president, we will confront these issues and tackle them head-on. As your president, I remain unsatisfied with the current state of our union. I will not stop here, but make no mistake about it, I am grateful to see this day. I am delighted to say that we have won against the NRA and against those who did not believe that a Democratic African American president and a Republican, an amazing woman from little ol' Georgia, could come together and accomplish this. I thank her, and I am very optimistic that we can, and will, commit to accomplishing more great things to come."

Vice President Bass said a few words, and then Stephen gave an overview of the new bill before signing it into law. Applauses erupted, especially when Stephen stepped back to give me a juicy kiss. I smiled wide, hoping that there were many more days like this in the White House to come.

30

President's Mother, Teresa Jefferson

Yeah yeah yeah . . . Everyone seemed happy, and everything was all good at the *little* White House. I was happy for Stephen, but in no way would I ever be pleased with that thing he called a wife. She had interfered and come between us. Stephen chewed me out, and I was in tears while driving, thinking about the way he had spoken to me that day.

"I will not stand by anymore and let you speak to Raynetta that way. The things you say are very hurtful, and you are not going to continue to upset my wife."

"I do not accept her as your wife, and I never will. And what about the way she speaks to me? Have you said anything to her?"

"No, but I'm saying something to you. Back off or you can go upstairs, pack your shit, and leave. It's your choice, Mama, and if you don't listen to me, you may as well consider me your enemy and not your son."

My eyes bugged. "Oh, so now we're enemies? She must've screwed you real good, because your mind is very twisted. But that's what tricks are good at. They make you forget about all that your mother has done for you. All the sacrifices I made and the twenty-seven hours of labor I went through to bring you into this world doesn't matter anymore. You've chosen her over me, and I never, ever thought this day would come."

Stephen shrugged, as if my words had gone in one ear, out the other. "I've never asked you for anything. But now I'm asking you to show my wife some respect. If you can't find the courage to do it, get the hell out of here and don't you ever call me again."

He left the room, slamming the door behind him that day. I left the *little* White House, vowing to do exactly what he said, which was to never call him again. I was so mad—angry because it didn't have to be this way. Raynetta was no good, and all I needed was for Stephen to see that. She didn't even want to give him kids, and what kind of man stayed with a woman who chose not to continue his legacy? I knew how to get to him, though. I knew how to wake him up and throw another monkey wrench in the program. I wasn't hating—was only looking out for my son who I always knew could do so much better than Raynetta.

I finally made it to St. Louis. Parked my car in Ina's driveway, hoping that she was home. Her car was there, but that didn't mean much. She had two or three cars, compliments of all that I'd given her over the years.

With my Louis Vuitton bag in my hand, I made my way to the door. Knocked, and several minutes later, Ina opened the door. She was always happy to see me, and as long as her house was clean, I was also happy to see her.

"Hello, Teresa," she said, opening the door wide so I could come in. "Why didn't you tell me you were coming? I would have cleaned up around here, and I definitely would have fixed you something to eat."

I liked Ina, but she was lazy. That was one of the reasons I never wanted her to be with Stephen. She didn't have her shit together, and Stephen being with her was a setback. She had gotten pregnant a few years after he graduated from college. He was well on his way to doing bigger and brighter things, and Ina didn't even have a damn job. Her family's background wasn't good enough for me, and with her mother being on drugs, I just didn't want Stephen to get caught up in the mix. Either way, Ina came to my house and broke the news to me about her being pregnant. I begged her not to tell Stephen. Told her I would take care of her and the baby for as long as I could. And over the years, that was exactly what I had done. Ina and I had gotten closer—she turned out to be a jewel, with a few flaws here and there. In addition to that, I loved my grandson more than life itself, and I would do anything . . . *anything* in the world for him.

"Come here," I said to my handsome grandson who looked so much like his father. "Come give me a hug, and give your sweet granny some suga."

He gave me a squeezing hug, showing me just how much he loved me. I wanted to tell Stephen about his son, but timing was everything. Fourteen years in, he still didn't know, but if Raynetta was ready to rumble, so in the hell was I.

ORDER FORM
URBAN BOOKS, LLC
97 N. 18th Street
Wyandanch, NY 11798

Name (please print):_____

Address: _____

City/State: _____

Zip: _____

QTY	TITLES	PRICE

Shipping and handling-add $3.50 for 1st book, then $1.75 for each additional book.
Please send a check payable to:
    Urban Books, LLC
Please allow 4–6 weeks for delivery